The Golden Gift of Silence

A séance, a bloody knife,
and a body buried under the gardenias

BOOK FOUR

AGNES MAKÓCZY

For information contact :
www.agnes-makoczy.com

Book Cover Image by
https://www.flickr.com/photos/lico43/8532415995/sizes/l/

Book formatting by Derek Murphy from www.CreativIndie.com

ISBN: 0-9774395-6-9
First Edition: August 2017

10 9 8 7 6 5 4 3 2 1

Contents

INTRODUCTION

The Salt Dunes in August

THE SAND IS PRISTINE, WHITE, SOFT, CLINGY. The old man sits for a while under the beating, relentless sun. This far south, there's no shade anywhere. From where he's sitting, he can see the first ruins of what was once the original settlement, the one they call Old Town, and very, very far away, what appears to be a restaurant, nothing more than a run-down shack, jutting out into the bay. Everywhere else, the vast expanse of Louisiana's Shark Bayou.

The sun beats down on the old man's head mercilessly, not that he's complaining, even though his bald spot is burning away. He pats his pockets and feels the bulge the many bills make in them. Won't be long now. He tries not to think about what all he had to do to get his hands on all this money, and focuses on the shining waters of the bay. Any minute now, the boat will show up on the horizon, bobbing on the water with determination, bringing him a most certainly better future.

But time crawls at a miserable speed in the humid, empty expanse, and forces the old man to get up and pace. He can't keep still, thinking that he's been had. Anxiety mounts. His contact should have arrived already. He must have been duped.

The sun's too bright to look at the shimmering water, so he uses his hands as a visor against the glare and coughs up with relief, muttering something under his breath. That's him. He's coming, he tells himself. He's really coming. There, so far away that he can barely see it with his rheumy eyes, a tiny rowboat comes into view and soon gets bigger. Yes, it must be him, the old man thinks and starts hobbling toward the shore.

There's a lot of money in his pockets, and it slows him down. The bundles loll from side to side as he tries to run on the dry sand and hit his thighs. What a sweet feeling, all that money on him. He grins a toothless grin and waves at the man rowing toward him.

The old man looks on anxiously. The newcomer throws down the oars and pulls in his boat onto the sand, and waves back in a cordial gesture as if they had always been friends. But they've only met once before. Briefly. The old man squints to take a better look at the younger man, but his eyesight is not what it once was. Still, he recognizes the voice and cries out.

"Good to see you. Did you get it?" he asks. He's not one to mince words. He can barely contain his impatience.

"You know I did. It was pretty easy, too."

"So, let's see it," he says quickly, and a spray of saliva spurts out of his mouth. He steps toward the younger, leaner man. The greed and the excitement have turned his eyes shiny, almost translucent. He puts a shaking hand out. His arthritic fingers are slightly curved, like claws almost, and the younger man recoils, disgusted. The old man's sour breath comes out in jagged strips, hoarse, barely human, distorted by years of solitary confinement in a jail cell, and by lack of human contact. He's almost forgotten how to talk to others, but the begging comes out clear. "I have to see it," he insists.

"Not so fast, old man. You have to show me the money first."

The older man knows that he should know better than to trust this stranger, but he has no choice in the matter. He looks at the young man's hungry smile and those long, sharp incisors that make him shiver with dread, and for a second he thinks about running away and forgetting all about this crazy adventure, but somehow, he feels that the matter is already out of his hands.

He sticks them into his pockets and pulls out the wads of money, all tied together neatly with blue fraying cord. He thinks about the years he's waited, the lifetime of suffering he still needs to redeem, and his hands shake. He shouldn't be here, he thinks. So much he could have done with this money. Why this obsession? Why?

"So how does it work?"

"I don't know," the old man says, shrugging. "I have to figure it out."

"Something tells me that you already know."

"No, no, I really don't. I've read about it somewhere, but they didn't know how to make it work either." The old man wipes the sweat off his brow and upper lip with the sleeve of his dirty, stained shirt. "Nobody does."

"If nobody knows, then you have no use for it, now do you?"

"What do you care if I have use for it or not? I paid for it fair and square."

"You paid me to steal it, but there was nothing fair or square about it." The young man laughs, sending a shiver down the old man's spine.

Before the old man can say anything else, the young man has already snatched the money out of his hands and is putting it away in his satchel.

When he sees that the young man is turning to walk away, he grabs him by the sleeve.

"Give it to me now, please. I've waited so long."

"You're naïve, old man. Did you really think I was going to give it to you? Then, you're a fool." And with that, he turns around and starts walking toward the shore, where he has left his rowboat sitting on the sand.

With a yelp of despair, the old man follows—as fast as he can—despair giving him the speed and the strength to keep up. He's sobbing softly now. "You have to let me see it," he says, catching up, and grabbing the man's arm. "At least let me see it," he begs. But the young man refuses to stop, refuses to acknowledge him.

Angry now, with the last bit of strength he has left, the old man grabs at the satchel and pulls. Surprised at his own strength, he pulls harder now and yanks the satchel off the younger man's shoulder. He's learned a move or two in his long, twisted life, and is pleased that he can still stand his ground if he has to. He clutches the unseen object to his chest possessively, unwilling to let it go. Over his dead body, he tells himself.

But the young man reacts with fury. His face gets red, and his eyes narrow. He lunges at the old man. This sudden violence terrifies the old man. He steps back, hanging on to his heart's desire, and turns to run, as if he himself believed that he would be able to. But it's pointless.

In the blink of an eye, he's rolling on the sand with the younger man, in a fight to the death. He refuses to let the satchel go. The more the other man pulls and punches, the harder he hangs on. There's sand in his eyes, and his nose, and in between his few remaining teeth. Again, and again, he questions his own sanity, but he will not let go.

All of a sudden, a strong, cold, burning, searing hot pain rushes into his chest, and he forgets to breathe. It takes him a few seconds to grasp that he's been stabbed. He grabs on to his belly—where the pain is worst— and tries to catch his breath.

As he turns on his back and looks up at the punishing blue sky, a feeling of confusion fills his soul, and he comprehends that something's wrong. He's getting colder, losing contact with his hands and feet. He's bleeding out. He touches his side where the pain is most excruciating and feels the hot sticky mess oozing out from between his fingers. He realizes, surprised, that he's dying.

At least the pain is subsiding now, but the world is fading around him. It's losing importance. He wonders if there's still time to believe in God and beg for forgiveness, you know, just in case, and thinks about how he's done too much evil in this life to be forgiven.

Then he remembers his mother. How odd. He hasn't thought about her in years. She was a kind woman, gone too young. At least she didn't live long enough to see him become this unloved, homeless mess. Then he has a glimmer of hope that maybe she'll be there on the other side, waiting for him. And finally, with tears of sadness and regret, he closes his eyes and prays, you know, just in case.

Chapter 1

The Murderer

THERE WAS THE OLD MAN, pacing on the shore. God only knew how long he had been waiting for him. Poor guy. He turned the artifact in his hands and pondered.

Since the beginning of this whole thing, he had been shocked by his own behavior. As an upholder of the law, he had never stolen anything in his life and never expected to be so exhilarated by it. But driven by an inexplicable impulse, he had slipped into a friend's library and stolen. He remembered touching the artifact for the first time, and the strange and wild thrill that rushed through his blood when he smoothly slipped it into his satchel. Not a pang of regret, shame on him. It was the most exciting thing he had done his whole life. He smiled wickedly to himself. He didn't expect anyone to ever suspect a respectable person like himself of the theft.

And then, as he turned around to slip out as quietly as he had entered, he saw the collection of knives there—right in front of him—in a glass-topped table cabinet full of antique wonders. He tried the latch and almost laughed out loud when he found it unlocked. Before he had a chance to rationalize what he was doing, he picked up a broad blade knife—a machette—sharp, etched with exotic markings that looked like Japanese *man'yōgana*, beautifully kept, and he turned it this way and that, admiring it. Then, he slipped it carefully into his satchel next to the artifact and hurried back to the door. He closed the door behind him, smoothed his hair with his left hand, and straightened his tie, and then he hurried back to the party to mingle with the other guests before he was missed.

Staring at the slowly approaching shore, he watched the bent figure pacing back and forth, and he felt sorry for the old man. He thought about turning back, knowing deep inside that he would do no such thing. So, he kept on rowing. It was hard work that he wasn't used to, the rowing. His shoulder blades and his arms were on fire.

At what point did he decide to keep the artifact? Hard to say. It just happened. A small school of colorful fish swam by his boat, and one of them lagged behind and looked up at him. It was at that moment he knew. Whatever it took, he was keeping the artifact. Whatever it took. And that was final.

But once he began rowing away from the beach and the murder, the enormity of what he had just done rocked his soul, and he began to shake. Did he deplore the killing of a harmless old man? Well, of course, he did, on some deeper level. He was no killer. But it was too late for regrets. He should have turned the boat around from the beginning, but he didn't. Instead, he talked himself into going ashore to explain himself, to let the old man know that he had changed his mind. Can't let him stand in the sun all day without an explanation, right?

And the whole thing had turned into a disaster. The old man had grabbed his satchel and refused to let go, so this horrible anger welled up in him, coming out of nowhere, and before he could figure out how to control himself, a hand—his own hand—had grabbed the Japanese machette he carried by his side, and buried it in the old man's chest. Still angry, he yanked the satchel from the dying man's hands, and by the sound of tinkering inside it, knew it was broken. It wasn't until that moment that he realized that in the scuffle for the knife, he had been slashed too.

He howled in anger and could have killed the old man again. He stomped away toward his boat trying to control his breathing and his fury. The old fool had not only wounded him but broken his precious artifact, and now what was he going to do? For now, he had to get away before he was seen. He looked around before jumping in the boat but saw that there was nothing to be worried about. He was all alone on this side of the universe. He looked down at his chest and the ever-expanding bloodstain on his shirt. It would be okay, he decided. It didn't hurt too much.

He rowed for a while before heading for the rocky bend that signaled the beginning of Old Town and stopped. The stolen machette lay where he had left it, in the bottom of the boat. He should toss it overboard, out here, so far from shore that nobody would even think to look for it. But he picked it up and held the beautifully etched piece, and something in him kept him from throwing it away. It was a beauty, and he was a lover of beautiful things. Maybe he could find a place to hide it until the unfortunate death got forgotten. It's worth the risk, he told himself. I'll store it, hide it, and then when it's safe, maybe sell it, maybe not. But I will never throw it away.

He grabbed the machette by the hilt and dipped it carefully in the water. For a second, the water ebbed around the blade, and it became tinted with the fresh blood. But there was so little of it really, that within seconds the red tinge got diluted, and it was gone. Then, remembering that there was blood all over his shirt, he took that off carefully because already the fabric was beginning to stick to the wound and rinsed it out in the water as well. Good thing it was a dark shirt. Good thing that it was a sunny day, and it would dry soon. As to the pain, well, it wasn't unbearable.

He stared at the shore for a while. He was so far now that he couldn't see the body any longer. The gentle waves lapped against the rowboat as he sat there, contemplating the enormity of what had just happened. But there was no point in sitting there. What was done couldn't be undone. So, he picked up the oars, and he rowed again. He navigated around the salt cliffs of the bend, careful not to hit the rocks that jutted out treacherously from under the water, careful not to make any sudden moves that would make the pain worse, and then he headed for home.

Chapter 2

Is That an Arm? The Next Day

THIS TIME OF THE DAY, and on a weekday too, the Parrot Joe Shack was rather empty. Sitting on what the locals were fond of calling *ze promontoire*, the ancient seafood restaurant teetered on the edge of a low salt cliff overlooking Half Moon Bay, the prettiest bay in South Louisiana.

Both the building and the décor were hundreds of years old. Parrot Joe had originally been built by pirates as a safe haven, a place where they could lay down their swashbuckling swords and enjoy a game of cards, and drink themselves into a stupor.

Said pirates were so fond of the location, of the protection offered to their vessels by the natural enclosure, that they settled there in their old age to raise their families. But after a series of bad storms, *Lor L'Anges*—as they called their settlement—was just about destroyed, and their houses blown away, so they moved their families to the less-exposed sandy side of the bay where they built the new and more modern town, and called it Half Moon Bay.

Margo Fontaine and Saffron Sigur sat at one of the tables of the Parrot Joe Shack by a window overlooking the gray, angry water, and ate their favorite seafood dishes and sipped on some iced-tea. They were watching fascinated as a small boat pitched up and down in the heavy swell.

"It's going to capsize," said Saffron, picking a crawfish daintily from her salad. "It's a good thing he's so close to shore."

"That's Manny's boat. He should have known better than to go out in this weather."

"Well, you know Manny. Always up for a challenge. At least he's wearing that bright red life vest."

"I think he enjoys both the danger and getting a rise out of his mother." Margo laughed. Manny was always in trouble. "I'm going to give her a call. He might have to be rescued again."

"I hear you're becoming quite the private detective," Saffron mentioned, flipping her fabulous mane of red hair out of the way of her crawfish salad. "How many cases solved with this last one?"

"Oh, I don't know. I'm not counting them," Margo answered bashfully, and she took a big bite out of her catfish burger. It would have been inappropriate to gloat or to look too pleased, but she had solved all her cases except for the one about the alligator's ghost—the one that was linked to the disappearance of numerous residents and had become a local legend more than anything else—so she simply said, "But I do love what I do."

"I'm glad you decided to stay in Half Moon Bay."

"Me too. After Jenny died, I seriously considered going back to school and never coming back. She was my best friend. Then, my cousin Robert's deceit, Aunt Beth's cruelty, and the murders of Rosa Nesta and Mr. Snail were almost more than I could bear."

"But then you decided to investigate."

"Because I needed to know how they had died to find closure."

"And on the plus side, you inherited an antebellum home by the beach."

"And Jenny's cats." Margo laughed softly. "Turns out that I'm a cat lover."

"And that brings me to the reason I asked you to come. It's about Beatrice Saint-Clair."

"The famous medium?" Margo looked at her friend, surprised.

"Yes. They say she has the gift. I know what you're going to say, Margo, but hear me out." Saffron leaned into the table and lowered her voice. "There have been so many frauds among the spiritualists that when a legitimate medium comes along, nobody believes anymore. Have you heard of Edgar Cayce, the American Christian mystic? He healed hundreds of people while in a trance and saved numerous lives. He became famous and was nicknamed the Sleeping Prophet. Never accepted a penny from anyone. And his prophecies and his medical diagnoses are well documented."

"But Saffron, everyone knows there's no such thing."

"Now don't be so narrow-minded, Margo Fontaine. President Franklin D. Roosevelt went to séances. So, did Arthur Conan Doyle, the creator of Sherlock Holmes." Saffron was ticking names off on her fingers. "Then there's long-distance radio and telegraph inventor Guglielmo Marconi, and Alexander Graham Bell, the inventor of the telephone. They all believed firmly in the possibility of communicating with the dead. And Beatrice Saint-Clair comes with plenty of references. You should look her up online."

"Well, I don't know her, so I shouldn't judge," Margo shrugged, feeling dubious. "What did you want to tell me about her?"

"She's been invited to come to town and give a séance. It was going to be in my house, but mom decided to come straight home after her European Opera Tour instead of taking a couple of weeks off, so I can't host the séance anymore. Mom would have a conniption."

"Hold on one second," Margo said, putting a hand on Saffron's arm. "Who invited her?"

"I heard it was Renata."

"Seriously? Renata, as in Mimi's daughter?"

"Yes. I believe so."

"Why would Renata ask a medium to come to Half Moon Bay and have a séance?"

"Well, I really don't know for sure, but it has to do with some dreams she's been having."

"I see. Well, that makes a lot of sense," Margo said facetiously and crossed her arms on her chest.

"So," Saffron paused and looked at Margo with her big, innocent green eyes, "can we have it at your house? It's a real antebellum mansion. It's so old and full of history. It would be the perfect setting for a ghostly night."

"Well…"

"Please, Margo, pretty please?"

"But why would you want to be involved in a séance anyway?"

"Oh, because of this exposé I'm writing for the Half Moon Gazette. Haven't you read my column lately? It's about true mediums and charlatans. If it's good enough, and it garners interest, I might turn it into a book."

"I guess…"

"You're such a dear. I'll owe you one."

Margo smiled to herself. Saffron—bless her heart—was always full of exciting schemes. To Saffron, everything was either an adventure or an opportunity. It was impossible not to love her and be carried away by her enthusiasm. She took a bite of her catfish burger and wondered which room to have the séance in.

Meantime, all of a sudden, Margo saw Rosalie, their waitress, come running from the kitchen, drying her hands on her apron and talking loudly a hundred miles an hour.

"Miss Margo, Miss Saffron, did y'all see that?" Rosalie was shaking with the excitement of her news as she pointed to another window, one that looked out to the back of the Shack, to the ruins of Old Town. "Look!"

Hearing Rosalie's yelps, everyone in the restaurant turned that way. At first, Margo could see nothing except for the dried-up vegetation rustling violently under the pre-storm wind, and the crumbling ruins of what had been the pirates' haven, their *bel abri*. Then she saw something move. It was big, and it was furry and pinkish brown, and it was the ugliest and scariest animal that Margo had ever seen. It wasn't in a hurry either. It walked at a steady pace, carrying something in its mouth, something long and stiff, something tinted a dark iron red.

"What is that?" she asked.

"That's a feral pig," Rosalie explained. "Pigs that have escaped their pens and run away, and now live in freedom. They're very dangerous."

"Are the doors locked?" Saffron asked, ever the practical one.

"They will be in a second." Rosalie ran to the doors and locked and barred them. The other customers approached the girls at the window, and they all stared at the wild pig in a hushed silence as it made its progress across the scrub. Margo remembered uncomfortably that that was about the place where they had found Buddy Mason murdered all those years ago.

"I think it's carrying a body part," someone said with a frightened cry, and everyone stepped closer to the window. It did really look like a human arm, but it was hard to tell. It was too far, and nobody was going to volunteer to go out there to find out.

"So, what do we do?" asked someone else. "We can't leave, not with that thing out there."

"Let's wait until it disappears, and then go," Saffron told them. "Meantime we're probably safe in here."

The room was absolutely silent. All you could hear was the big clock over the fireplace, ticking the silent seconds away. They watched huddled by the window as the feral pig sauntered across the ruins of Old Town, breaths fogging up the dirty window panes, fear overcome by excitement. Margo and Saffron moved over to a corner to talk without being overheard.

"I called Sam. That did look like an arm, which means there has to be a dead body nearby."

"Yes, but where? This whole area is enormous. You've lived here all your life, Saffron. You know that."

"Dogs could probably find it."

"Cadaver dogs? Are there even any, here in Half Moon Bay?"

"I don't know, Margo. I have no idea."

"Look, it's coming back. What if it left its dinner in one of the caves and is going back for more? We should follow it."

"I'm not going anywhere near that thing. It looks vicious. Look at those tusks."

"Oh, come on, Saffron. You can't let me go all by myself. Besides, if we find the body, you'll have a great story for the paper."

"I don't have my camera."

"But you have your cell phone."

"Oh, all right, but if it kills us, it will be your fault."

Chapter 3

"It's a dead body"

MARGO PULLED SAFFRON ALONG, and they followed the enormous pig. It didn't seem to mind being followed, and Margo wracked her brain, trying to remember if she'd ever read anything about wild pigs. Would it turn around and attack them? As far as she knew, wild animals don't go and attack humans unless they're hungry, or they feel threatened. Well, she and Saffron were following very respectfully, so there was no reason why it should feel threatened.

The beast had a route, and with determination crossed the empty expanse of Old Town, climbing over clumps of vegetation with tight little steps and circling around crumbling walls. At one point, it stopped and turned around to stare at them with beady eyes, and Margo saw Saffron whip her phone out and take a picture.

"Don't do that," Margo said, alarmed. "You're going to make it angry."

"It's for Sam. I'm texting him."

"Is he coming?"

"Yes. He's waiting for Andy—his deputy—and the animal control guy, and he'll be here soon."

"Nice to have a sheriff for a friend."

"Sure is."

They had cleared Old Town, and the pig vanished behind some shrubs. It was heading downhill, toward the other beach, the uninhabited one. There was nothing pretty about this stretch of sand, so Margo wasn't surprised that nobody had bothered to build anything on it. For one thing, it was too low-lying, and it probably flooded with the tides. For another, it was as inhospitable as a stretch of Saturn, full of wildly growing camphor daisies and seaside purslane, and, at the moment, it was being battered by gusts of stormy wind coming in from the angry sea. Margo shivered under the whistling wind. If they were going to find a dead body, this would be the place.

Margo peeked over the shrubbery and saw that the pig had reached its quarry. Far enough for them to be in safety, it was almost at the edge of the water. It was poking at what seemed to be a pile of rags from afar, but that could very well be a dead body. The odor of death wafted toward them, carried by the wind. It didn't seem to bother the pig, who was on the verge of grabbing another arm to take home.

Then—all of a sudden—the police siren broke the silence of the barren beach, and the feral pig looked up at them, startled out of its rêverie. And then, it took off running in a powerful, dusty stampede, and even from so far away, you could see its strong muscles rippling as it went. Well, that was that. But deep down, Margo felt relief. She didn't want to see the big beast being hunted down. By the time Sheriff Sam Stark, Andy, his deputy—who was bringing the dogs—and the animal control guy got there holding a gun that looked like a harpoon, the pig was long gone.

The dogs approached yelping and sniffing. They pulled at their leashes, dragging the skinny Andy behind them like he was a rag doll. They wagged their tails and got more out of control as they got closer. And then, they broke loose. They took off, their leashes flapping behind them, their tongues lolling with excitement, leaving an embarrassed Andy to run after them, to try to catch them.

Finally, they were all down by the water, by the dead body, and Andy said, "It's a dead body." He bent down and picked up something small and blue from the sand and slipped it into his pocket. Then he scratched his head.

No kidding. The body was a bloody mess. Margo, who by now had seen her share of dead bodies, felt sorry for Saffron, who had turned around to throw up. The animal control guy, more used to gore, bravely held on to the yapping dogs and pretended to be immune to the stench.

"You guys," yelled Sam at Saffron, and at Andy who had gone over to help her. "Y'all are contaminating the crime scene."

"Oh, Sam, what's the point of worrying? Between all this sand and what the pig has done to it, a little vomit won't make a difference."

"I guess you're right. Let's see what we have here. And Andy, don't tell me again that it's a dead body."

Margo and Sam got closer. The body was covered in flies and beetles, but their buzzing was drowned out by the incoming storm. The man was old, emaciated, with a big bald patch on the dome of his head.

"Not from around here," Sam said. "He does look kind of familiar, though."

"You think?"

"Yes. Come to this side. Look at how long and angular the face is. Thick eyebrows, big ears."

"Now that you mention it, yes, maybe. He kind of looks like Mr. Snail, my aunts' old butler, the one that died in the fire. Do you remember him?"

"Sure do. Could be a relative. Could be a brother."

Sam pulled a pair of disposable gloves from his pocket and snapped them on. With a look of disgust, he tried to shoo the bugs away, and he went through the dead man's pockets. Finding nothing in the front, he touched the back pockets reaching from the sides. He triumphantly pulled out a wallet and lifted it for the girls to see.

"Now let's find out the man's name." There was dried blood on the wallet, caked and sticky, and Sam struggled to open the case and find identification. "Aha," he exclaimed all of a sudden. "We're right. His name was Snail. Jerome Snail, from Oklahoma, recently let out of Jess Dunn Correctional Center. An ex-convict. Well, well, well. How interesting."

"But what was he doing here, out here? And what did he do to get himself killed?"

"That, we're just going to have to find out."

Margo looked around her. Good luck finding any clues in this barren wasteland. She looked out to sea and watched the storm as it rumbled over the open water, approaching fast. She hoped Manny was home safe already, or at least close to shore, and no longer struggling with the waves. Then, she returned her attention to the body.

This was a very lonely stretch of land. Anything could happen out here, and nobody would ever find out. If it hadn't been for the pig, this dead body would have rotted away, swallowed by the ever-shifting sands without anyone being the wiser. What was the old man doing out here, all by himself?

"Okay, we've got to get out of here before the storm hits." Sam started directing his deputy to lock the dogs away in the animal control van and get a move on the ambulance. "Go back to the Parrot Joe Shack and show them the way."

The dogs howled, and the storm threatened with dark clouds and a rumbling sky. But soon the two guys from the ambulance jogged down to the beach with a stretcher, and without raising an eyebrow in surprise, they smoothly carried the mangled body away.

Margo and Sam squatted by the spot, and Sam poked about the sand with a stick. A momentary ray of sun shone among the dark patches of dry blood, and something picked up the light and sparkled. Sam picked it up with a tissue paper and they both looked at it.

"I wonder if this is evidence. I better bag it." He pulled an evidence baggie out of his pocket and carefully placed the ever-so-slightly curved shard of glass in it. It was thick and milky and looked very old.

"Can I see that?" Margo asked. "I won't touch it. Just hold it up." She stared at it for a while. "I think I know what this is from. I've seen something like this before."

Margo's memory went back to a visit she had once accompanied her aunts on. It had been years and years, but she remembered it clear as day because Aunt Beth was visiting a friend who was dying. Mr. Snail—the butler—was wearing squeaky shoes, or maybe they got wet in the rain that kept falling, and maybe that was the reason they were squeaking. But anyway, as he shuffled forward behind the aunts, carrying something in a big box, Aunt Beth kept wincing with every squeak, and Margo couldn't help herself and she giggled, and at that moment Aunt Beth turned around, absolutely furious, and lifted her cane. Margo watched—horrified—as the tiny old woman hit the immobile chauffeur over and over again, with unmitigated violence. Mr. Snail never winced, never complained, but that look of hatred in his eyes, that murderous silent rage, she would never forget that, ever, as long as she lived.

Then, unexpectedly, Aunt Beth's cane caught on something as she twirled. It hit a ship in a bottle sitting on a side table, and the impact lifted the thick bottle in the air, and it shattered against the tiles on the floor of the living room. It was in a million pieces, the glass, and startled and embarrassed, Margo bent down to pick the pieces up. But they were small, and one of the shards cut her finger. While she sucked the blood to make it stop the bleeding, she saw one larger piece that had skidded on the tile and had landed under the breakfront. She picked it up and marveled at the glass, which was unlike any glass she had ever seen before. It was thick and milky, and full of air bubbles, and you could tell right away that it was very old.

At that moment, the sky opened with an angry rumble, and the first big, fat, wet, drops fell, and Margo and the sheriff ran to the patrol car for shelter. Thunder and lightning shook the empty expanse, and Margo sighed with relief to be under cover. And then she remembered what she had been about to say.

"I know exactly where this piece of glass came from," she told Sam Stark. "You're not going to believe it."

Chapter 4

Margo and Saffron Look for a Ship in a Bottle

"WE'RE LOOKING FOR A SHIP IN A BOTTLE," Margo said with conviction.

"How's that? Did you deduce that from that sliver of glass you found under the dead man?"

"Well, yes. Look at it, and I'll explain." Margo pulled the plastic evidence baggie from her purse and smiled when she saw Saffron's look of horror.

"Isn't that evidence?" she asked. "Does Sam know you have it?"

Margo chuckled. "He wouldn't know what to do with it. Besides, he'll be pleased when we solve this little mystery for him." She slipped the piece of glass into Saffron's palm. "Don't worry. It doesn't have any fingerprints that we'll be smudging. I checked. Now hold the glass up to the light. Careful, don't cut yourself."

Saffron held the glass up toward the window. "What am I looking for?" she asked.

"Bubbles."

"Bubbles?"

"Yes. The older the glass, the more bubbles it has. Two hundred years ago, even one hundred years ago, the art of glassmaking hadn't reached modern levels. When they made glass, it was thicker, milkier, and it was full of air bubbles."

"Okay, I do admit I see a lot of bubbles, and the glass is thick and milky, but this shard could belong to anything, a pitcher, a wine glass, anything."

"True. But what else do you see?"

"A white smudge. It's painted in brush strokes, it seems."

Margo rummaged in her purse and pulled out a portable magnifying glass.

"Here. Look at it with this."

Saffron examined the glass shard carefully with the magnifying glass and exclaimed suddenly.

"It's a cloud. I can't believe it. It's a cloud. It even has a tiny bird painted on it. I thought it was a spot of dirt."

"So cool, right? I've been reading up on ships in bottles. Many of the older European bottles have quaint villages and small towns painted inside to serve as a background for the ship itself. You sometimes even find trees, clouds, or a lighthouse."

For the next couple of hours, Saffron's sleek and ambitious looking young new intern—wanting to prove that he was indispensable—made dozens of trips downstairs to the archives of the Half Moon Gazette to bring Margo and Saffron the last ten years' worth of the Gazette's Society Pages.

"So, who's the new intern?" Margo asked. He was good-looking, well built, with a modern minimalist hair cut that regardless, allowed Margo to admire his reddish, blondish hair.

"His name is Jimmy Falgout. His parents own the tractor dealership by the mall on East Storm Petrell. Good Cajun folks. They want him to go places. You know how it is with parents who want their children to be better than they are."

"But I hear a but in your voice."

"Um, no. He's okay. He's a bit overanxious. He tries too hard, maybe? Anyway…"

They went through the Society Pages one by one, looking closely at the photographs with magnifying glasses, hoping to spot a ship in a bottle in someone's home. After an arduous morning of hard work, they narrowed their list down to the following: the politician, what was his name? Jefferson Renard, and a couple of others.

"I've seen the one in Jefferson Renard's house," Jimmy Falgout said unexpectedly. Margo hadn't realized that the intern was standing so close behind her back, and she moved away discreetly. As he pointed his finger toward the photograph, she noticed that his index finger had an ugly brownish, yellowish stain on the fingernails, and she cringed. "It's right by this really ugly painting of a girl with a cloth doll."

"According to this list, my neighbors have one as well," Margo said. "But I barely know them because they aren't the friendliest people on earth. Still, I guess they wouldn't mind if we asked to take a look at their ship."

"The president of fundraising from the Opera House Committee has one she purchased recently at an auction," Saffron said and sent Jimmy Falgout to make some phone calls. After a while, he came back and reported that the Maritime Museum, the one behind the Fisherman's Wharf, had numerous examples, and feel free to come see them any time. Just give the curator a call, he said, and handed Saffron a piece of paper with a phone number on it.

Now all that was left was to call and make appointments to find out if anyone was missing a ship in a bottle, and while Margo waited on that, she went to visit Sam, to find out if there was any new information on the dead man.

Chapter 5

Madame Mansard

MADAME MANSARD STEPPED OUT of the airport terminal building in New Orleans jetlagged, disoriented, blinded by the strong afternoon light. Her lungs wheezed as she inhaled the moist air thick with the droplets of water and the fetid miasma blowing in from the swamps, and with the sudden lack of oxygen came a sense of panic. She should have never come.

Everyone who had arrived on the same flight with them had already left. Only she stood by the curb, with Haruki and Yuna, waiting. She looked at the empty road, disappointed. Initially, there had been a flurry of cars, and a rush of people lugging bags and suitcases, but they were all gone. By now, even the taxis had left, and all that was left for her was to stand there and wait for the hired car and its chauffeur.

She willed her heart to slow down its erratic gallop. Breath, Presence, and Tranquility, she reminded herself. She would be of no use to anyone if her heart gave out before her business was finished.

"We can still turn around and go back home," she told the stoic young Japanese man standing next to her. He carefully read her lips and then let out a litany of guttural words in his native language.

"I guess you're right," she told him. "We have come this far, after all."

There was no breeze, just that blazing sun beating down on them. Madame adjusted her Japanese kimono jacket. The armpits of the silk jacket sported dark sweat spots. Haruki, always attentive, handed her a pristine white handkerchief, and she wiped the wet strip above her upper lip.

Poor Haruki. He was being hounded by mosquitos. She watched him squash one with a lightning-fast slap to his neck and then look at his hand. There was blood on it. His sister stood next to him, impassive and unaffected by the bloodsucking bugs, and he growled at her with annoyance.

Yuna stared at the empty horizon, pointedly ignoring her and Haruki. Her silent hostility grated on Madame's nerves, but she couldn't really blame her. A long time ago, she had promised the girl the magnificent family heirloom around her neck as soon as she was old enough to wear it. But Madame Mansard had changed her mind and never mentioned the pricey gift again. Yuna openly resented that she had broken her promise, and in time they stopped being friends altogether.

It hadn't always been an effort to love Yuna, though. As a baby, she had been adorable, cuddly, and loving, but she turned in her teenage years. The affable girl became unpleasant and belligerent, and Madame stopped liking her. Not having children of her own, Madame just didn't know what to do with the disagreeable young woman.

She stared—bewildered—at the wild expanse of unfamiliar, dusty vegetation around her, the neglected shrubs, the random flower patches, so different from the Katsura and Sento Gosho narrative gardens of Kyoto, with their exquisite stepping-stones, the charming arched bridges, and the dark, limpid pools where fish swam in carefree harmony with nature.

Where was that driver? Local bums—looking dirty and ill-tempered—had begun gathering in small, hostile groups—inching ever so slightly closer, and stared at them. Haruki stared back fiercely, ready for a fight. His hand touched his chest as it always did when he wanted to check on his Enyo blade. But Madame reminded him that the blade and its Kydex sheath were in the luggage, safe from the wandering eyes of Customs, and not under his shirt, and she told him that there was nothing to worry about.

But Haruki insisted on looking apprehensive. He had made it very clear that in his opinion it was folly to dig up the dirt of the past now, so late in her life. She chuckled grimly. He had no qualms about calling her old. And he was right. She should be more worried now about spending her last years with her friends and relatives who loved her and enjoyed her company instead of chasing ghosts long gone. We're being watched, Haruki signed. Too many people know we're coming.

Madame Mansard fanned herself nervously with her little sensu fan desperately trying to cool the air she was breathing in. She turned toward Haruki and said, allowing him to read her lips.

"I'm afraid, Haruki. I keep having the same nightmare. They begin digging, and they dig too deep, and they find a bone, and then another, and then a skull, and rotting pieces of cloth. And then someone says we should have buried them deeper. Why did I not listen to your honorable uncle and let this unpleasant quest go, why?"

"Grandmother must remain calm," Haruki told her in his guttural Japanese, adding a flurry of sign language words. "These are just dreams. They will find nothing. There is nothing to find."

"What if the medium receives something incriminating, and then tells?"

"We can skip the séance, Grandmother. We don't have to go."

"I have to, Haruki. I have to find out what happened. And if possible, repair the damage that's been done."

Haruki bowed deep. His heart was full of affection for this troubled and stubborn old woman. "I will do my best to keep you safe, Grandmother. You have my word."

Madame Mansard smiled at the young man and patted his arm fondly. She just had to stay alive long enough to right all wrongs, and then it wouldn't matter anymore.

The driver zoomed through the rutted highway disregarding the speed limit. In the back seat sat Madame Mansard, deep in thought. Stretches of empty roads lined with frondous trees that seemed to reach to the sky alternated with tracts of neglected roads. A few random houses dotted the dry countryside. Decaying barns, lonely horses tied to posts, cows standing under the merciless sun watching their car zoom by. At times, they took substandard roads full of potholes that the driver seemed unable to evade. At other times, she had to look down into her lap to avoid looking at roadkill, and she sadly prayed *Se pou volonte ou fèt sou tè a tankou nan syèl la.*

At an intersection, they stopped at a red light in the middle of nowhere. A gas station to the left, and a diner to the right. Nothing else. Abandoned railroad tracks meandered parallel to the highway, the weeds between the joints and the ties growing almost knee-high. No houses, no town, no inhabitants, except for one lonely beggar sitting on the floor in front of the empty diner, playing a beat-up saxophone with a vacant stare. Bits and fragments of the mournful tune reached her ears while they waited for the light to turn green, and then it was gone.

So, this was the land of her ancestors, she thought despondently as she looked out of the window. This was the land where her life had begun, where her mother had lived briefly, just long enough to give birth to her before running away to Japan—to the other side of the world—to escape those who wanted to hurt her. And now she was back.

She wished her mother had told her why she had run away. But her mother had insisted on keeping her secrets to herself, so here she was, not really knowing what she was doing, but here anyway, hoping to find out the truth.

Her hand went to the chain around her neck and she touched the cross hanging from it for comfort. *Beni mwen Bondye,* she prayed. *Pwoteje m 'anba sa ki mal.*

Chapter 6

Margo Visits Sam for Information

MARGO APPROACHED INDEPENDENCE PARK through the quiet streets behind the Opera House, driving slowly, enjoying the graceful abandon of the aging homes and the rambling disorder of the overgrown yards. There was this one place where she loved to park, an empty lot—small, hidden, and paved with cracked gray flagstones, a space barely big enough to fit her car and allow her to open the door on the driver's side and squeeze through.

She turned the ignition off and smiled with pleasure. This was her secret spot. She was under an enormous centenarian oak tree whose powerful roots had lifted the iron fence that separated the empty lot from an old, mysterious house with shuttered windows and peeling mauve paint. She walked to the tarnished once-black wrought iron fence and peered between the pickets, careful not to squash the spiders and their delicately woven webs that fluttered like lace in the gentle breeze.

Margo headed at a leisurely pace toward the park with her hands in her pockets, enjoying the balmy weather. The last few months had been too quiet in Half Moon Bay. The dead body and the mystery of the missing ship in the bottle were a welcome break in an otherwise enjoyable but monotonous lifestyle. Not that she was pleased that someone had been murdered, she reminded herself. But other than singing in the choir at St. Quintian's or awaiting her boyfriend Pierre's infrequent visits, there was little to do to occupy the time. She was just pondering whether she should take up painting or needlepoint as a hobby when she noticed a movement from the corner of her left eye, and her attention was drawn to it.

She stopped. Her heart skipped a beat. Something had disrupted her inner peace. An animal? No. Too tall. Probably just a shadow. Or her imagination. She shook her head at her own foolishness. She did have a very vivid imagination.

She looked quickly around to make sure but saw nothing unusual, so she continued walking. But her mind wasn't on the pleasure of the walk anymore.

Every few steps, she looked behind her left shoulder. She couldn't shake the feeling that someone was watching her. And, sure enough, right before she got to the end of the block, she saw movement again. There. There, behind that tree to her left, on the other side of the street. She knew it. It sounded crazy, but she was absolutely sure this time that she had seen—just for a few seconds—a mop of blondish, reddish hair, and the wide shoulders of a tall man. Her eyebrows scrunched.

Was she being followed? Should she be afraid?

A pang of anguish assaulted her. Of course, she should be afraid. The street was empty. Deserted. And she was all alone, and at least three long blocks from the next busy street. The old, rambling, eclectic houses around her suddenly looked scary. Threatening. Too many shrubs and bushes. Too many dusty, rusting cars on both sides of the street. If she were to scream, would anyone hear her? Would anyone even come out of their house to protect her? Probably not.

She must not panic. Act natural and get out of there fast, that's what she should do. Walk faster. Quit getting distracted. Quit wasting time looking back. Just get out of there.

With her heart pounding wildly in her chest, she considered her options, not that there were many. She couldn't backtrack. Her car was already too far. Best to reach the corner of South Anchor—a busier street—where there would be at least some random traffic. And from there on, it was just a couple of short blocks to the park, which was always crowded. Unless the person came right out and attacked her, she would make it. Meantime, she should just keep on walking.

Pretending to mind her own business, she glanced sideways, nonchalantly as she hurried on, watching from the corner of her eye how the individual moved sleekly from tree to tree, following her, keeping up with her. Still hiding.

Margo's hands clenched and unclenched. Anger, fear, and indignation, all welled up in her chest. I refuse to panic, she told herself. I'm not going to allow this person to terrorize me. I should take care of this right now. What if I confronted him? Find out what he wants?

She almost turned around to face her stalker. But no. That would be stupid. The individual could have a gun, or a wire, or a knife, or be so big that he could easily overpower her. She, herself had a gun in her purse—and she finally thought of taking it out—but causing a shootout could result in her or someone else being wounded or killed. So, she slipped the gun into her pocket and carefully held on to it. At least, if push came to shove, she could defend herself. In the meantime, the only thing to do was to keep going, continue on to Independence Park, where the Opera House, the Police Station, and St. Quintian's Church, all converged and stayed busy.

Ignoring her aching feet, Margo picked up the pace. She knew only one person with reddish hair, tall enough to be a man. The young intern at the Half Moon Gazette. But she hated the thought of suspecting Saffron's assistant. Why would Jimmy Falgout be in this part of town? And why would he be following her anyway? It made no sense. Surely it had to be someone else.

She was still a block and a half from the South Anchor Street intersection, and already she was getting tired. She glanced quickly to her left and noticed that the shadow had moved again. A black cat ran across the street, and she shivered with foreboding, and then all the dogs in the neighborhood began barking, breaking with a ruckus the eerie silence. Still, nobody came to their door. Still, she was all alone on this empty street. And realizing that the individual was closing the distance between them, she broke into a run.

On her side of town, all the houses and all the yards were properly maintained. But on this street, chaos prevailed. And she usually loved it. But today, that meant that every untrimmed bush, every run-down garden shed, every derelict car, could provide a potential hiding place for someone following her. And she was in the open air, a moving target in an empty street. She tried to run faster, but the high heels on her shoes kept getting stuck in the cracks in the pavement, and in the clumps of weeds that grew in them. She took quick shallow breaths and struggled on. Almost there.

At the end of the block, Margo darted across South Anchor without stopping to look either way and jumped back quickly when a small sports car zoomed by in a rush and almost ran her over. Once it vanished around the curb, Margo kept on running.

She reached the crooked house on the corner. Painted a barn red, every single door and window frame was crooked. It was a lovely house with no concept of parallel lines. Window boxes in every lopsided window were always full of colorful, well cared for flowers, and always a pair or two of multicolor rubber gardening boots by the door. Sometimes, toys were strewn about on the well-cut lawn.

On impulse, and almost too tired to keep on running, Margo decided to knock on the door. She had often seen a friendly woman gardening around the house. They had waved at each other several times. Maybe she was home. Maybe she would help. She opened the little wrought-iron gate and hurried up the walkway panting, struggling to catch her breath.

She took the front steps two at a time and rang the doorbell with a shaking hand. While she waited and counted to ten, she rummaged in her purse for the cellphone. Where was it? Where was it? Quivering with frustration, she rang the doorbell again, but when she saw the shadow make another move, she gave up. She sprinted back down the steps, hating herself for having wasted so much time and she took off running again.

Little more than two short blocks to go. It seemed like she was going to make it—if she didn't die of exhaustion. She quickly looked behind her. She was still being followed. There he was, slinking between tree trunks and bushes, the coward, carefully keeping out of sight. At least she hadn't been shot at. Small thanks for that. Maybe he didn't have a gun after all. And if he was planning to kidnap her, or to garrote her, he was about to miss his chance, because she was almost in the clear. Margo gulped hard and ran faster, clutching her purse with one hand, keeping the gun safe with the other, wishing she was wearing tennies. Less than a half block now.

As she passed the rambling house with the swampy swimming pool at the end of that street, she hesitated. Shouldn't she try and find out if it was really Jimmy Falgout who was following her—while she had the chance? Bounded by flagstones, the pool behind the house had long been abandoned to nature. Its water green with algae, bubbling like a stinky brew, was probably teeming with frogs, water snakes, and turtles. Enormous half barrels around it were crowded with overgrown red geraniums that seemed to enjoy the miasma rising from the fetid waters of the pool.

It was the ideal place for hiding. The yard was not fenced in, and the neglected garden was full of bushy azaleas that could easily camouflage her. She could duck behind one of them, and then wait for him to go by, and maybe see his face. But what if something went wrong, and there was nobody home, and nobody came out to help her? What would she do then?

She quickly discarded the idea and kept on running. At long last, trembling with exhaustion, she reached Jamaica—the busy road that circled Independence Park. She almost wanted to cry with relief. The street was full of people walking by cheerfully, as usual, pushing strollers or pulling dogs on leashes, and she knew she was safe. She wiped the sweat off her brow and around her eyes and willed her heart to slow down. She filled her lungs with the clean warm air redolent of the aroma of the flowering honeysuckle bushes she was standing by. She was going to have to call Brooks to come and get her car because she was never going to walk down that street again.

The traffic was heavy on Jamaica, and she waited impatiently while all the cars came and went, taking quick looks behind her back, until the walking light turned green. She was right behind the Opera House, by its famously inconspicuous back door entrance. A few benches, a Magnolia tree that was always shedding its leaves, and a small newspaper stand on the corner of the walkway. This was where the musicians gathered for their rehearsal breaks. They were an extravagant lot, the members of the orchestra. And all they ever talked about was music. The men tended to dress like French bohémiens, the jacquard vest, the rolled-up sleeves, the beret—always the beret—and pencil-thin *moustaches*. The girls smoked, with long, slender filters holding up their cigarettes. All *Très Cliché*.

A small group of musicians had brought their instruments outside and were playing Baroque. A girl with stiletto heels and tight black dress was drinking something out of a silver flagon, and some of them recognized Margo from singing in the Opera choir and waved at her. Margo, feeling safe at last, happily waved back. She quickly turned around in the direction that she had come from, and saw nothing but an empty street. But she had to wonder. The stranger would have had plenty of time to catch up with her and hurt her—had he wished to do so—yet he hadn't. Anyway, she gratefully remembered to send a prayer of thanks to St. Nicholas Owen, the overworked patron saint of narrow escapes, who was fast becoming her favorite saint and hurried through the park.

She gazed at the long line of customers at the Cajun Dog stand with regret. She was ravenous, but she had no time to stop. Once upon a time, the young man who worked the stand had been sweet on her friend Jenny. Jenny had never paid for her hot dogs or her sodas, and she and the young man had always giggled a lot and looked into each other's eyes with longing. She wondered if he had moved on since Jenny's death. He noticed Margo walking by and waved. Margo sighed. Gosh, how she missed Jenny.

The park—as usual—was full of lovers, sitting on benches, kissing, or strolling while holding hands. She thought for a second of Pierre, her faraway boyfriend—who never had any idea of the dangers she kept getting herself into—and thought about the pointlessness of a long-distance relationship, which was like no relationship at all. There was no sense in planning a future together. Pierre had a good job at an Engineering firm in Lafayette, and he was working on another Master's Degree. He wasn't going to leave that, or his ancestral plantation home. She had her own life here in Half Moon Bay, and couldn't envision living anywhere else. But Margo shook off her wistful mood and hurried on.

She said hello to the marble lion in front of the Opera House, skirted the musical fountain where children were always playing with the water, and walked up the steps of the City Hall. She turned right and entered the freezing-cold environment of the Police Station, that tiny station that was part of the elegant new City Hall building. She waved to Maurice, sitting at the front desk taking his job so seriously, and asked him to buzz her in.

People at the station had given up a long time ago trying to teach Margo correct procedure. It all slipped off her back like so many droplets of water. Maurice grinned, shrugged, and said go ahead. She knocked on Sheriff Stark's door and entered without waiting for an answer.

"I'm starving, Sam. How about some lunch? I have some stuff to tell you."

"Can't it wait? I was just about to leave. We found out where old Snail was staying, and I would like to check it out before I sit down to eat."

"Oh, okay. We can talk on the way there."

"You're not coming, Margo."

"Please let me come. You know you never regret taking me with you. Besides, someone followed me to the park today. Don't you want me to tell you all about that?"

"All right, but you stay out of my way," Sam said, wagging an angry finger. "And no talking to the perps. I'll be the one asking the questions this time."

"Got it. Has the autopsy report arrived yet?" Margo asked as they headed for the police car.

"Yes. The old man was dead when the pig tore his arm off."

"Oh, good. That was really bothering me. Anything else?"

"Yes. He was killed with some sort of knife. Doc hasn't figured it out yet. He says it's different from the knives he's familiar with. The hilt mark is very distinctive. He'll let me know when he's found a match."

"So where are we going?" she asked as they drove through the back streets of Half Moon Bay avoiding the traffic, skirting first the Golf Course and then the Marina.

"To the *Quai des Pêcheurs*."

"What's that?"

"That's the Fisherman's Wharf. He was staying at a flea-bag motel out there."

Sam took a sharp right down the incline to where the anglers kept their boats and the spacious market where they sold their catch. At the end of the main street, overlooking the tiny enclave that harbored the fishing boats, they found the motel. It was a dirty, three-story, peeling, and neglected edifice that had seen much better days. Ironically, a faded wooden sign—hanging from rusty, screeching hinges—announced it as the Best Stop Holiday Motel. Margo shivered with disgust but followed Sam in through the slimy front door.

Chapter 7

The Best Stop Holiday Motel

THE OWNER, A SHORT, OVERWEIGHT, dark-skinned Cajun woman with wiry white hair and chatty attitude, wiped her hands on her dirty apron and approached them with a friendly smile.

"*Bonjour*, y'all must be Officer Sam and um, hello." She looked at them expectantly, waiting to be introduced.

"Bonjour, Madame. Thank you for seeing us. This is my friend Margo Fontaine. She's helping me investigate the murder down by the beach."

"Ah, *oui* oui. *Pauvre vieux salaud.* Please come with me to ze kitchen. My food is going to burn."

Sam and Margo followed Madame through a warren of dusty hallways and dark, shady corners where the paint was peeling, and the wallpaper hung in moldy strips. Dimly lit and dank, and almost claustrophobic, the smell of old dust and mildew was soon replaced by one of spices and food aromas, and Margo remembered that she was very hungry.

The kitchen was enormous, open, with wall to wall opaque windows that let in a cascade of cheerful light into one of those old-fashioned kitchens that had once served as day rooms as well. Many pots of foods bubbled on the stove at once, and steam rose from them bringing the spicy smells to them by cascades. Madame ran to her pots and began a round of vigorous stirring. A large serving plate full of piping hot boudin sat next to a pot of white rice, next to a stacked pile of dishes and silverware. Margo salivated.

Faded old posters of local festivals alternated with those of Mardi Gras parades long gone, and a neon sign for crawfish boudin by the door blinked on and off. A couple of guys, sprawled lazily on a grimy yellow sofa watched football on an ancient black and white cathode ray tube television set. The table in front of them was full of empty beer bottles. A mangy dog Madame kept calling Marcel sauntered up to them and showed a minimum of interest by wagging his scrawny tail. He briefly scratched himself here and there, and then went back to where the guys were watching TV, to the tiny piece of grimy rug at their feet.

"Don't worry," Madame said. "*Pas de fleas*. Pas de fleas. He just likes to scratch himself, zat Marcel."

Finally done with her stirring, Madame wiped her hands on her apron again and pointed to the wooden table and benches by the stove and told them to come sit, and placed a freezing-cold, frosted bottle of beer in front of Sam. When she saw Margo decline with a gesture, she poured her some coffee from the percolator bubbling on the stove.

"He was scruffy, *mais* he was a nice man. Polite. Paid in advance. Liked my cooking. Don't know what else to tell you, *sha*. He was quiet. Some guys try to smuggle in girls, mais he didn't. Then he just never came back. I figured he had gotten in some kind of trouble because he paid for two weeks mais he was gone in five days."

"Would it be okay to see his room, Madame?" Sam asked very politely. He had a way with old ladies. He had a way with the young ones as well. None of them ever told him no.

"*Mais oui*, of course. I haven't touched anything, seeing as how he still had days left." She gave the boiling pots one vigorous stir each, wiped her hands on the apron again, and waved at them to follow her to the back of the house where a narrow stairwell led to the second, and then the third floor.

The stairs that had once been carpeted were now just covered by the remnants of rotting fabric. Madame climbed the steps slowly, with little grunts, and Sam and Margo followed in silence. The stairwell wall was covered by some kind of wood paneling that in spite of the neglect was still intact and shiny. While Sam and Madame chatted about inconsequential things on the landing, Margo looked up and admired the ornate Victorian chandelier at the top of the stairs. Even with missing light bulbs—and she could really not fathom how Madame would be able to reach the high ceiling to change the light bulbs, the chandelier was magnificent. With its delicate rope tubing and its curling tendrils, it bespoke of prosperous times long gone.

The room of the pauvre vieux salaud—as Madame had called him—must have once been regal and imposing, but was, like the rest of the house, quite run down. She sat down cautiously on a threadbare French Provincial armchair next to a grubby coffee table and watched Sam examine the room looking for clues. He went through the clothes in the armoire, barely a scant pair of pants and a couple of shirts, and said, there's nothing here. In a drawer, he found the bus ticket with a return date for a couple of days later and held it up for all to see.

"He obviously didn't expect to stay in town very long," Sam said. "Did he meet up with anyone?"

"I don't think so. Pepe ze taxi driver came and got him a few times, and then brought him back. Mais nobody came to visit him."

"Where can I find this Pepe?"

"Downstairs, drinking beer in front of ze football as usual."

Indolently, Margo picked up the pile of magazines on the coffee table and looked at them. Other than a couple of dated entertainment magazines that had obviously belonged to Madame, there was one newspaper, brittle with age. Margo looked around and observed that nobody had noticed the newspaper. She wouldn't have paid any attention to it either had she not seen the grainy photograph of a ship in a bottle on the front page under the masthead. As swift as the wind, the newspaper vanished into Margo's oversized purse. Then she sat back in the chair and pretended to mind her own business while Sam finished looking around.

Downstairs, back in the kitchen, Pepe explained.

"I drove him to the Half Moon Bay Public Library. You know, the new building by the high school." Sam nodded. "I went back for him in the afternoon. He didn't say nothing. Then, another day, he wanted to see the Maritime Museum, where they have all those old ships and stuff. I went in with him at that time. Neat place. Never been before. He went upstairs with the officer dressed in white uniform, and he was gone a while. I didn't go with them on account of my knees. The stairs, you know. Instead, I looked around. Very interesting. He came back down after a while, and we drove back here."

"Did he say anything?" Sam asked.

"Nope. He wasn't much of a talker." Pepe shrugged, uninterested. "But he paid in cash. He paid well."

"Was that it?" Margo could tell that Sam was getting frustrated. Pepe wasn't one to volunteer information. It had to be dragged out of him.

"Actually no. I took him to the beach."

"What beach?"

"The one that's real hard to get to? The one behind Old Town? I asked him what he wanted to do way out there by himself, but he just grumbled and told me to mind my own business."

"Did he ask you to go back for him?"

"Nope. He said he had his plans. And how are you getting back to the motel? I asked."

"And what did he say?"

"That he would call someone. But how? You don't have a cell phone. That's what I told him. And I mentioned how it was a very long walk for a very old man all the way to the Parrot Joe Shack."

"Why the Parrot Joe?" Sam asked impatiently.

"Because out there it's the only building with a phone, but he got angry and told me to just leave him alone and go away. So, I did. Never saw him again."

"If you remember anything else, will you call me?" asked Sam handing Pepe a business card. But Pepe shooed his hand away.

"I'm not going to remember nothing else," he said. "But I will tell you this. He was excited. He could barely sit still, and his eyes were real shiny like. He looked like he was mighty pleased with himself." And with that, Pepe picked up his bottle of beer and turned his attention back to the football game on the TV.

Chapter 8

The Article

MARGO COULD HARDLY WAIT to be alone. With Sam safely back at the police station, she hurried to the park and—more ravenous than ever—picked up a Cajun Dog and a soda, which she placed on an empty bench next to her. Then, she took the newspaper out of her purse and gently unfolded it in her lap.

Goldcrest Boy Wins Fourth proclaimed the headline in enormous letters over the masthead of the Daily States Vol. 37 No. 1, published in New Orleans, Louisiana, on Saturday, January 1st, 1916. Just about one hundred years earlier. Wow! It had only cost 2 cents.

The paper was divided into three well-delineated columns. The one on the left was an article about the war. "1916: Hundreds sink with the Persia, torpedoed and sunk by an enemy submarine; hundreds die." And the article on the right detailed the Goldcrest Boy win. She shrugged. What she was really interested in was the article in the middle. She took a big bite out of the hot dog and read.

FROM HAITI TO HALF MOON BAY

Judge Renard is a man of contradictions. Autocratic, yet modest, he's considered one of the richest men in Louisiana. And yet, he doesn't "condescend" to talk with newspapermen like so many self-important men do. He either talks with them or—if he doesn't have the time or the inclination—he does not.

Today, the Honorable Judge Renard has invited me to his home to show me his newest book entitled Pirate Treasures: From Haiti To Half Moon Bay. I'm sitting here in his fabulous ancestral library, admiring the thousands of books on the shelves, and the numerous paintings on the walls. I ask about one in particular: one that portrays a child holding a straw doll with its mouth sewn shut, but he reminds me politely that it's the book that he wants to discuss. Chastised, I sit down and begin to take notes.

"Your Honor, tell us about your book."

"It's actually the biography of the Dominican priest Monsignor Lafontaine, who hid my grandmother in his church in Saint-Marc when the slaves came for her during the last revolts of the end of the 18th century, and the narrative of their escape by sea from Cap-Saint-Marc, and their safe arrival to the shores of Louisiana.

"As you probably know, in April 1791, a massive black insurgency turned violently against the plantation system and racial slavery. With the cooperation of their former mulatto rivals, black slaves defeated the French army at the Battle of Vertières. During the following years, all the local white families were lynched one by one. Ours was the last one standing, saved from certain death only because of Monsignor Lafontaine's quick thinking."

"And how did your family manage to escape in the end?" I asked.

"You'll just have to read the book to find out, young man. This, I can tell you. My grandfather, a very reputable judge himself, was murdered, but his wife—my grandmother—and his only daughter—my mother— escaped, and moved back to Half Moon Bay."

"Moved back, Your Honor?"

"Yes. This is where my family originally came from."

"The title of the book includes the words Pirate Treasures. Would you care to give your readers an idea of what you mean?"

"Well yes, there were vast treasures, of course. And there were paintings, as, for example, the one behind me, the one you were curious about. They also managed to bring numerous journals that chronicled their life in Haiti before the revolt, back when it was still called Saint-Domingue."

"I am very intrigued by this painting, Your Honor, and I would be very grateful if you would allow me to take a photograph of it for our readership."

"In due time, young man. In due time. As you can see, it's the portrait of a young child holding a straw-filled doll, whose mouth has been sewn together with a crude piece of red twine. Come closer. You can see for yourself the name of the painting—at least we assume it's the name of the painting—above the lintel, in small letters."

"Your Honor, does it say The Golden Gift Of Silence?"

"Indeed, it does."

"What does it mean?"

"To tell you the truth, I have no idea. This painting has been hanging in this room since it was brought over by my grandmother from Saint-Domingue. She used to tell stories about those times, and often mentioned that there was some secret connected to it, but alas, by then her memories had faded and she didn't always make sense. Hence, the true meaning of those words has been lost to time."

"And the numbers?"

"Which ones, son?"

"Those, Your Honor. The ones under the words. You can barely see them."

"Well, well. I had never noticed them."

"They are 19.10493 and -72.69494. What could they mean?"

"Your guess is as good as mine. Maybe it's some secret cipher. As I said, there's no way to find out what they mean anymore."

"Do you talk about this family secret in your book?"

"Yes, indeed, what little is known about it. I also mention the story of this ship behind me."

"The one in the bottle, Your Honor?"

"Yes. It was brought over with the paintings and the journals."

"Does it have a history as well?"

"Apparently, it does. There was a legend. The ship was carved after a real-life brigantine, *La Concepción*. But something happened, and the name was changed to *La Decepción*."

"That is Spanish, is it not?"

"Yes. Decepción means Deception, as you might have guessed. At any rate, the legend said that whoever figured out how to unlock the secret of the carved ship would unlock the truth about the real one."

"Meaning what, Your Honor?"

"Your guess is as good as mine. Now back to the book."

"Just one more question, please, Your Honor."

"What is it?"

"The doll. Does the doll in the painting not look to you like a Haitian Voodoo doll?"

The judge turned around and faced the painting. As I stood next to him in the library, I saw in his eyes the sense of dread and disgust that he felt. He shuddered. He answered with a shaky voice. "It sure does, son. It sure does. I try never to look at it."

Margo took her portable magnifying glass out and stared at the faded, blurry pictures in the article. One of them was a ship in a bottle, indeed. But it was impossible to see it in any detail. The writer of the article had managed to photograph the painting as well. Even in black and white, even grainy and faded, it was a disconcerting sight. An evil-looking young girl stared at the painter with beady, unsmiling eyes. In her hand, hanging limp, a crude cloth doll with an x for each eye, and a wide mouth sewn shut. She shuddered and looked away.

The last picture was of a portly man, middle-aged, maybe a little older, wearing what seemed like a three-piece suit and a cravat. He had a beard and a moustache, and he stared at the camera with a disconcerted frown. He looked familiar. Even with the beard and the extra years on, even though the photograph was grainy and unclear, Margo could tell right away whom he reminded her of. The man in the picture was the spitting image of Jefferson Renard, Half Moon Bay's own backstabbing, greedy politician. Go figure.

Chapter 9

The Politician

JEFFERSON RENARD WAS SHORT IN STATURE but tall in pride. A receding hairline gave him a lot of grief, especially when he noticed Renata watching other men, younger, more handsome men. He took his glasses off and wiped off the sweat and the fingerprints that forever seemed to get smeared on them.

He had some quick thinking to do. He turned the blue envelope in his hands for the hundredth time without opening it. There was no way to avoid the séance anymore. Everyone knew he was going, and tongues would wag if he didn't show up. A big sigh escaped his chest. An accident? He could fake an accident and escape the commitment.

Jefferson Renard had inherited the family homestead, but not the ambition that should have come with it. He would have preferred to go to his camp down at Cypremort Point and spend a week or two fishing. He hated being a politician. But the terms of the will were clear enough. Follow the family tradition of service to the country through politics, or give up the mansion, the homestead, and all the financial security that came with it.

He was no fool. He knew well that Renata wouldn't go out with him if he was a simple man. Glamorous and exotic, Renata Savoie was not the kind of woman to spend quiet weekends in Cypremort Point, fishing. Nope. She wanted to date a politician. She had her own ambitions. And he was desperately in love with her, so the answer was simple. Hang on to his job, thus hanging on to Renata.

He adjusted his tie, splashed on some cologne, and headed for the fireplace over which hung Grand-père's portrait in full uniform of some kind—not that he cared—posing for a painter who had been talented enough to make him look taller, younger, and much more imposing than he had been in real life. He hated Grand-père and the preposterous terms of his will. Yet he couldn't help imitating the posture in the painting, subconsciously wishing he had the guts and the courage to bribe, confound, and steal, as his ancestor had done before him.

Well, it is what it is, he told himself. After all, it was nice to enjoy the fruit of the old goat's labors. Besides, there would be no Renata without them. Gosh, how he wished to marry her. He would even be willing to go to government functions and political commitments if he had her for a wife. What a joy it would be to show her off in front of those nasty, jaded politicians with their nasty, jaded wives.

The séance. That was what it always came back to. There would be no peace in Renata's heart without it. And he'd heard that Beatrice Saint-Clair was good—too good. She could make the ghosts tell tales. As long as the ghosts didn't talk about his family or the skeletons in his closet, he didn't care. Then suddenly, he wondered if there was a way to bribe Beatrice to say nothing about him. He pulled his cellphone out of his pocket and dialed a number he knew well by heart. Maybe the bribe wouldn't work. But there were other ways. There were so many other ways. Jefferson Renard smiled as he closed the door behind him. Oh yes. There were so many other ways.

Chapter 10

In the Public Library

MRS. T., MARGO'S FAVORITE LIBRARIAN EVER, came back from her search empty-handed. Mrs. T, comfortingly plump and always patient, wore her long, wavy hair in a loose bun on top of her head, held up with pins in the shape of butterflies that seemed to have nested in her hair.

Mrs. T. knew every single book in her little library: where it was located, what it was about. If she couldn't find it, it wasn't there.

"I'm sorry, sha, but we don't have Pirate Treasures: From Haiti To Half Moon Bay anymore."

"But you say you did have it at one time."

"Oh, yes. We used to have one copy. Funny thing. That book sat in the front stacks for years, taking up space, and nobody ever showed any interest in it. So I decided to move it to the back where the rest of the unread books are. I remember thinking that nobody seemed to care about pirate treasures anymore. Anyway, then, two weeks ago, two different people asked for it."

"And what happened?"

"The first time was on my day off. Alma didn't know I had moved it, so she told the man that she couldn't find it."

"And it was a man for sure?"

"That's what Alma said."

"And the second time?"

"I was here then. I went to the back and brought him the book. He sat at the table by the window and read it for a while. Then, I had to go to the bathroom for a few minutes, and by the time I returned, he was gone, book and all."

"Wasn't there anyone else working that day?"

"In a teeny tiny library like this one? No. It's just Alma and me. Occasionally—for the busy season—we get a volunteer or two, but it's August. People are back at school and work, and we hardly have anyone come in. There has never been a need for more people."

"So, he just walked out with it? I guess that without a library card, he wouldn't have been able to borrow it."

"No, he wouldn't. There are rules to get a library card. You need an ID, and you need to be local, which you have to prove by showing a bill in your name with your local address."

"So, if he really, really, needed the book, he had no other choice than to walk out with it."

"That's what I'm thinking."

"Did he ask any questions when he first came in?"

"Yes. We chatted for a while. I sat down at the table with him, and we talked about Louisiana coastal life and pirates, and he was particularly interested in the ship in the bottle that's in one of the photographs in the book. We looked at it, and we talked about it."

"What specifically did he want to know? Do you remember?"

"I sure do. He wanted to know if anyone had ever cracked the code. I had to tell him that I had no idea what code he was talking about."

"Did he explain himself?"

"Yes. Apparently, if you do something to the ship model—the one in the bottle—it discloses how to decipher the secret of the painting."

"Sounds a bit farfetched."

"It does. I confess that I laughed at him. Not unkindly, you know, just, well, he sounded so childish. But he laughed too and said he was just curious."

"What if it actually uncovers hidden troves and secrets from Haiti's past?" Margo asked wistfully. "I wonder if anyone has tried."

Mrs. T. laughed and patted her arm. "To what? To tinker with the ship? But how? It's in the judge's house, somewhere."

"But imagine, Mrs. T., a family legend of a fantastic treasure trove of artifacts and gold, smuggled out of Saint-Domingue and brought to the United States around the year 1800. Imagine that the treasure is now lost and that the clues to finding it are in that painting on the wall in the Judge's house, but its secret has been lost in time, and now nobody understands the clues the original owners left behind."

"You have a fertile imagination, my dear."

"Yes, but, can you imagine the family, escaping from the former slaves hunting them down, hiding by day, traveling by night, through ravines and across rivers, doing their best to avoid the snakes and other deadly wild creatures, carrying untold treasures on their backs through an unsafe land, and finally reaching their ship anchored at the bay, where they are rowed to safety? And now they still must travel far on unsafe waters, risking an attack by pirates, or going down in a storm. Always carrying their secrets, and their treasures, and finally reaching the Louisiana coast. And then they lose their treasure? How cruel is that?"

"But you don't know if the treasure was lost."

"True. We don't even know if there was a treasure, to begin with."

"Anyway, I don't see his family allowing a stranger to go into their home to nosy about in their past. But surely you don't believe in all this as well?"

"Oh, I don't know. Someone seems to have been murdered for a ship in a bottle, and that's too much of a coincidence."

"Are you talking about the murder out on the sand dune?"

"Yes. An old man stabbed to death. Do you remember what this man looked like by chance, the one who ran off with the book?"

"I sure do. He was tall, skinny, old, and bald. Not much to look at."

Margo nodded. "Sounds like the same man. Did he say anything else?"

"Now that you mention it, yes. There are numerous photographs in the book. We looked at them. They were grainy and of very bad quality. The writer of the book included a few photographs of Maritime paintings, all of them apparently showing the same ship. Were they really the same ship? I can't tell you. I'm no expert. They did have different names. Some of them were named Concepción, some Decepción."

"Same ship, different name?"

"I don't know. It sounds to me like one of those crazy conspiracy theories. Although, now that we're talking about it, I seem to remember a presentation on sunken treasures."

"When was that?" Margo sat forward, her eyes big with expectation.

"It must have been at least a year ago."

"Did they mention the Concepción and the Decepción?"

"I wouldn't know, my dear. I didn't attend. Not my cup of tea, you see."

"So, you wouldn't know who gave the presentation either, would you?"

"Sorry, no. I don't. But I did see the poster advertising the lecture. And there was a photograph of the professor giving it. I'll never forget it because he was wearing the fanciest bow tie. I didn't think men wore those anymore."

"And how about the famous painting about the little girl and the cloth doll? Was there a photograph of it in the book as well?"

"There sure was. Even in a grainy photograph, that Voodoo doll was as ugly as sin."

"And did you get the feeling that there was anything sinister about the doll, with its mouth sewn shut?"

"Oh, I'm not so sure. To me, it seemed more like a warning. I believe that the doll tells us that a secret must be kept. That's all. It could be a completely harmless secret too, for all we know."

"Maybe. Maybe not."

Margo sent Sam Stark a text informing him about the stolen book, and everything Mrs. T had told her. So far, Sam seemed almost reluctant to proceed with this investigation. "We find ourselves at a dead-end," he told her and suggested that she let this one go. Frustrated, on her way out, she couldn't help having the feeling that there was a lot more to this story than Sam kept saying, so she decided that—if he was not going to do anything about it—she would have to. Someone had to.

Chapter 11

Father Armand Looks to the Past

FATHER ARMAND CLOSED FIRMLY THE DOOR to his office and turned the key in the lock. He welcomed the absolute silence, but the disquiet in his soul remained. He shook his head, forlorn.

He'd heard about the dead man on the beach. It was heartbreaking. An old man murdered, passed away alone—all alone—on a hot day, under the cruel heat of the August sun, no last rites, no prayers, no ministrations, nobody to hold his hand as he lay there dying. Father Armand's throat tightened, and he wiped away the moisture around his eyes.

Then, he reflected on the old man's connection to the ship in the bottle. This couldn't be a coincidence. Like most old-timers, he'd heard rumors about a brigantine from Saint-Domingue, abandoned and rotting around the South Louisiana coastline somewhere, that—like the Flying Dutchman—appeared to treasure seekers out of the fog at random, only to disappear again. He rubbed his chin. He remembered reading about Monsignor Lafontaine, that self-righteous, cruel scourge of the innocent. Hadn't he arrived at Half Moon Bay on that same ship? Something told him that there was a connection. But what?

He paced for a few minutes, watching his feet pensively as they moved the cloth of his soutane. He was going to have to talk to Margo Fontaine, Half Moon Bay's own private investigator. This was precisely the type of mystery that would fascinate her. Let's face it. Albeit being a nosy and sometimes quite annoying young woman, Margo was good at solving cases that baffled everyone else. And her stubbornness and persistence were a good catalyst for Sam—the local sheriff—who was the last great procrastinator. Otherwise, no murder would ever get solved around here. Father Armand shrugged. Sam liked being the Small-Town Sheriff, taking care of *les petites choses,* the little stuff. He was no mighty murder investigator. And who could blame him? How much joy could there be in looking into the often-sordid lives of murderers and their victims?

Now, where was that book? He looked at the wall lined with endless shelves of books across from his desk. He was sure he'd seen it somewhere. Ah! There it was: Monsignor Lafontaine's autobiography. Monsignor Lafontaine, that arrogant, tyrannical, cruel, so-called man of God. Oh, how he hoped that Monsignor was burning in the pits of hell. It gave him the shudders to even touch the book, but he had to be sure.

Father Armand poured himself two fingerfuls of Glenfiddich Single Malt Scotch, and with the whisky in one hand, he pulled the moldering leather tome from the shelf and sat down in an armchair by the window. Then, he took one big gulp of the whisky and began to read.

Saint-Domingue, 23 August 1791

An unwelcome sound disturbed my sleep, and I stirred. Bastien—my faithful dog—was barking loud enough to wake the dead. I yelled out to him to quieten down already and managed to doze off again. But a few minutes later, the fidgety beast started up again, even more insistently. He hustled back and forth between the bed and the window, restless, agitated, trying to tell me something.

I jumped out of my bed and ran to the open windows. *Qui va là?* I asked of the darkness on hearing suspicious noises in the shrubbery. A deep, angry voice like thunder answered me: *Ç'est la mort.* It is death! Completely awake now, I noticed the hundreds of torches with their tiny lights dancing in the gloom. This must be then, the slave rebellion everyone was talking about.

Pistol shots echoed in the night, coming from afar, and what horrible sounds! At first, a low murmur, almost a growl, that grew louder and more menacing as a boundless crowd of angry slaves got closer and closer to the church and the *grand'case*—my house. And before I had time to do much thinking, we were surrounded. I watched them mesmerized, by the moonlight, and by the light of their torches. Hundreds and hundreds of them, milling, shoving and pushing each other, shooting their stolen pistols wantonly into the air, excited, drunk with madness and with pilfered rum.

Suddenly, I was torn by indecision. Not every night does one wake up to an unexpected insurrection. Like everyone else, I had heard of the lynchings, the rapes, the hangings. But I never thought they would dare attack their own priest in his own home.

Meantime, Bastien whimpered next to me, his bark all exhausted. What to do? Oh, what to do? But when I heard the front doors being beaten with violence with something big and powerful, and the rhythmic litany of encouraging screams that accompanied the pulsating pounding of the massive front doors, I knew I had to do something. It was just a matter of time before they tore it down.

I ran to get my own pistols. First, I was going to shoot Bastien rather than allow him to fall into cruel hands. Then, if I had to die, at least I would do so defending myself, and hopefully, I would have a chance to send some of these animals to hell before they took me down.

Sadly, I found my pistols unloaded, so I had no choice but to escape like a coward. And bidding my dog Bastien to follow me, choking on the smell of gunpowder coming in through the open windows, I pulled the lever to the secret tunnel behind the fireplace, and the dog and I escaped into safety, right as I heard that they had torn down the front doors to my house. And in the blink of an eye, my life changed.

5 September, I think

My eyes hurt. I've been writing by the light of one slender candle, my nose stuck to the page. Who knows how long I'll be forced to stay in hiding? What will I do when my candles and my food supplies run out? Domine Miserere! It's been about three weeks already.

I can tell when daylight breaks because of the narrow slits in the paneling behind the altar. Like small colored pinpricks that reflect the multicolored glass in the rosette window across from it, they suddenly come alive with the shine of the morning light, and I know I can make another notch on the wall, like a prisoner in a dank cell. Thus, I count my days—my lonely days.

This is my cue to enter the sanctuary while the world still sleeps, and get down on my knees and beg God to send an army of dragoons to skin these beasts alive and let me be free. But every time I set foot in the church, I wonder if this is going to be the day that they find me out and slit my throat.

God's house has been desecrated. Everything that had any value is now gone: the statues and the silver, and everything that could be carried, stolen. The pews, those beautifully carved, well-made wooden benches. And the statues of the saints. Everything gone.

21 September

My faithful Bastien isn't happy. We can't go for walks like we used to, but occasionally—despite the danger of being discovered and killed— we step out of the shadows of the underground rooms to spend a short while in the woods behind the church.

For the most part, the insurgents seem to be gone. I don't hear screams or shots anymore. Having sacked this part of town down to its foundations and murdered all the white folks who lived in it, they must have moved on to more profitable areas.

28 September

The stench of death wafts this way, carried by the wind. Not even hiding under the church am I completely free of the stink. Today, hoping to discover what all's going on, Bastien and I decided to venture further out than usual.

What we discovered goes beyond any horror I had imagined. The insurgents have turned death into a new art. We came to a clearing where they had piled the decomposing bodies of their victims one on top of the other and made walls of flesh with them. We saw dead Frenchmen hanging from the trees around us like ripe, rotting fruit. Fires from the burning plantations and the fields of crops fill the distant horizon with smoke. The reek, the bugs, and the decomposition, they don't seem to deter them. Like a plague, the rebels have destroyed everything in their path.

Tonight, I was walking with Bastien among the trees when I heard the rustle of fabric in the bushes and the unexpected sound of voices coming closer. Domine Miserere! I became terrified. Bastien—who has learned to be as quiet as a dead dog—threw himself down on the ground and played possum, and I froze in panic.

The strangers were carrying lanterns kept at low fire, which helped me follow their progress among the trees and bushes as they approached us. I was too indecisive and remained frozen in my spot. I waited. By the time I realized that they were not the enemy, they were right in front of me. If these had been the insurgents, I would long be dead.

30 September

There are five of them: the wife of the local judge—not a young woman anymore—her two slaves: man, and wife, and a mulatto. Then, there's the judge's young daughter. She's with child. Madame, the judge's wife, told me in confidence that the mulatto forced himself upon her and left her pregnant. And now, he refuses to let her go.

The three don't talk to one another. It's rather awkward. The young woman hates the mulatto, and I can't say that I blame her. The older woman refuses to look her daughter in the eyes. She too hates the mulatto, I think. And the mulatto just sits stony-faced staring at the walls with determination, his enormous hands tightly clenched. I can't tell whether it's love or greed that keeps him vigilant of the young woman, but he will not leave her side. It's an ugly business.

5 October

They should be here to rescue us any day now. The judge's wife sent word to her cousin in Gonaïves that they were in peril, and she calculates that it's a matter of days, if not hours, before they get to us. Gratefully, Bastien and I have been invited to go to Louisiana with them, not only because I'm a man of the cloth, but because they've found sanctuary in my tunnels. It's a question of gratefulness.

As food has dwindled, her slaves have ventured out into the darkness to replenish such things as clean water and foodstuffs.

The first few days, I was terribly worried that those two would give away our hiding spot, but Domine Miserere, I have seen the devotion with which they treat their mistress and her daughter, and I feel safe now among them. They too are coming with us, I believe.

6 October

Sitting by the flickering candlelight, finishing off my stash of wine and fine spirits—rather than leave it behind—Madame and I share our stories. The daughter usually sits morosely to one side, while the mulatto watches over her like a hungry wolf. The slaves stay in their corner, modestly aware of their status, even though the ancien régime has fallen, and this revolution was fought to liberate them from their slavery.

Madame's story is very similar to mine. Like me, she was surprised by the uprising of the slaves. "My acquaintances were being kidnapped, raped, or killed with their whole families," she said, "but my husband hesitated, so instead of escaping while we still could, we stayed on. He insisted we should all remain calm. The soldiers would come and rescue us. Surely, we would be safe until then. Surely we were too powerful to fall."

But fall they did. They broke into Madame's house in the middle of the night. With a trace of remembered panic in her eyes, she told me how she had barely enough time to hide behind her bed, and there, shivering with anxiety, she waited to be discovered. Meantime, like an angry beehive, the malcontents buzzed about her private rooms, opening drawers and armoires, chortling with elation when they found something they liked, and encouraging each other to leave nothing behind, to steal it all.

As she crouched behind the bed, she heard that her husband the judge had been shot. At least he went fast. But her sons, they pursued them across the sugarcane fields, hunting them down like rabbits, and they cut their throats. They told this with glee, and several of them laughed. But they never mentioned the daughter, and she realized that they hadn't found her. It seemed like she had managed to escape.

Later, with the insurgents gone, Madame roamed her devastated plantation home looking for survivors. She found the daughter in the back kitchens with the mulatto that had ravaged her, and with her slaves Aimée and Barthol, who had remained faithful. It had been the mulatto that had kept them safe from his comrades.

In the end, together with her slaves Aimée and Barthol, with her poor dear daughter, and with that Jacques Boukeman—the man who had defiled her—Madame managed to escape into the darkness, and to safety.

"And that's how we ended up in your church, Monsignor," she said. "As we escaped, I tore off my pearls and gave them to Barthol's brother. 'Take word to my cousin in Gonaïves to come and rescue me. You know the way,' I told him. I had no idea that you were still alive, but Monsignor, my family built your church, and I knew exactly where the entrances were to your secret tunnels. In my request, I let my cousin know that we were going to be here as it was the only place nobody would find us in. And so, here we are."

Father Armand took another gulp of the Glenfiddich. Monsignor Lafontaine had been a notoriously cruel man known for his excesses in his parish of Saint-Marc. Quick with the whip and the chains, he never had any compassion for the blacks that worked the church's coffee, sugarcane, and spice plantations. Father Armand had read the priest's *Life Of A Christian Man Among The Beasts of Cap-Saint-Marc* as an assignment way back in seminary, and still remembered the nausea and disgust that had made him end up throwing the book in the fire. He had failed that school assignment but felt like he had saved his soul. And here he was, all these years later, reading about him again.

8 October

Bastien raised his head and growled. I carefully opened the door a crack and peered out into the night. A whistle and a swaying lantern at low light signaled that we were finally being rescued. We hurried to the clearing, where a detachment of dragoons stood at the gates of the cemetery, waiting armed to the teeth. As we ran toward them, I abandoned myself to joy and gave thanks to God. We quickly summed up the events of the last few weeks to our rescuers who—horrified at the loss of so many good citizens who had been massacred without pity—promised to protect us, swearing that they would never allow anything to happen to us.

Avoiding the main trails, we kept to the darkest, most rugged parts of the wooded area on our way down to the coast. I often tripped over my habit, the hem of which was by now torn, soiled with mud, and with the green algae of shallow brooks. Mademoiselle, the judge's daughter also complained. Numerous times she ran into a quiet spot to throw up what little food she managed to consume. And the mulatto, this Jacques Boukeman, would scurry after her, and hold her while she heaved. Unpleasant man. I wish we had left him behind.

9 October

I can see the square-rigged brigantine Concepción already. Beautiful in the morning light, sails at half-mast, and barely a short distance from shore. The dragoons will accompany us to the boat that will row us to the ship, and then turn back and continue to fight the insurgents. The distance is short, but the danger is enormous.

Last night nobody slept. We sat quietly waiting for the first light. We didn't dare light a fire, so we sat, shivering, cold, wet, and hungry. At least the rain kept the mosquitos away.

We were very uneasy. We sometimes saw, by the light of the moon, rogue bands of brigands rushing by on the main roads, hooting and hollering, drunk with revenge, celebrating the death and destruction they were leaving behind, and we remained silent, fearing that they would come to find us and put us to death despite the protection of our dragoons.

12 October

Arguments, fighting, and threats can constantly be heard from the Captain's cabin. Jacques Boukeman insists on sharing quarters with Mademoiselle, the judge's daughter. The Captain has refused. This is his ship, and he's a Catholic man and a man of honor, and he won't be allowing any sin to transpire on his guard. So, the mulatto sleeps outside Mademoiselle's cabin, rolled up in a ball, protecting the door. The sailors often kick him as he lies there, and then they laugh with self-satisfied glee.

In the meantime, the Quartermaster, who seems like an evil and untrustworthy man, has been following with dark eyes the Captain and his arguments with the mulatto. What he's thinking about is anyone's guess.

I say nothing, simply happy to be rescued with my dog Bastien. We keep out of everyone's way.

Madame's slaves stay out of sight too, well aware of their precarious position. I haven't seen them once since we set sail.

14 October

A brief storm has blown us slightly off track. We reached the limestone outcrop of Cayman Brac early this morning. Quite a sight as we sailed by. The white bluff rises steadily from the sea along the length of the island and almost seems to touch the perfectly blue sky. From the brigantine, it seems to be some sort of paradise. Small huts scattered on the stretch of sand, and tall palm trees that sway from side to side. We saw numerous dark-skinned people jumping up and down, waving to us. Perhaps not with glee, as some of the other passengers would like to think, but with menace.

To my surprise, a small boat was lowered onto the water, and Mademoiselle and her mulatto were thrown into it with a few barrels of beer and some dry food. 'I've had enough of you,' I heard the Captain bellow. 'Now you two can live here together in sin forever. And good riddance. May God have mercy on your souls.'

Madame, the judge's widow, threw herself at the Captain's feet and cried and begged, and Bastien my faithful dog barked and barked until a sailor threw a piece of driftwood at him. But the Captain refused to change his mind. As we set sail, I looked down at the translucent sea and at the pitiful boat bobbing so forlorn on its tranquil blue water. I wondered whatever would happen to those two among all the savages. I had wanted to be rid of that bully, Jacques Boukeman. But I do feel almost sorry for the girl.

Father Armand put his hand on the open pages. He needed to give Margo Fontaine a call. There was something he had to show her at St. Adelelmus, out beyond the Fisherman's Wharf. It might have some bearing on her investigation, even if it couldn't tell her who killed the old man.

There was a knock at the door. Father Armand looked up from the book, annoyed at being interrupted, and drank up the last of the Glenfiddich before answering the door.

Chapter 12

Renata

RENATA PULLED ON HER FLOOR-LENGTH lace nightgown and ran. The house was mired in foggy darkness, and the silence was hollow, absolute. Disoriented, she ran through the endless corridors barefoot, unsure of where she was, hesitating at the end of every hallway. Finally, exhausted, she stopped to lean against a wall and catch her breath.

She closed her eyes and listened. The house was as cold and silent as a mausoleum. She must have left him behind. Renata put a hand on her wildly beating heart and begged it to slow down. Her breathing quietened down some, and the murkiness in her brain lifted. She stuck her head out from behind a corner and ventured a peek.

What had happened? What was she doing here? She gasped, terrified. She wasn't sure. She clung to her nightgown with shaking hands. All she remembered was hearing the violent banging of a large echoing front door being opened and then slammed shut, and knowing that a man she was afraid of was home.

The dogs barked and broke the ominous silence. Then, one of them yelped painfully. The man must have kicked it. This man, this dangerous man that she was running from, he liked to kick the dogs. His boots had painfully sharp tips, too. Somehow, she knew that, and she shivered with dread. Then, she heard the heavy footsteps of the rugged boots on the stairs, echoing in the dead silence, and then on the landing, getting louder as they got closer.

With a struggle, Renata fought the desire to give up and throw herself on the floor. She was too tired to keep going. She was almost too tired to care. She sobbed to herself softly. Her bare feet were bruised and bleeding, and they hurt. But how could she give up?

With a groan, she willed herself to move. She had to keep going. She had to get away from him. She knew he wouldn't let her live if he caught her, and she didn't want to die.

She straightened her back and grabbed her nightgown with determination. She stepped out from behind the armoire and turned toward the sound of the approaching footsteps. She was going to have to hurry. But it was too late already. There he was, barely a few yards away, just turning the corner. She inhaled sharply, surprised. She had wasted too many precious moments making her decision, and now he had caught up with her. Their eyes met for a brief second, and she saw him grin. He had found her.

Renata took off—propelled by the sudden panic—fear giving her strength to keep on running. But he had long steps, long legs, and while she scrambled to get away, he pursued her slowly, relentlessly, with a maniacal chuckle, sure to catch up with her eventually. Renata knew she was doomed. But still, she kept going.

She ran blindly through the empty house and its endless corridors, banging into walls, stubbing her toes on loose floor planks, at times tripping on the hem of her long nightgown. But no matter how fast she went, the echoing footsteps of the heavy boots were never too far.

Just when she was about to give up and throw herself at the man's mercy, she felt a glimmer of hope. She stopped. Her hand went to her throat, and she felt nervously the throbbing of the veins. This wasn't another dead-end corridor, she told herself. She recognized the place. She knew somehow that she had been in there before. It was the library. Had to be. Those thick, heavily carved wooden doors, they could only belong to the library. Renata looked around, pleased with herself. She could see that the massive doors were ajar, and she hurried toward them and pushed them open.

But she soon realized her mistake. Inside the library, she was trapped. There was only the one long corridor that led to it. If she tried to backtrack her steps, she would surely encounter him again.

She stood in the middle of the dark, quiet room, trying to think what to do, trying to find a place to hide. But it was not the kind of room where one could hide. There was nothing more in it than dainty carved chairs and low tables, and all those walls, covered with endless rows of books.

She looked around in a panic. The windows were open to the warm night, and the lace curtains billowed in the breeze. An owl hooted. And then the dogs barked again. She thought about escaping through the open window into the night, but go where? She knew no one. She had no one. He would eventually hunt her down and punish her for trying to escape. She had no courage left for that.

Standing in front of the barren fireplace—despondent and heartbroken—knowing that she was about to die, she stared at the painting above it, that horrible painting of the little girl with beady eyes and the straw-filled doll that reminded her of everything that was evil and twisted in the world, and she wished that she had never been brought to this horrible house. And all the while she could hear those heavy footsteps approaching, getting closer, closer. Boom, boom, echoing evilly in the hollow halls. She covered her ears with her hands and closed her eyes tight. Still, the footsteps got closer, closer. And there was nowhere to go. All was lost.

Then, a noise made her turn around and look. There he was, this unknown, dangerous man standing in front of her, his eyes wild with hatred, the hunting knife in his hand, its silver blade glinting in the meager moonlight. There was blood dripping from it. And she wondered if he had killed one of the dogs.

But there was no point in thinking about any of that anymore. She might as well face her doom. This was the end. She could only hope that death wouldn't be too painful, and as she walked backward awkwardly, tripping over the furniture and the rugs behind her, she began to cry. She didn't want to die.

Then, suddenly, she had a moment of lucidity, and she realized that she was dreaming and that she had had this dream many times before. She willed herself to not be afraid, to wake up, and the room disappeared, and the man retreated, back into the nightmare.

With a start, Renata opened her eyes to the sun flooding in through the sheer curtains, warming the room. She wiped the tears off her face and gulped in the fresh air. She had had a terrible night, tormented by the eerie noises of the torrential rain and the howling wind. But the storm was over, and all that was left of it was the drops of dewy water, sparkling on the window panes.

She shook her head. Even with her eyes open, wide awake, she could see him standing there nonchalantly, that tall, rather handsome looking guy wearing canvas trousers, mid-calf boots, and a dirty Club Collar shirt with its sleeves rolled up. He was smiling at her with malice, an arm over the mantel, a hand holding the dripping knife. She wondered who he was, and why she kept dreaming about him.

She jumped out of bed. She wasn't going to tell Jefferson, not this time. For one thing, she didn't want to burden him. But mostly, she didn't want him looking at her in that special I love you anyway way. She hated that. He probably thought she was going crazy.

She put her robe on and went to the balcony door. She needed to breathe in the fresh air, and she went outside, barefoot. It was one of those rare, perfect mornings. Not warm, not cold, not humid. Just placidly sublime. The floor on the balcony was still wet from last night's rain, and she walked carefully to the railing, making sure she wouldn't slip.

The breeze was comforting, and it played with her long, black, wavy hair. From where she stood, in her private apartment in the Pirate Bay Hotel, she could see the Marina at her feet, and further out, the Boardwalk and the beach, and the sailboats that glided on that perfectly blue, perfectly pristine water of the bay. One day, all this would be hers.

By all accounts, she should be happy. Jefferson wasn't Jack, granted. Jack had been the love of her life, but she had lost Jack twice. Once to Margo, and then again to war. He hadn't really loved her, anyway. As soon as he met the richer, younger, Margo Fontaine, he had been charmed away by the lure of the good life. Jefferson—on the other hand—loved her and only her and their future looked good. And after a long and painful inner struggle, she had finally let Jack go. Now, it looked like she could have everything anyone could dream of. So why wasn't it enough? Why couldn't she be happy?

Chapter 13

Ice and Fenway, Cautiously Optimistic

THE EQUIPMENT FOR THE SÉANCE began arriving on Monday, at noon. The room in which it would take place was an octagonal sitting room at the back of Margo's house with a soaring sixteen-foot ceiling and ancient rafters laid bare. It was an unused, dark, and forgotten room. If there was any place in the house that could be haunted, this was it.

Built before the 1800s in the opulent antebellum plantation style, the house had originally boasted an outhouse out back, and a big wooden tub in the kitchen to take baths in by the fireplace, close to the water and the heat. Back then, ladies sat in the double parlor in cold weather, or on the verandah in the summer heat drinking mint juleps with real crushed ice, and men ran the world while their slaves occupied themselves with the day to day operations of their house.

Two hundred-some years later, the outhouse was gone, and proper bathrooms and electricity had been installed, but even when Margo had first moved into her ancestral home—barely four years earlier—it had been in a serious state of disrepair. Hurricanes, floods, and neglect had caused parts of the roof to cave in, and wood rot to destroy some of the loveliest examples of its antebellum architecture.

The octagonal room in which the séance would take place hadn't been restored yet, but being at the back of the house, it had survived most of the onslaught of the endless cycles of storms and hurricanes coming in from the sea. Upon opening the heavy, moisture swollen doors to the room, they had discovered more or less a hundred years' worth of dust and dead bugs.

Wasn't this the room where Grand-Mère had sat by the fireplace on that stormy night when the stranger walked in from the rain to claim his house, and Grand-père François shot him in the chest and killed him? Lila, who had been young then, had to help Perrier the butler wash up the blood and the spilled guts in the library, and then Perrier and Grand-père had rowed the dead stranger out into the middle of Shark Bayou somewhere and dumped him there. His body was never found. Her aunts Beth and Tilly were still small. Lila said that they had cried.

Margo looked around the neglected room with longing. She felt the emotional pull of a family history that she knew nothing about. The meager overhead lights of the ancient chandelier cast long shadows on the mildewy wallpaper and brought a sparkle to the tarnished gold-leafed frames of the paintings that filled every one of the eight walls: life-sized portraits of the ancestors—the men in sober uniforms, the women in long, elaborate formal dresses, long out of fashion, their hair up in gentle waves, artfully framing their faces. Once, someone had known who all these people were, but not anymore. They hung on the walls in their anonymous beauty, looking silently down at her, the women always smiling, the men very stern and self-important.

Four years living in this house, and Margo still felt like a stranger. Four years deciding what color to paint the parlor walls, or what shrubs to plant in the back garden, all by herself. Nobody to talk it over with, nobody to please. It was overwhelming at times to have to make all the decisions, to be the responsible adult, and she regretted not asking her aunts Beth and Tilly, or Madeleine—her cousin's wife to stay on with her for a while. It was such a big house, and sometimes it felt so empty. What gripped her heart the most was the loneliness of the lost years, thoughts of her dead mother, and no family to share the day-to-day little nothings that added up to a life lived. Jack gone. And Pierre, never there.

Ice, who could always tell that she was moping, sauntered over to her and brushed his shiny white body against her leg, and little Fenway, who did everything her big brother did, hurried over and rubbed against her legs as well. Margo smiled, forgetting her sorrows, and bent down to pat the soft little bodies.

Thick, blood-red velvet drapes would replace the numerous diaphanous, dusty, rotting, lace curtains in the room, and the exotic carpeting was rolled up and taken to the attic temporarily, to allow the natural echoes of the wooden flooring in the room to come through.

Ice and Fenway proceeded to sniff everything carefully—as cats usually do—sneezing from the dust. They supervised the workers as they moved the furniture out of the room, and brought down a large round table from the attic. Hard-backed chairs, long forgotten in dusty corners were cleaned, and polished, and placed around the table, and new, softer and more tenuous light bulbs replaced the old ones in the crystal chandelier above their heads.

Saffron had sent over a list of requests. At Beatrice's urging, candles would be used instead of overhead lights if possible, so Lucy and Brooks had hunted down a handful of old candelabras in the attic and around the house. And she needed a large glass bowl. No explanation had been given.

The cats shivered with excitement. Their little mouths chattered as if they were carrying on a conversation among them. Their tails stood up, curled, like question marks. The house was enormous and had plenty of corners to explore, but in the end, it was an enclosed environment. Anything new was always exhilarating. Margo smiled at their antics as she stood in the doorway with Lucy—her housekeeper—watching the workers' progress with her arms crossed on her chest.

"Why are we having the séance here, Miss Margo?" she asked. One of her eyebrows shot up dubiously. Margo could tell that she didn't like the idea one bit.

"Because Saffron had to back out. Her mom is coming back home early from her concert tour, and she would be really angry at Saffron for bringing strangers home. Besides, look at how spooky this room is. Isn't it the perfectly ghostly environment to call upon the dead?"

"Oh, Miss Margo, I really wish you wouldn't talk like that. Aren't you even a little bit spooked?"

"Not really. Well, maybe a little bit. But I'm also curious. If you had the chance, wouldn't you want to talk to a dead loved one? Maybe ask them how they are? Maybe find out what the afterlife is like?"

"I try not to think about death and all that, but I guess I wouldn't mind finding out how my Mimaw was doing. I miss her very much."

"You see? That's the point. What if the séance works and we can communicate with our dead loved ones? What if?"

"What if she's a fraud? Mediums usually are, aren't they?"

"They probably are. But there's no real proof either way. I don't know, Lucy. We'll have to see it for ourselves, and then make up our own minds."

Lucy's penetrating eyes bored into Margo's suspiciously. She always could guess what Margo was thinking. "So, that's it, isn't it?" she said. "You're hoping to get a message from someone you lost."

Margo looked away and sighed. It was ridiculous, and she knew it, to expect a medium to get in touch with her mother. But if Beatrice was truly capable of communicating with the dead, where was the harm in trying?

"Miss Margo, Beatrice Saint-Clair might turn out to be a perfectly nice, decent lady, but there's no such thing as communicating with the dead."

"I know, Lucy. I know. Don't judge me. But this is my mom, my dead mom we're talking about. If it could be done, I would never forgive myself for not trying."

"When will it take place?"

"Thursday week."

"Why Thursday?"

"I have no idea. Beatrice told Saffron that Thursday was a good day for a séance." Margo shrugged, pretending nonchalance. But it wasn't true. She cared. She cared a whole lot.

Chapter 14

The Historian—Tuesday

HARRY LOUVIÈRE WAS ARGUABLY the most talented man of Half Moon Bay. As a matter of fact, he was quite famous. Author of numerous history books, treatises on South Louisiana naval shipwrecks, and other obscure subjects, he was not only relatively well off, but he was extremely handsome.

Women flocked to Harry Louvière like flies to honey and tried unsuccessfully to catch him, but by now it was obvious to all that he was not the marrying kind.

Harry Louvière stood in front of his hallway mirror and adjusted his newest bowtie, a recent acquisition from an exclusive menswear boutique in the Champs-Élysées, created from exotic red and silver silk, crisscrossed with an embroidered pattern of real gold thread.

Bowties were Harry Louvière's weakness. He had more of them than rich women have shoes. His walk-in closet boasted an armoire especially built of precious aromatic woods where each bowtie was encased in a small drawer with a glass front, on a gentle bed of dark felt. That was how much Harry Louvière loved his bowties.

While he admired himself in the mirror, he brooded about his sins and wondered if he would be able to get away with them. It was that greed, that desire for those things that didn't belong to him that burned in his chest late into the night. So what, if he had a guilty conscience? He could live with it—as long as nobody ratted him out. But of course, nobody would, because nobody knew unless that meddlesome Beatrice told. He had been staring at the blue envelope on his desk for days, torn between the desire to know what was in it, and the dread. But come on, didn't he know already?

He thought about Beatrice, how she was always so accurate with her readings. He had looked her up online and admired her long list of accomplishments. The police swore by her gift of second sight. Hadn't she helped find that little girl who was kidnapped a couple of years ago, taken out to that cemetery out beyond Houma, and buried alive? At first, the police had refused to listen to her when she went to them with her nightmares. Everyone has nightmares, the police told her, declining her help.

But time was running out. For every hour that they didn't find the little girl, the chances of her dying increased horrendously. In the end, it was the little girl's mother who had gone crying to the police, falling on her knees in front of them, begging them to listen to the medium who had seen her baby in her nightmares. They almost found her dead, too, because they got there almost too late. But the little girl was alive, and whatever was broken on her could be fixed. And that was the first time that Beatrice's gift made it to the news, and that was how she had become famous.

Before he left the house, Harry Louvière picked up a piece of blue twine from the floor by the front door and wondered where it had come from. Then he grabbed his car keys and closed the door quietly behind him.

Yes, Beatrice was extraordinary, but she was breakable, like everyone else. Maybe he could pay her off. Or maybe he should scare her. Yes, so she could see that he meant business. He couldn't allow her to tell on him, now could he?

Chapter 15

The St. Adelelmus of Flanders Chapel and Monastery—Wednesday

MARGO PARKED HER MERCEDES next to a wild hedge of flowering lantana and stepped out of the car. The decaying chapel, the crumbling campanile, and the newly renovated monastery, all rose from a foggy mist that hovered over the bayou like the beginning scene of a haunted movie. The heavy air smelled of rot and mildew.

Built on a narrow strip of dry land, the chapel was surrounded by centenarian cypress trees with hanging, cascading clumps of Spanish moss that stuck out of the swamp water and seemed to reach all the way up to the sky, floating against the moving clouds.

The morning sun shone slanted on the sluggish water tinting it a bright orange. Patches of duckweed had invaded every inch of available slough, growing right up to the trunks of the old trees, trying to strangle them, to suck the life out of them. Someone had nailed a warning sign to one of the trees: Danger! Tourist, do not put your hands out of the boat. Well, that was reassuring.

She looked sideways at Father Armand, walking next to her quite unperturbed, looking ahead, crunching with gusto the crushed oyster shells that served as paving under his feet. She loved watching Father Armand take those long, dignified steps.

"It used to be called St. Adelelmus of Flanders, named after the saint, who was famous for his hermit way of life," Father Armand said.

"What's it called now?"

"I'm afraid it's become the Maritime Museum."

"How unpoetic."

"Yes. But it had such a glorious start. According to the local legends, a fisherman was rowing home from a nearby town on a quiet moonlit night when from the shore, a cloaked stranger signaled to him and asked the fisherman to row him across the swamp. The stranger sat quietly as the fisherman rowed. All you could hear was the hooting of the owls and the stirring of night creatures in the silence.

"As they approached the opposite shore, the moonlight illuminated a dry patch of land and revealed a translucent, shining angel hovering on that spot. When the fisherman turned around to tell the stranger what a wondrous sight he was beholding, he realized that there was nobody in his boat.

"He told his friends the next day what a strange thing had happened to him, and they all marveled and called it a miracle, and they decided that they would erect a modest chapel on that same spot. Once the chapel was built and word spread, missionaries began arriving, and right after hurricane season, they undertook the building of a monastery that was annexed to the chapel and the building of the campanile.

"The monastery flourished. Novices, followers of the hermit's path of contemplation came from all over the South, attracted by its isolation. In time, the chapel and the adjacent buildings were considerably expanded, and, in the process, the floor level was elevated a number of times because it had a tendency to sink back into the swamp.

"There used to be a cemetery behind the chapel, but with time, the caskets and the tombstones have either sunk or floated away. The important members of the order and the more prosperous people of the surrounding towns were buried in vaults inside the chapel. For a while, they recycled the vaults by emptying them every few years and reusing them as needed. But after a few decades, they began to take the bones and the dead bodies up to New Orleans, where there was plenty of space."

"I feel like an interloper," Margo said with a big sigh. "Like we shouldn't be here."

Father Armand laughed and gave her a pat on the back. "I wouldn't worry if I were you. We're not really breaking and entering, or committing any particular sin. We're just coming to visit an old chapel that was once an important part of a community that has died off."

"You make it sound so sad."

"It is sad. This was once a thriving collective of monks. There was a school here. That large charred remnant of a building at the back was the dormitory. Children ran and played in these gardens. Parishioners came to this chapel on Sundays for Mass. But after the dormitory burnt down in a fire, it was never rebuilt because of a lack of funds, and soon thereafter, the school closed. By the 1970s there was barely a handful of monks left, and they were so old that they needed a lot of help just to get by. After the last one died, the weeds took over. It's a miracle that this much has been recovered."

Margo and Father Armand walked in amicable silence. The morning was mild and noisy. All kinds of birds and bugs twittered in the bushes around them. The monks that had chosen to live in quiet contemplation in this secluded part of South Louisiana must have been very happy.

As they walked around the buildings, heading for the front where the chapel was, Father Armand pointed out—with commentary—what he remembered about the place.

"Here they had a kitchen garden. They even grew Muscat grapes for making their own wine." Margo looked in direction of the pointing finger and noticed remnants of trellises aligned in parallel lines still holding up the twisted branches of those grapevines that had managed to survive. A raggedy scarecrow stood silently standing guard over them, slowly rotting away.

"They had citrus trees, look. Maybe kumquats. Maybe lemons and oranges. But look at the fig trees. They've become enormous. They've been here at least a hundred years."

"Undisturbed."

"Undisturbed, yes. But what a blessing! Birds like figs, and so do raccoons and other wild critters." Father Armand sighed. "But eventually, everything dies. Even these bountiful fig trees will die."

"Maybe I shouldn't have asked you to come, Father Armand."

"No, no, my dear. I'm glad you did. I haven't been back here in years and years. Besides, it was my idea. There's something I want to show you."

They reached the heavily carved front doors of the chapel. The wood was swollen and distended, but you could still distinguish carved cherubs, palm trees, and flowers in bloom, and there were remnants of the copper strip that must have coated some of them. Margo touched the wood delicately with her fingertips and exhaled.

"This is beautiful," she said.

"It was carved with cherubim and palm trees, and a palm tree was between cherub and cherub, and every cherub had two faces," Father Armand recited, and Margo looked at him, surprised. "It's from Ezequiel," he said. "They carved these doors after that verse from Ezequiel. Look at the cherubs. They all have two faces."

Decades of rains and humidity had left the front doors warped and next to impossible to open. They put their shoulders to the doors, and after some struggling and a lot of pushing, one of them budged. And then, they were inside.

Whatever it was that Margo had expected, it wasn't at all what she found. The massive door opened with a dusty bang, and a cloud of black birds, startled, took flight and flittered noisily about over their heads until they escaped in a single wave to the outdoors.

Most of the ceiling had collapsed. The thick wooden rafters that had once held the roof up still remained, and the sunlight poured into the abandoned sanctuary obliquely, brightening up the gloomy interior and pointing out those details that were still lovely inside.

The altar, probably marble, shone under this light. The frescoes that had filled the walls with images of the saints and the life and adventures of the Holy Family had just about peeled away, but you could still see a face here, a halo there, a donkey peering at a baby in a straw pallet.

There had originally been four stained glass windows, two on each side of the altar. Now, only one of them had any colored glass in it. The others had been barricaded with plywood. The remnants of an organ lay rotting in one corner. Rusty and tarnished, some of its pipes still stood at attention, covered with a dark green growth. And the floor was buried under everything that had fallen, or died, or crumbled.

"Come this way," Father Armand said, and Margo followed, stepping carefully around bricks and rotting wood. "There's a statue that you must see. It might have something to do with that story you were telling me about."

They veered left before the altar and entered a tiny side chapel where a forlorn marble statue of the Virgin Mary stood, sadly contemplating her empty chapel, holding her precious baby. Facing her, toward one side, a sailor wearing an old-fashioned cap and buckled shoes kneeled, seemingly sculpted out of the same mildewy white marble. His one arm was extended toward the Blessed Virgin and he held something that looked like a half bottle. It was the offering of a gift.

Father Armand dusted the object in the sailor's hand, first with his own hand, then impatiently with his soutane. "Come closer and take a look at this."

Margo stuck her face to the object trying to understand it. Then, the realization hit her.

"Oh, how clever. One side of the object seems to be a bottle. The other side is the carving of a ship."

"Yes. It seems like that was the only way the artist could sculpt a ship in a bottle. And I think there are tiny letters carved on it, but my eyes are not good enough to see them."

"I have a magnifying glass in my purse."

Father Armand laughed. "Why am I not surprised?"

Margo stuck the glass to the letters as close as she could. The morning sun had shifted, leaving part of the chapel in the shadows, but the letters were still visible after all these hundreds of years.

"What does it say?" Father Armand asked.

"I can't believe it. I really can't believe it. It's the name of the ship. It's the Concepción. What in God's name is it doing here?"

Father Armand chuckled. "I think there's something else," he said.

Chapter 16

The Catacombs

FATHER ARMAND WALKED TO THE WALL across from the Virgin's statue and stopped in front of the remains of a faded fresco. Some of the plaster had crumbled and fallen into uneven little mounds on the floor and exposed rudimentary brick-and-wood work. Barely visible, small carvings embedded into the plaster still survived. Primitive images depicting tiny, tiny ships with unfurled sails and coconut palm trees and straw huts mingled with religious symbology and a scattering of just as tiny free-standing letters.

Margo approached Father Armand. "What are you looking at?" she asked. Father Armand's nose was stuck inquisitively to the wall. It was so damaged and so decayed that unless you were looking at it directly, the carvings were almost invisible, hiding in the details of the vanishing painting, and in the random areas in which the mortar hadn't crumbled away.

"It's something I read. One of the Abbots of this monastery arrived from Saint-Domingue roughly two hundred years ago. Called Haiti today. By then, the monastery was in bad condition. As you know, no construction lasts very long in these swamps. He wrote in his diary about having the monastery repaired and about some underground tunnels the monks discovered when shoring up a crumbling wall."

"And this made you think what?"

"Well, since in his church in Saint-Marc he had a secret passage that went from behind the altar to the private rooms of his house, he might have wanted to replicate that arrangement here. Back then, priests were really into safe escape routes. I remember thinking about that the last time I was here, years ago."

"So, you think the entrance to the tunnels could be somewhere around here?"

"Yes, perhaps behind the altar. But it's nothing more than wishful thinking. It's not even a hunch."

"Wishful thinking? More like illogical expectations, Father. The deltaic soil of South Louisiana doesn't lend itself to underground tunnels. Not even underground graves. You, yourself just told me that the caskets had sunk or floated away."

"Yes, I know. But I have no reason to think that the Abbot was lying. Those tunnels could date from thousands of years back, from before Louisiana started sinking. Sea levels have risen almost a foot in the last two hundred years, and there's all that coastal erosion. But there's no telling what the terrain looked like back then. Besides, I've always been fascinated by secret tunnels. And look at these letters and pictures. How can they be meaningless? So, don't spoil the fun, and help me find out what they mean."

"Okay, then. Let's press them all, see what happens."

After a while of pushing and prodding, Margo and Father Armand realized that only the letters C, D, E, I, N, O, P and the S, allowed themselves to be pressed down, and the rest of them remained firmly embedded in the solid wall. It was a no-brainer. It spelled out Concepción or Decepción, and little else.

"What now?" Margo asked after a while. "We've been pressing letters for an hour, and nothing."

"I'm so disappointed. I was so sure that we would find a secret passage. But it seems like you're right. There's nothing." Father Armand sat down on a pew dejectedly and pulled out a handkerchief. The humidity and the exertion had made him sweat. His soutane and his handsome, handmade Italian shoes were covered in dust.

"Don't be discouraged, Father Armand," Margo told him kindly. "Maybe we're missing something." Margo made an effort to sound cheerful even though she wondered if Father Armand was about to have a stroke. The elegant priest was more used to comforts and pampering than to roughing it in the swamps. And he looked too red in the face and too breathless. "Let's check the letters on the marble ship again."

"I've tried that. I've tried pushing them. I've tried to rotate the ship in the sailor's hand. You name it, I've tried it. The marble won't budge."

"Okay, then it has to be something else. Like for example the S. Why the S? Neither Concepción nor Decepción are spelled with an S, right? You know some Spanish, don't you, Father? What can that S be for?"

"Concepciones?"

"Or maybe Decepciones? Come on, Father. Let's give that a try."

Father Armand got up from the pew with a grunt. He stared at the wall with a wistful look while Margo punched in the letters for Concepciones. But again, nothing happened. "One last try before we give up," she said quickly before he could start complaining, and she spelled out Decepciones. Then, sounding as if it was the bowels of the earth itself rumbling, they heard chains and wheels moving with a rusty effort, screeching and struggling to move. The ground and the walls shook with the effort, and some of the stucco dislodged from the walls and plopped on the ground lifting little clouds of dust. Then, after a few grunts, the machine went quiet and stopped.

Father Armand looked around. His eyes shone with excited fervor. "It came from behind the altar, didn't it?"

"Yes. Maybe just under the cross." They rushed to the back wall of the church and palmed the paneling, looking for a wedge, a crack, a change in texture.

"There's a narrow fissure down here, and I'm pulling, but it won't open any wider. Can there be a tunnel behind it?"

"Maybe. But I don't see a way to open it."

"Do you have a flashlight?"

"Father Armand, you know I do." Margo ran back to the pew where she had left her stuff and rummaged in her purse. She found her J5 Tactical V1-Pro flashlight and hurried back with it.

As soon as Father Armand directed it through the narrow crack, the powerful 300 Lumen gadget produced an intense beam of light and illuminated the inside of the space behind the paneling, but the fissure was so narrow that they still couldn't see anything. It was very frustrating.

"Should I get the tire iron? We could try to force it open."

"I'm not sure we should do that. The whole building could collapse on us. It's old and unstable."

"Then what do we do?"

"I don't know, Margo. Let me think about it. I'll make some phone calls. Come on. Let's go home."

The day that Margo had bullied Father Armand into burying her friend Jenny in St. Quintian's Churchyard four years earlier, embarrassed about her behavior, she had sworn to herself to never argue with him ever again as long as she lived, so she dug her nails into her palms to appease her frustration, and she followed him quietly. But she didn't go willingly. She had an aching desire to see what was on the other side of that panel, even if she had to tear the wall down. She promised herself that she would be back at the first opportunity to continue her investigation. Maybe all you needed to do was to try the sequence of letters again, and the machine would come to life. She was angry at Father Armand for giving up so easily, but she couldn't blame him for being prudent. He was probably right. In a decaying building like this one, there really was a danger of total collapse. Ugh.

Clenching impatiently the car keys in her hand, she stepped over the debris, and she walked behind him. Unaware of her disappointment, Father Armand chatted on in a soft monotone about the tunnels under LSU, the Louisiana State University campus. "Some people claim they're haunted by the indigenous people who built the nearby mounds five thousand years ago," he said.

But Margo didn't care about those tunnels. These were the ones she cared about. She turned back toward the altar and toward the fissure that was now just about invisible. Suddenly, a slender stretch of cold blue light emanating from the space behind it lit the dark slit, but before she could tell Father Armand about it, as fast as it came, it was gone.

Chapter 17

The Gypsy Woman

RENATA STARED AT THE BLUE ENVELOPE sitting on her dresser as she did every morning. The whole séance thing was her own doing. She had hunted Beatrice Saint-Clair down, she had begged and cajoled. She had said I'll do anything for you if you come to Half Moon Bay. But now that she got what she wanted, the regret set in. She was repelled by the idea of attempting to get in touch with the dead. There was something so revolting about it. She imagined the departed all lingering on in some sort of purgatory waiting for the living to want to contact them. She shivered with dread.

She combed her curly, unruly black hair slowly, methodically. She sighed. She lived in a world that didn't believe in clairvoyance, telepathy, intuition, psychic healing, or anything like that. And yet, many years earlier, a friend of her mother's had been struck down by an impossible disease. From one day to the other, she had begun to waste away—without any medical explanation—almost as if she had been cursed, a steady trickle of blood dripping from her eyes and her nose, and as the days went by, she became weaker and weaker until she could barely hold herself up.

Money was no object to the family, so the most famous specialists were consulted, but none of them knew what to do. The blood wouldn't stop dripping, and the weakening of the body couldn't be reversed. In the end, everyone gave up and went home, and Mimi's friend was left alone to contemplate her own relentlessly slow, agonizing death.

It was about a month later that the fair came to town. By then, Mimi's friend was said to be at death's door. She no longer sat up in bed, nor could she even turn from side to side without help. Bedsores festered, the rosary was prayed, and eventually, a priest was called out to give her the Last Rites.

Then, Mimi—Renata's mom—had an idea. Maybe it was something she saw in a movie, or she read in a book or even an irrational impulse, but Mimi suddenly had the urge to go to the fair and find someone to help. She walked around the fairground, wondering whom to turn to when she saw the tarot reader's tent, a fantastically colored tent adorned with mythical signs and astrological symbols.

She entered the tent hesitantly. An old woman who looked exactly like all gypsy tarot card readers do in the movies sat at a small table covered in multicolored brocade shawls, her hands on a crystal ball. It was so cliché that she almost laughed out loud. But the gypsy woman gave her a deeply profound look that seemed to have a layer of meaning that went way beyond the generic I've been waiting for you greeting she was given, so, despite the surrealness of the moment, she nodded and said hello. Mimi always said that this was the defining moment when she knew that all would be fine.

Mimi brought the gypsy woman to see her friend. They walked upstairs and entered the dying woman's room, and—as if they had been handling a lifeless rag doll—they propped her up with pillows. The poor woman was pale, sallow, and unresponsive. From time to time, a nurse wiped the sad drops of blood from her eyes and her nose. Her face was raw from the wiping, and from the blood. Those open sores must have hurt beyond words, but the friend showed barely any signs of life. She just stared at Mimi and the card reader with empty, dead eyes, as someone who had given up on living.

"I see a man in your recent past," the card reader said as she set the tarot cards one by one in front of them, on the blankets that covered the sick woman. "You once had a complicated relationship with him. You know who he is." The woman nodded to herself and shuffled the cards, and picked out the Queen of Wands.

"The Queen sits upon a throne decorated with lions facing away from her. Fire and strength. In her left hand, the sunflowers symbolize joy and satisfaction. The wand in her right-hand blossoms with life. But the Queen of Wands also has a dark side. Look at the black cat at her feet. The black cat means magic and occultism. The Queen is interested in occult powers and the energy of magic."

The card reader showed Mimi's friend the Queen of Wands and pointed to it with a long, curved nail painted a vivid red. "This is her. She's a tall, dark-haired woman. She has very long hair. She's laughing at you. Her mouth is open and wide. She's the one who has done this to you. She needs to be stopped." The woman mumbled some unintelligible words and shuffled again. Then she looked straight at her mom's friend and told her, "I can help you."

Renata's mom often told this story, and it had become part of the family lore. The card reader had visited every day for a while and taught Mimi's friend how to block the evil directed her way, and eventually, the bleeding stopped, and after some time, she healed completely.

And therein was the lesson. It didn't matter if you believed in such things or not. The truth was that there were people out there—very few people—who had the Gift, whether given by God or given by the Devil. And sometimes they cared enough to help others. She hoped that Beatrice would be one of those who cared.

Renata exhaled and looked down at the table, and at the book that was to her right, the one that she had picked up at a garage sale, from a stack of 50 cent books in a dusty corner. It had stared right at her—the strange book—as if it had wanted to go home with her. It was so beautiful, and she remembered the jolt of electricity that passed through her as she touched it the very first time, and she had known right away that it had to be hers.

At home, she had opened the crisp white tissue paper they had wrapped the book in. It was old, crumbly, the cover in tooled leather. With her fingertips, she touched the indentation where the gilded words of the title had just about faded away. The title, La Concepción y La Decepción meant nothing to her, but there was a mystery to it that tugged on her imagination. She had seen those words before.

She remembered turning the pages for the first time, surprised at the feeling of familiarity that they stirred in her. There were tiny drawings of groups of people traveling in ships, across mountains, and walking in the woods. They depicted some of them dead, being buried, others traveling on. Wars were fought, more dead portrayed, and always the little figures kept going. As if a story was being told. And accompanying the figures and their story, unknown words that seemed so familiar scrawled in all the empty spaces of the pages.

The book was also full of maps with captions written in Spanish, old, unfamiliar Spanish. She didn't understand the words, and yet they struck the chord of a memory long gone from her mind as if she knew what they meant. Except she didn't.

That had been the night she had dreamed of the stranger for the first time. He was standing in the library holding up the book, telling her in a foreign language that it was his livre des trésors, his book of treasures. Then, the nightmares began. Every time she saw the stranger in her dreams, he became more and more violent. More abusive. Every time it was harder to run away from him. The last couple of times, there had been a knife in his hand, and it was stained with blood. Her blood.

And this was her circle of torment. Anymore, she was scared to go to sleep. They said that if you died in a dream, you died for real. Could that be possible?

She held her head in her hands, trying to understand. Who was this man who delighted in tormenting her night after night? What did he have to do with the painting in Jefferson's library?

She could hardly wait for the séance. If Beatrice was legit, she might be able to help. But if Beatrice was a fraud, then, she would have nowhere to turn. She could already imagine herself slowly going mad from the lack of sleep and the horrors of the nightmares. She could imagine the pity in the eyes of Mimi—her mother, and the forceful cheerfulness of Jefferson telling her it would be okay, and it was just a bad dream, as he patted her hand kindly. It was the kind of behavior that made her want to gag. No. She couldn't let that happen.

Chapter 18

Margo and Saffron Talk—Thursday

"WAS THAT ALL?" Saffron asked with her exquisitely melodious voice, arcing a perfect eyebrow.

"What do you mean, was that all? it's the Concepción. The ship we're looking for. In the hands of a statue. Sculpted out of marble. Don't you find that strange?"

"Yes, maybe unexpected. But did you see anything else out of the ordinary? Because a ship in a statue's hand doesn't sound like such a big deal."

"Actually, yes. The whole place was unusual. How many churches have I ever been to, especially with my mom when we traveled around the world? Hundreds? More than hundreds? I know what a church is supposed to look like. This one was different."

"Different how?"

"Well, the first thing that hit me was the smell. The place has been empty for decades, but it still smells of decay and death. It felt unholy. Wrong."

"Like an animal died in there, or something?"

"Yes. Or something."

"After all this time?"

"Weird, right? But Father Armand didn't notice, so I didn't mention it."

"What else?"

"Oh, I don't know. There were iron rings cemented into the walls, like the kind they chain prisoners to in the movies. I wondered about that, but couldn't figure out what they would have used those for. The pews were in bad shape, rotting away. Some of them looked like they had been hacked with axes. As if there had been an uprising or a revolution. I was surprised that nobody had bothered to take the debris away."

"Maybe there was nobody left alive to clean it up," Saffron said and chuckled morbidly, but Margo gave her a worried look and continued.

"There's a pretty stained glass rosette over the altar. Its colors are still beautiful. The altar on the other hand seemed stained with blood. I don't know. Maybe they were having Black Masses out there, the kind where they have blood sacrifices."

"Like animal sacrifices?"

"Yes. Or worse."

"They don't have those anymore, do they?"

"I don't know, Saffron. I'm just telling you what I saw." Margo closed her eyes, trying to remember. "Several statues were missing from their recesses. They were on the floor, broken into pieces. There was a lot of rust on the walls, flaking off. For some reason, I keep thinking that it was dried blood, and that's where the smell was coming from."

"You know, Margo that for ages there were rumors of human sacrifices out there. Nobody ever corroborated them. But I've heard old people talk."

"Oh, come on, Saffron. This is a Catholic chapel. Not a Pagan one."

"I know, but think about it. The monks were completely isolated from the world. Especially after the school was closed down. Nobody must have gone out there. Who knows what all they entertained themselves with when nobody was looking."

"People still went to Mass on Sundays."

"Did they? Do we know this for a fact, Margo?"

"I guess not."

"Haven't you heard stories of children disappearing from a town or another close to this chapel and never being found again?"

"No, I haven't," Margo said, angry.

"And people would talk, but nothing was ever proven?"

"No, and no. This is a Catholic chapel we're talking about."

"Are you sure?"

Margo just nodded. She felt like she was about to cry.

"I'm sorry for upsetting you, Margo dear. Please forgive me. I do that to people sometimes." Saffron patted Margo's hand fondly.

"And they always forgive you?"

"Come on, I did apologize. Now tell me what else you saw."

"The vaults."

"What vaults?"

"The transept is built like a cross, with the altar in the center. To the left is the alcove where the Virgin's statue is—with the sailor and the ship. Across from there, in the opposite alcove, there's a series of burial vaults that covers every available space on the wall. I wonder how many dead people are interred there. So many rotting skeletons."

"That sounds creepy."

"We need to go back and check things out."

"I don't think so. We're going to leave this mystery alone."

"How about the space behind the altar? Don't you want to know what it is, and what the blue light was?"

"Oh, Margo. You could have imagined that."

"How about the machinery that moved the paneling?"

"I don't know. That gap could have been there all along, and go unnoticed. You do have a very vivid imagination."

"At least let me show it to you. And then you can decide if you want to believe me. Just one quick look-see. It would be a great photo op, for your newspaper."

"Oh, okay. But we have to go to the Maritime Museum first. Have you forgotten we're looking for a ship and a bottle, and a murderer?"

"No, I haven't. But we'll be right there, so after the museum, we can walk over to the chapel, can't we?"

Chapter 19

Rain and Blood—Thursday Night

THE RUMBLE SHOOK THE WINDOWS, and the dog—afraid of storms—barked at the night. Annoyed, the murderer walked over to the windows and closed them. He told the dog to settle down and walked back to the bathroom. The knife wound hurt like hell, and he was anxious to clean it and get it covered. Fortunate thing that he had all that gauze that he had bought with the first aid kit a while back. Never thought it would come in handy.

He rolled and rolled the gauze around his chest and thanked his lucky stars that it was nothing more than a flesh wound, probably no big deal, but it still hurt a lot. A big glass of rum and a handful of painkillers was either going to kill him or get rid of the pain.

Once he was done, he picked up after himself and cleaned the blood off the stark white porcelain. No need to give the maid an excuse to gossip.

He looked at himself in the mirror, pale, startled, but not contrite. Did he hate having killed? Not really. Life was ephemeral. Nobody was here for very long anyway. With a shrug, he finished putting his first aid kit away and walked back to the living room where he poured himself a generous shot of rum.

The dog jumped up and ran to his side, and they went and sat next to the unlit fireplace where a small wooden ship, no more than six inches long, sat waiting for him, the dog on the rug, the man, cautiously in an armchair.

It hurts like hell, Ruff, he told the dog and patted its head. The dog, he loved. Humanity, not so much. He chuckled as he remembered Father

Armand's sanctimonious sermon of last Sunday about brotherly love. The good padre had no clue about true human nature, ensconced as he was in his pretty colonial church. He had to wonder how much of their sins the parishioners actually confessed. No wonder Father Armand had that stilted, optimistic view of humanity.

Once the pain of the wound subsided some, he leaned forward and picked up the little ship, and the magnifying glass that sat next to it.

As you see, Ruff, it's a plain wooden ship model. But it has a secret. He turned the ship around and around and examined it from every angle with the magnifying glass. No, Ruff, I have no idea what the secret is. It's something to do with the name. But what?

The night quietened as the storm passed, and the big glass of rum and the handful of pills finally dulled the pain in his side. His eyes slowly closed, and before he knew it, he was dreaming.

The brigantine tossed and tumbled on the stormy sea. Angry clouds had gathered overhead and let out a torrent of icy cold rain, and the ship hands were running around, pulling chords, adjusting sails, and yelling to each other in a language that he couldn't understand. It was obvious they were scared, and he looked out to sea and saw that an enormous funnel of water churned near them and was almost certain to swallow them whole.

Then he heard some anguished cries and asked a couple of powder monkeys scurrying about what was going on, but the sailors rushed back and forth around him as if they couldn't see him. He turned toward the prow of the ship and he noticed the gangplank. A man and a woman were standing on it, begging, screaming. The woman's drab, dirty skirt billowed violently in the wind, slapping against her legs. The man kept darting terrified looks about him, his eyes pleading for mercy. Somehow, he knew that those two were about to be thrown overboard.

Then he heard someone calling him Monsieur, Monsieur, over the roaring winds, and he turned. A young girl wearing a white dress with pink and yellow flowers was staring up at him. She held in her arms a cloth and straw doll, big, ugly, with its mouth sewn shut with a crude red thread. Then the girl opened her mouth and began laughing. He shivered in horror as her mouth grew larger and larger and he saw in the black maw that the little girl had no teeth.

He woke up in a sweat. Ruff was watching him with a worried look in its eyes. Ruff always knew when there was something wrong with him. One more reason to love that dog. He patted the dog's head and talked to it kindly. Don't worry, Ruff, he said. I'm okay. It was just a bad dream.

Chapter 20

The Maritime Museum—Friday

FRIDAY MORNING THE SUN CAME OUT. All traces of the storm had vanished as if it had never existed. Margo and Saffron sat in plush comfort in the back seat of the Mercedes, and they looked indolently out of the window as Brooks drove past first the Marina, and then the Golf Course.

It was a warm, pleasant day, and the water in the bay shimmered under the burning sun. The fishing vessels bobbed on the sea, surrounded by clouds of seabirds flitting expectantly around them, and following them as they glided on the water, waiting for the fishermen to clean their catch and toss the chum overboard.

Probably nothing much had changed in the world of fishing in the last who knew how many hundreds of years. The boats, old and peeling, the fishermen, old and rheumy, and the hungry birds, always following. Fishing was not lucrative anymore. Much of the catch came from bigger fishing centers, and certainly not from Shark Bayou as it once had.

They zoomed by Fisherman's Wharf without slowing down, and Brooks took a sharp left turn at the intersection, and they left the coastline behind.

It didn't take long for the view to change. The landscape became swampy and dark. Bald cypress trees appeared out of the shadows, very graceful, with their reddish bark, their exquisitely bent branches, and delicately fine leaves. Here and there, a dead stump stuck out of the wet swamp like a ghost extending its dead branches to the sky. Small houses on stilts, semi-hidden behind clumps of vegetation, cypress dugout pirogues bobbing on the dull greenish water choking with duckweed, tied up to posts to keep them from floating away.

Brooks stopped all of a sudden and pointed ahead. An enormous alligator, at least ten feet long, sunned itself on the baked mud of the road. Brooks drove by slowly, careful not to anger the beast or run it over. But it woke up and looked at the car with calculating beady eyes, and sauntered toward the water. Then, with one smooth movement, it was gone.

"The Monastery that now houses the Maritime Museum once flourished as a beacon of Catholicism," Margo read the pamphlet to Brooks and Saffron. "But, as with so many religious orders around the world, fewer young men were interested in being ordained. By the end of the 20th century, only a handful of aging monks were still alive, and they spent their last days in the nursing home adjacent to St. Hildegard.

"In time, the gardens became a wilderness. The walls crumbled, and the once beautiful colonial buildings were invaded by raccoons and feral cats, who found it more pleasant to live and breed within their walls than without, in the wild outdoors.

"At that point, the council decided to tear the whole thing down. It would be cheaper than to continue trying to keep up with it, they said. Besides, it was too far from town. Nobody ever cared to visit anymore.

"It was Father Armand, priest of St. Quintian's Church of Half Moon Bay, who convinced the council that a building of such important historical value needed to be preserved. Eventually, the Maritime Society moved its treasures from a warehouse to its new home in the monastery. Today, the income from tours that promote a visit to the Museum—combined with boat tours of the swamps—has allowed for a revival of the old buildings, and restoration work is ongoing."

The first thing that came into view was the chapel with its campanile, the bell tower. The stone of the restored bell tower had recently been sandblasted and shone with sparkling whiteness. As for the chapel, it looked as dark and foreboding as it had when Margo had come with Father Armand.

Brooks parked in the shade of a sprawling oak tree and decided to stay with the Mercedes, to keep an eye on things, he said. Margo and Saffron walked up to the museum door that said Entrance and rang the doorbell. While they waited, Margo commented on the quiet and the serenity, and she inhaled happily the out-of-doors air. After a few minutes, they heard heavy footsteps, and the door was opened by an efficient looking navy officer in a spotless white uniform.

He walked with heavy steps, clicking the heels of his white boots on the uneven flagstones, keeping his hands tightly clasped behind his back. Once in awhile—as they followed him through an endless corridor full of exhibits on each side and reeking still of the spicy smell of gunpowder— he would lift an arm and point toward something particularly interesting.

The first room was dedicated to famous explorers like Louis Joliet and Jacques Marquette, who explored Upper Louisiana in 1673. Then there was, in 1682, the Chevalier de La Salle and the Italian Henri de Tonti, and in 1699, Pierre Le Moyne, Sieur d'Iberville, and so on. Their life-sized portraits, and paintings of their expeditions, were interspersed with large maps of the time, colorful posters, and cabinets full of their medals and their commendations as well as small scale models of the flimsy ships they navigated, that brought to point—poignantly—how desperately dangerous these expeditions into the unknown were, and how utterly brave the men who undertook them had to have been.

"Ships in the 1700s relied on sails to propel them, so the length of the voyage basically depended on the wind," said the officer without slowing down, never looking back, absolutely confident that he was being followed and he was being listened to. "An average voyage between Europe and the New World could take anywhere between two and three months.

"Of course, to this, you had to add periods during which ships remained anchored in a harbor in either England or the American colonies while they were being filled with cargo. Sometimes ships remained anchored at a port for as many as three weeks at a time.

"As to the passengers, they couldn't always afford to pay their passage fee. So, they were usually required to remain on board the ship until they were sold into indentured servitude, forced to work for some colonialist for a number of years to pay for their passage fee."

Margo shuddered at the thought. Enlarged drawings on the walls, and early sepia photographs, portrayed these indentured victims—hungry, with terror in their eyes—as they were being hauled off the ships upon their arrival to the colonies.

"Those early journeys across the Atlantic Ocean were very difficult," the officer continued unperturbed. "Imagine the men, women, and children, crammed into the belly of a small wooden ship, rolling and rocking at the mercy of the sea. Imagine the stench, the fumes, the horror, the vomiting due to seasickness. Then, the miserable passengers would come down with fever, dysentery, headache, and heatstroke. They got constipated. They got boils, scurvy from lack of Vitamin C, cancer, mouth rot from excessively salted food and meat, and the contaminated water. Because people think that water remains fresh forever. But oh, no, it doesn't. Water rots like everything else.

"And as a final indignity, when passengers died, their bodies were simply thrown overboard because there was no way to store them on the ship. Ah, here we are." The officer stopped, turned around, and smiled at the girls. "Please come this way," he said, jovially.

"Is that where the ships in the bottles are?" Saffron asked, taking the cover off her shiny black Leica Q camera. "It will be okay to take some pictures, right?"

"Absolutely. The bottles are upstairs. The air is cooler and less humid. Besides, we only have a handful of them." The officer walked proudly as he told the story of each ship. "Here's the replica of the American Privateer Corsair Rattlesnake. It's from the American War of Independence." While Margo admired and Saffron photographed, the officer gave them a quick rundown.

"Ships in bottles are an ancient maritime craft. They used to be called Patience Bottles, obviously, as it would take sailors months, or sometimes years, to whittle down and build them.

"This one is a Black Ball Clipper. Clippers were fast and dependable. Ships in bottles were already known by the end of the 16th and beginning of the 17th century. Made of anything they could get their hands on—like for instance wood, ivory, or even human bones, they were usually given as presents to family, or to sweethearts.

"Occasionally they were used to settle debts. This four-masted French Polka Barque you see here was acquired in the settlement of a debt about one hundred years ago and was donated to the museum upon the death of the owner. Since glass bottles were so rare, ships in bottles were very valuable items.

"Look at this beauty. It's a replica of the Spanish Galleon San Mateo that sailed in 1670. Galleons were the ships that brought treasures from the New World back to Spain.

"So, visitors to the museum aren't so interested in them?" Margo asked.

"Not that much, no. They used to be downstairs in a small room, but visitors just rushed past them. Besides you, only two other people have requested to see them in months."

"Really? Do you remember them?"

"Yes, I sure do. Funny thing, they both asked the same questions."

"That's odd, right?"

The naval officer laughed out. "It sure is. They both wanted me to explain how they were built, and they both wanted to know about the Decepción.

"And what did you tell them?" Margo held her breath.

"That I had never heard of it, and to look it up online. I also suggested a couple of books I know about offhand. They both mentioned some secret related to it, but I told them, look around, we don't have—nor have we ever had—a replica of the Decepción, especially not in a bottle."

"So, you've never heard of it? That's disappointing."

"Well, after all those questions, I became intrigued and asked around." The officer had a big grin on his face. "It turns out that everyone around here has heard of the Decepción."

In the meantime, Saffron finished with her photographs, approached Margo and the officer, and gave the man a big shiny smile. "I haven't," she told him.

"It's an unusual story," he said, and he walked to the windows, his hands clasped at his back. "The Concepción was a brigantine flying under

French flag that carried members of a prominent Louisiana family to safety after rescuing them from the Haitian Revolution of 1804. They docked in Half Moon Bay. We know that much for sure.

"The rest of the story is kind of sketchy. The Captain was in town visiting when he got into an argument with a local plantation owner, and, as a result, got himself killed. The sailors—who were not too fond of their Captain—saw this as a sign and decided to steal the ship, taking off in the middle of the night. They lynched the cook and the navigator, and, some of the passengers who were still on board waiting for the ship to continue its voyage, were kept as hostages.

"They must have realized that they had a problem on their hands. They would be hunted down. So, they decided to change the name of the ship. By then they were on the high seas in uneasy waters, and reaching the lettering of the ship proved harder than they expected. According to the one lonely, emaciated survivor, they managed to scrape off the first three letters of its name before the seamen fell to their death. After that, they decided to add just two letters to the beginning of the name and call it a day. Even that cost them two more men. That's how it ended up being called the Decepción."

"What happened to the hostages?"

"That I don't know. Except for the lone survivor, the ship was empty when it was found. And the man died shortly thereafter. It's anyone's guess whether he said." The officer crossed his arms and looked pensive. "There was more to the story, I think. But I can't recall."

"If you do remember, would you give me a call?" Margo handed the officer a business card. "It might help us solve this murder."

"Margo can't stand not knowing the solution to a mystery," Saffron added pleasantly, and the officer chuckled. They slowly walked downstairs, avoiding the pitfalls of the treacherously worn downstairs.

"What did the two men look like? The ones that came to look at the ships?"

"Let me see," the officer said, rubbing his chin. "One of them looked like an old beggar with a mean eye. For all his appearance, he was a congenial fellow. He came first. Then, a few days later, a young man showed up. He was well dressed, but there was something wrong with him.

His hands shook, and he seemed feverish. He was sweating a lot. He constantly wiped his face with a handkerchief. I couldn't stand him. He was a know-it-all, one of those types."

In front of the Entrance sign, Margo, Saffron, and the officer shook hands, and the girls had already started walking toward Brooks and the car in the shade of the oak tree when the large wooden door opened behind them, and they heard the officer yell for them to hold on.

"I remembered," he said. "I knew there was more to the story. It was said that when the ship sailed from Baye-Saint-Marc, it was carrying a treasure worth a king's ransom. But when the ship finally docked in Shark Bayou, there was nothing. The treasure had vanished. The ship sat rotting in the docks for years. Then, the mystery took on a life of its own, and explorers tore what was left of it apart, panel of wood by panel of wood. But the treasure had vanished. Just like that, it was gone."

Chapter 21

The Chapel in Ruins—Friday Afternoon

MARGO PULLED SAFFRON ALONG and waved to Brooks to join them. Overhead, a noisy flock of black-bellied Whistling-Ducks flew by low, easily recognizable by their boisterous whistles and their brilliant pink bills. They briefly looked down on Margo and her friends, but cheerfully continued on, flying above the cypress and the oak trees, riding the wind.

They crossed the yard in haste. What during the daytime could have been considered quaint and touristic was at this time of the afternoon just plain creepy.

As they approached the derelict chapel, Margo turned around and saw the naval officer walking slowly to his Jeep. He never looked their way and probably never noticed the Mercedes still under the shady trees, or the three of them about to enter the chapel. He slammed the Jeep's door, and the sound echoed in the clearing and reverberated. Then, the tires hit the pebbles and the crushed oyster shells, and their crunching receded into the distance, and, with the officer gone, an ominous silence fell.

Margo couldn't shake the feeling of being watched. She looked around, trying to penetrate the shadows in the shrubbery. The place was so desolate, so lonely, that now that the sun wasn't shining so brightly anymore, the chapel in ruins and the burned-out building in the distance gave the monastery an eerie, dangerous feel. It reminded her of the time that someone had followed her to the park, and she scolded herself for not having made more of an effort to find out who had been shadowing her.

Suddenly, Margo wasn't so sure that it was such a good idea for them to be all alone in the middle of nowhere. She looked sideways at Brooks who was young and strong, but probably too inexperienced to protect them all. And Saffron, well, Saffron was wearing her pretty shoes and had just had her nails done recently. That didn't inspire much confidence either. She thought about the gun in her purse and considered briefly going back to the car for it, but the car was far, and she didn't want to admit that she was scared to go alone, so she rejected the idea.

Nobody spoke a word as they put their shoulders to the warped, peeling door. And when it opened with a groan, Margo's nostrils were assaulted again by the surprising remnants of the scent of incense, and that lingering one of old dried blood.

The light—what was left of the afternoon light—shone inside the decaying nave in an oblique angle that intensified and deepened the shadows of the rafters and the skeletal remnants of the broken windows projected onto the opposite walls. But it left the back of the chapel in darkness, and Margo felt an evil in the air that she couldn't explain. Just two days earlier, she had been in here and had only smelled the dust and the mildew from the rotting wood, and maybe the rusty scent of ancient dried blood.

Yet, this smell was different. It was fresh, wet rot, and she saw new smears on the walls, and a terrible foreboding gripped her, and she ran forward, followed by Saffron and Brooks who kept asking what was wrong. It was the transept and the vaults she wanted to reach in a hurry, and she jumped over the debris and tried to see into the darkness, but it wasn't until she got there that she found what she knew to be there, a dead body, in the center of the alcove to her right. She ran to help the creature lying there, but she knew before getting there that it was hopeless. Right there on the floor, right in front of her, young, with a cruel-looking knife in hand, the face stared up at her with blank, swollen, dead eyes. Bugs were buzzing about the body furiously, breaking the silence with their violent presence, and anger welled up in Margo at the injustice. What profanity, what sin, to murder someone in a house of God and leave them behind like that and walk away.

Then, when she looked around, she noticed that the vaults had been broken into. Barely visible in the penumbra, the skeletons they had contained—and the rotten rags that still stuck to them—had been dumped unceremoniously in a corner like so much trash, and the stone facings of the vaults, well, they had been hacked off and left where they had fallen.

Saffron must have thought that Margo was about to faint because all of a sudden, gentle arms were directing her toward the front pew. As she sat down and was told to put her head between her legs, she heard Brooks on the cellphone telling Sam to hurry up, because there was a dead body in the chapel.

Chapter 22

Sam at the Chapel—Friday Night

SAM SLAMMED THE DOOR of his pickup truck and looked around. He had never been out here, this far out into the bayou. He didn't expect the place to be so desolate. He sure was glad not to be alone. The warm humid air was a shock after the cold air-conditioned inside of his vehicle. And he hadn't taken the first step, and the mosquitos were already after him.

Above his head, the first stars were beginning to twinkle in the darkening sky. The penumbra was unfriendly and unfamiliar. He had heard the stories about this sacred and yet not so sacred place, and the Rougarou and the missing children, and some stuff he preferred not to think about, and the hair on his back stood up on end. Next to him, Andy walked dragging his feet, with an unpleasant gait, in a nervous mood.

The path that led to the chapel must have once been a nice walkway, connecting the different buildings and the road. But time and neglect had upended some of the flagstones, and they were unpleasantly uneven under his feet, unreliably uneven in the dark. There were no lamp posts anywhere, so they went back to the pickup, and Sam rummaged in the back seat for a flashlight.

"Hey Andy, are you okay? You look like you were in pain," said Sam, frustrated at Andy's shuffling gait. He was making too much noise. He would have preferred silence, to get a feel for his surroundings.

"I'm okay, Sam. Just a stomach bug. Must be something I ate."

It was impossible to explain Sam's annoyance without hurting the feelings of his deputy. Andy, limping next to him, was nervous and chatty, and he really wished that Andy would shut up already, but he wasn't an unkind man, so he said nothing.

"Shh," he finally told Andy when he couldn't take it any longer. "Listen. Quit talking and quit making so much noise when you walk. There might still be someone in the bushes. We have to be alert." And it was true. The murderer could still be lurking out there. He grumbled. Friday night, and having to investigate a murder instead of watching some pre-season football with a cold beer and a slice of pizza.

Then, all of a sudden, something rustled among the leaves in the shrubbery, something big, and he stopped. He grabbed Andy's arm and put a finger on his lips. They listened for a full minute or so, but whatever or whoever had been out there was gone. Sam shivered. Out there, among the cypress trees, an owl hooted and then something barked.

The wind had picked up some, and the last of the daytime clouds were swept away as the sky became darker and gloomier. There was nothing left of the day but a sliver of yellowish-red tingeing the edge of the horizon behind the sprawling trees as the sun went down for the night. And everything around them was so deeply and completely silent. It was the aloneness out here, in haunted land, and the whistling of the wind, that gave him the spooks. Everyone had heard—growing up—the stories of children stolen and eaten by the Rougarou, the creature with a human body and the head of a wolf, the one who lived in the bayou, prowling the swamps, waiting for the children to misbehave so that it could come and get them and take them to its lair to feed on them. And even though adults didn't believe in children's tales, the ancestral fear remained. Sam shivered.

As soon as he stepped into the chapel, he was assaulted by the unbearable stench of death. He stood in the doorway looking in, his eyes adjusting to an even deeper darkness. The sound of the wind was muted inside the walls, barely a whisper left behind, a soft rustling among the leaves, a crackling like dying embers in a fireplace.

He forced himself to put one foot in front of the other and entered the gutted space. The moon shone meekly through the rotting rafters, and their silhouettes reflected on the walls. He felt as if the air had suddenly become cold with evil, and his breath was coming out in a chilly mist with every breath, but he knew it was his imagination. It was a warm night, and there in front of him, in the front pew, sat three possibly scared people that he had to be strong for. So act professional, he told himself, and don't show any fear.

Sam walked around the crime scene, close enough to see, but not close enough to contaminate it. Andy, his deputy, stayed near him, taking photographs of the body and the walls.

Sam felt queasy from the scent of blood. That was one thing he could never get used to. He hated murders. Plus, there was this underlying stench of rot coming from those skeletons dumped in the corner, white bones sticking out from under the layers of rotting soutanes, shining malevolently in the brightness of the flashlight. After this macabre scene, he figured he was never going to get another wink of sleep as long as he lived.

He walked back toward the pew where Margo, Brooks, and Saffron, sat, and he looked at them with frustration.

"Why did you have to come out here? And on a Friday night?" He asked them and swatted a mosquito on his neck. He set his flashlight on a piece of stone and took his notebook out. The faces around him stared back at him with big, startled eyes, looking ghastly pale in the uneven light of the flashlight.

"Sorry, Sam," Saffron said. "It wasn't our intention to inconvenience you. Margo wanted to show us the statue of the Virgin Mary in the back. And we came in, and it smelled like an abattoir, and she had to see where the stench was coming from, and well, here you are."

"Have any of you met the deceased before?"

"No, I don't think so," said Saffron. "Not that you can see much in this light."

"What time did you get here?"

"Right after six. We were at the Museum next door," answered Margo, pointing her thumb to her right. "Can we go home?"

"Well, Doctor Gabe is on his way. Why don't you wait until he gets here in case he has any questions?"

"He's not a medical examiner," Saffron said.

"I know, but he's the closest we've got. Man, we are way over our heads here. We're going to have to call in the State Police. I don't think we can do this on our own."

"Wait, Sam," Margo objected, and put her hand on his arm. "You know what they're like. Let's give ourselves a couple of days first, to see what we can find out."

"Okay then. Tell me everything you know," Sam said, thinking quickly. Maybe Margo was right. Maybe they could figure this out by themselves. It was way better than having the town invaded by those bullies from the State Police.

"He didn't drive. The Mercedes was the only car in the lot."

"Unless he parked out back as we did."

"I don't think so, but I can't be sure," said Brooks. "I walked around while I waited for y'all, and I didn't see any cars, or any car tracks either back there. And the ground is soft and moist, and a car would have left tracks."

"Did anyone touch anything?"

"Are you kidding me? Who would be crazy enough to even get close?"

"Okay, then. The murderer must have broken the vaults open."

"Probably looking for something."

"Inside the vaults? That sounds a bit creepy."

"Yes, why not? Something hidden a long time ago."

"Unless the deceased was the one who broke into the vaults and was surprised and killed."

"Could the naval officer have done it?"

"Maybe. We'll have to find out if he has an alibi."

"Would a naval officer have left a body behind to be found, instead of getting rid of it? That sounds so inefficient."

"Sam, the deceased is holding some kind of combat knife. And there's a lot of blood splatter on the wall, did you see it? They must have had a fight."

"In which case, the assailant could be wounded."

"It could be related to the murder of old Snail."

"Why do you say that?"

"I don't know. Because of the knife, I guess. Nothing ever happens in Half Moon Bay, and then suddenly two murders, and a suspicious knife."

Meantime, Dr. Gabe had quietly entered with his crew and with powerful flashlights examined the scene of the crime and the body. He walked up to the group.

"Sam, the kids might have a point. Death by knife, just like the old man."

"Dead how long?"

"I'd say sometime yesterday afternoon. But I'll know more after the autopsy."

"I told you," said Margo. "These two deaths are related. Will you be able to say if it was the same weapon?"

"I might. I'll let you know."

"Was the murder committed here?"

"Most definitely. And I'd say the other person was wounded as well because there's blood on this knife all the way up to the hilt, which is lucky. Because we probably have the murderer's DNA on it."

"Anything else, doc?"

"Nothing I can think of. I found no papers, no identification. Pockets are empty. We'll look for fingerprints. Hopefully, they're on file somewhere. By the way, the clothes are unusual."

"Unusual how?"

"Why, they are foreign. Didn't you notice that the dead person is Asian?"

Sam looked back toward the body and noticed that a male nurse was carefully wrapping the cadaver's hands in plastic bags. He looked surprised at Dr. Gabe. "That's to keep them from getting contaminated. Don't worry, Sam. I might not be a real medical examiner, but I know what I'm doing. Talk to you tomorrow."

Sam watched Dr. Gabe and his medical entourage take off with the body. Then, he asked Andy if he was done with the photographs. He should at this point go back to the enclosure and check the vaults out, and the skeletons that had been dumped in the corner. But he just didn't have it in him. They'd been dead for decades or more. They could wait another day.

"Who needs a beer?" He asked, and walked towards the outside without looking back.

Chapter 23

Renata's Nightmares

RENATA FLEW BAREFOOT through the gloomy corridors of the big house where a man she didn't know was trying to kill her. Mid-conscious in her sleep, she tossed and turned as she struggled to wake up. But always she kept getting pulled back into the nightmare.

The house was a maze of halls and corridors. Here and there, shallow recesses in the walls marked the entrance to mysterious rooms, locked behind ancient carved doors. Diaphanous curtains billowing in front of open windows looked like ghosts rising to touch her, and not knowing if the man was behind one of them—hiding, waiting for her—she ran on, navigating in the melancholy darkness without end.

In the main parlor, she stopped to listen. Her heart thumped unevenly in her chest, and she clutched nervously at her skirt, so inconveniently long and bulky. Every small sound felt like the harbinger of doom. The restless whistling of the wind echoed through the eerie house. She thought she had heard him calling out to her with his familiar, hostile, cajoling voice, and she shivered with dread. "There's no point in running, ma petite," he often said. "You know I'll catch you." But it must have only been her imagination. She was all alone. Still, tonight was the night, and there was no time to lose. She took off running again.

At the bottom of the stairs, she tripped on the hem of her skirt and missed her footing, hitting one of the stone steps, and she stumbled. Pain exploded all over her body as she fell over the stairs, hitting her knees, her elbows, and scraping her hands on the rough stone. But she pushed away the urge to yelp, got back up on her feet, and kept on going, grunting with pain as she took the steps one by one.

Choking back her despair, she rushed along a hallway that she recognized and stopped at a small oak plank door. She grabbed the brass door handle with force and entered the quiet room that she somehow knew was her own.

She closed the door quietly and bolted it, and she leaned her shaking body against it, with an ear to the wooden planks, listening carefully for the sound of footsteps. But all was quiet. The house was silent, and it appeared that she was safe.

She sighed with relief. This was her chance to escape. But she had to hurry up. Banging drawers open, she dragged clothes out of them and began shoving them carelessly into her carpetbag. If she could just get out of the house and make it to the stables, she could ride out of there— saddleless if she had to—in time to catch a train somewhere, anywhere.

She brainstormed. She had seen the horses. She was pretty sure that she had ridden them on numerous occasions, although in the midst of these recurring nightmares, it was impossible to be certain. She tore some dresses off their hangers while she continued thinking about her escape, and she tried fitting them into her carpetbag, but they were too voluminous. Ugh. These enormous dresses only fit in trunks. Should she leave them behind? She grew more and more frustrated as she struggled with the indecision. This was about her life. The clothes, the carpet bag, these packages she wanted to take, they were all hindrances. They were going to slow her down and get her killed.

Renata paced. Was she brave enough to leave everything behind? All her precious belongings? She couldn't make up her mind. But she was wasting time. She had to get out of there. Immediately. He was going to be back any minute. He was never away for very long. She heard a door bang shut, and wondered if it was him. Because, who else could it be?

Discouraged, she realized that she was fighting a losing battle and she would never make it. He would never let her go. She was so naïve. How many times had she tried to escape and failed? This time would be no different. And she just didn't have the courage to fight.

In a haze, the nightmare shifted forward, and the man was banging on her door now, in a nearly uncontrollable rage. He was yelling something, but she covered her ears so that she couldn't hear him. She didn't want to know. She knew that what came next was inevitable, and that she was trapped in her destiny like a bee in a spider web, and that she would never escape.

When the door broke down, he entered her room as angry as a rabid bear and smashed her mirror and swept the long row of perfume bottles that stood on her dresser with his arm. Her precious bottles hit the stone floor and shattered into thousands of pieces, and the overbearing, heady mix of perfumes choked the air out of her lungs. She was furious and terrified at the same time. All her little bottles of perfume broken, shattered just like her life, into pieces on the floor.

"What do you want from me?" she asked him, her voice shaking with fear. "Why won't you leave me alone? Why won't you let me go?"

"Because I want you dead. Dead, you understand? I want you dead," he said, taking measured steps toward her. And then slowly, with a deadly determination, and with that look of madness in his cruel dark eyes, his hands lifted towards her throat and began choking her. She couldn't breathe, she stopped struggling and everything went black around her.

Then the dream shifted again, and for a while she saw herself sitting in a boat, dressed in a pretty flowery Sunday dress, placidly holding a lace umbrella to protect herself from the sun. A young gentleman rowed the boat and told her sweet nothings as he smiled. They glided gently on the river. She wondered if she was dreaming or if she was awake, but pleased, she smiled back. The boat glided gently on.

But in the next scene, she was back in the nightmare, beating with her fists on the walls of the narrow chamber in which she had been locked, beating with her fists until they bled. And she could hear the man laughing maniacally behind the door.

She sat down in a corner of the small chamber, her soul broken down, and she put her face in her hands and began to sob aloud in the empty house, knowing that nobody but the man could hear her, and nobody was going to come to her help.

All of a sudden, the nightmare stopped, and Renata was awake, back safely in her room in the Pirate Bay. She sat up in bed, disoriented, startled by some noise that had awakened her. Her heart was pounding erratically, and she took deep breaths to quieten it. The remnants of the terrible nightmare ran through her mind, and she felt a rush of relief, thankful that it had only been a bad dream.

She listened for the noise for a few minutes, but her room was silent. The sound of music floated up from the Marina, and some people were arguing in the parking lot, but that was all. Finally, realizing that it was nothing, that it was probably part of the nightmare, she laid her head down on her pillow again, and by and by, fell into a restless sleep.

Chapter 24

Bleak and drizzly—Saturday Morning

SAM, MARGO, AND ANDY looked up forlornly at Saffron as she walked through the doors. Jimmy Falgout—limping visibly, and with beads of sweat above his lip—followed with a cardboard tray full of coffees. Outside, a soft drizzle beat against Sam's office window. Raindrops slowly slid down the pane, distorting the outside view. Saffron's hair was wet.

"Why the faces?" she asked, distributing the coffees and hanging her jacket on the coat rack. Then she turned around and told Jimmy to go back to the office and finish going through some files.

"We didn't think to secure the crime scene," Sam told her, and he sighed. "I'll be in all kinds of trouble."

"Maybe you shouldn't tell anyone."

"But, how are we going to investigate the murder if all the evidence has probably been washed away?"

"Well, didn't Andy take like five hundred pictures last night? Let's check them out."

"Oh, I don't know. I hate investigating murders."

"Margo doesn't," she said. "Margo loves them. Cheer up, everyone. She'll figure it out."

"I could send y'all the picture files, and we could each take a chunk and check them out," said Andy, and Margo looked at him surprised that he had managed to come up with that idea all by himself. Although a sweet and loyal guy, Andy wasn't the sharpest crayon in the box.

"Has Dr. Gabe called yet?" Saffron asked.

"Yes, like half an hour ago," said Margo. "He did a preliminary exam. He's with Dr. Wayne Richard from Lafayette now. They were about to begin the actual autopsy."

"And what did he say?"

"That they will send the fingerprints to the FBI. And that Dr. Richard took a quick peek and declared that both victims had been killed with the same knife. But we knew that already."

"Is that all?" Disappointment showed on Saffron's pretty face. "I've nothing to report either. I called the hospital and both pharmacies, and nobody has turned up with a knife wound. Nor has anyone shown up to purchase first aid supplies. I even called all the little mom and pop stores."

Everyone sipped their coffees, watching the rain beat on the window pane. An oversized clock on the wall ticked loudly the seconds away.

"So basically, we have nothing," Saffron said with a gloomy voice. "Have we even checked out Mr. Snail's belongings?"

"Of course, we have," Sam defended himself. "Andy and I went through his clothes and his luggage with a fine-tooth comb. And you know how thorough Andy can be. There was nothing interesting. At least nothing to tell us why he ended up in Half Moon Bay."

"Well, I might have some information on that," Margo said uncomfortably. "I might have forgotten to mention that there was an old newspaper in his room at the motel that points to his previous knowledge of the bottle and its legend."

"And again, you kept evidence to yourself?" Sam was angry. He got up from his chair and began pacing. "How many times have I asked you to leave evidence alone?" His voice kept getting louder and louder.

"I was just trying to help."

"But you have to understand, Margo, that even though I don't know what I would do without you, I can't see the greater picture of a puzzle if I can't see all the pieces."

Margo got out of her chair and went to stand next to Sam by the window. The gentle patter of the rain was barely audible above the roar of the air conditioner. Still, Sam stared into the drizzle with a concentrated frown, as if there was something crucial to see out there. She stood next to him for a few seconds, giving the anger time to dissolve, and then she put a hand gently on his shoulder. "I'm really sorry, Sam. I just wanted to help. Look at all the things Saffron and I have already uncovered. Please don't get so upset about it."

But Sam didn't answer and continued staring at the drizzle. As Margo grabbed her purse and got ready to leave, Andy stepped close to her and grabbed her wrist. "You shouldn't have done that. Where is it?"

Margo pulled her hand away and looked at him. All of a sudden, Andy didn't seem like his usual friendly self. His eyes were dark and menacing. The acrid smell coming from his sweat-stained uniform shirt assaulted her nostrils and offended her. She shivered with dread and walked out. She never looked back.

Chapter 25

The Autopsy

DR. GABE WATCHED DR. RICHARD get ready to work with a slight annoyance. The old geezer reeked of alcohol again, and his hands shook with age and palsy. It was frustrating that he had to step back and watch someone do a job he knew himself to be so much better at. Dr. Richard was a thorn at his side. He really wished the old guy would retire already or drop dead.

The funeral home attendant rolled the gurney in with the body and left saying he'd be right back. Gabe stepped up to the body in front of him and looked on sadly. So young. She had been quite pretty, in an androgynous sort of way, with the typical features of someone whose one parent was white and the other one Asian. Very slender, narrow hips, almost no breasts, and an ambiguous haircut that could have made it very easy for her to blend into a masculine-dominated society. It seemed very contrived as if she had tried to efface herself on purpose. Poor child. Couldn't be any older than twenty-four or twenty-five years old.

Following Dr. Richard's succinct orders, he began filling out the paperwork. Then, he assigned the young woman an identification number, and tied a toe tag to her big toe, admiring the perfect beauty and symmetry of the dead woman's feet. So incongruous that despite her understated appearance, her toenails were painted a bright pink.

Poor young woman. Not from around here, he thought, having never seen her around town before. Never having seen her in the hospital before either. Maybe a tourist caught in the wrong place at the wrong time. Young enough to be her mother's baby. This was going to break her mother's heart.

Dr. Richard bellowed at him to get on with the photographs, and he picked up the camera and focused on his job for a while. He proceeded in an organized fashion, head to toe, front and back, in the clothing the young woman had been wearing when she was brought in to the funeral parlor, just like the autopsy manual instructed.

When they peeled the blood-soaked clothes off, already completely dry and stiff, Gabe inhaled, surprised. The young woman's body was crisscrossed with superficial cuts as if she had been in many fights. All the cuts—except for the one that killed her—were antemortem, old, and completely healed. Then, he remembered the combat knife she was holding when she was found, and baffled, wondered if this young woman had been some kind of warrior or martial arts practitioner.

Get on with it, Dr. Richard fussed, so he continued taking the photographs like before, head to toe, front and back, but now with the body completely naked.

Dr. Richard scampered about, busily weighing the body on the scale, measuring it, and taking the fingerprints. Gabe watched his hands shake and wondered if the old geezer was going to botch something. He promised himself to take those fingerprints again.

The young woman was sinewy, light, almost underweight, but even dead, exuded health and vitality. She was slender but tall for a girl, and breathtakingly beautiful. Her short hair had slipped back, exposing perfectly even ears, and again the anachronism, two small pearl earrings. The words so not a robbery popped into his mind. There was even a trace of makeup on her eyelids. That gave him the idea of asking young folks around. A pretty, modern, young tourist, someone must have seen her around.

While Dr. Richard and the morgue attendant X-rayed the body, Gabe examined the clothes. He lay them out as best he could and took some photographs, with some for research purposes on his own cellphone. The clothes were edgy, sophisticated, and looked expensive. But probably purchased overseas. Never mind. He discreetly extracted a few fiber samples anyway, and put those in a plastic baggie in his pocket. Then he approached the combat knife and took as many pictures as he could next to a 12-inch ruler before he was called to attention again.

Have you taken notes of the wounds, tattoos, and scars? Yes, of course, he said, and he continued taking notes, mentioning that there were no needle marks on the legs or arms. Three broken nails on the left hand were noted, and he took pictures of that. He clipped a tiny sliver of nail and placed it in another baggie. He looked up to make sure that he hadn't been observed. Then he cut a few strands of hair, and he stashed those away as well.

The morgue attendant extracted blood and urine for comprehensive toxicology tests, and Dr. Richard nonchalantly picked up a scalpel and began the full body-length Y incision that opens up the entire front of the body. His cuts were jagged, rough, and unemotional. Gabe knew well that the young woman was beyond caring, but it made him sad to see how callous Dr. Richard's cuts were.

The old doctor proceeded with haste. Organs were removed, diced, and tested. Dr. Richard muttered to himself and to the morgue attendant that the young woman hadn't been sexually molested or had had any relations prior to her death. No need to examine stomach contents, he said. Death by knife wound, yes? Gabe debated arguing with him. Knowing what she ate or where she ate right before the murder could help find the killers. He finally spoke up and Dr. Richard told him, you do it then if you're so curious.

Gabe sighed. Dr. Richard was done, already signing the death certificate, and yet there was so much more that he wanted to know. He signaled to the morgue attendant to leave the body and told Dr. Richard goodbye.

He was mostly interested in the wound. He examined it and tested different types of knives, hoping to find one that fit. His resources were limited. This was a mortuary embalming room. Half Moon Bay had no autopsy facility. Still, he had a modest collection of knife wounds and hilt impressions on a computer program, and he could check those back at his office.

It had been an upward thrust, by a right-handed person. He was sure of that. The hilt of the knife had a small irregularity. Perhaps a tiny corner had been chipped off. He took numerous photographs with his cellphone. It wasn't much of a clue, that tiny chip, but it was better than nothing.

He retook the fingerprints, not trusting Dr. Richard's shaking hands, and added that to the list of clues he was carrying in his pockets.

Dr. Richard had been hasty. Probably had a date to play golf. He shrugged. In a way, he was glad the old geezer hadn't bothered with the skull. It was small comfort, but if he ever got to meet the young woman's mother, he could tell her at least that her beautiful head had been left alone.

Gabe put everything in its place and snapped his gloves off. On his way out, he told the morgue attendant, thanks, man, and patted his back. I owe you a bottle of something for not ratting me out. Then they slipped the body into the refrigerator and turned the lights off. And then, they each went on their own way.

Chapter 26

Margo Looks for Clues—Saturday Afternoon

SATURDAY AFTERNOON THE SUN FINALLY CAME OUT, and the vegetation sparkled with drops of leftover rain. Margo sat in the back seat of the Mercedes, watching the Marina and the Fisherman's Wharf zoom by, but seeing nothing. Her mind was somewhere else.

She took her phone out and looked at the picture Andy had taken. It was clear and crisp, and when she enlarged it, she could see perfectly well the square object sticking out from under the dead monk's rotting robe, the only even and square object in the jumble of bones. It had to be either a book, or a journal, or some kind of document.

Brooks knew the route well enough by now, and he mechanically took the sharp left turn toward the Maritime Museum without looking at the GPS. The Spanish moss clung deep from the cypress trees rising from the swampy soil, welcoming them, hanging like the hair of long-dead ghosts, reaching out, wanting to touch you, to grab you. It wasn't so much that she was excited to go back to the chapel. It was more like she had to. She had to know.

"I still don't understand why you want to go back, Miss Margo," said Brooks looking at her through the rearview mirror with a worried frown.

"I told you. There's something about those skeletons in the corner that bothers me."

"You're not planning on examining them, are you?"

"How else am I going to find out what I need to know?" Margo chuckled. "No, seriously. There are two things I want to check out. One, is there anything left in the vaults?"

"I'd be surprised. If it was something of importance, the murderer must have taken it—whatever it was—if that's the reason why he was there."

"True. But I can't get Sam or Saffron to come with me, and it's nagging at me, so I have no choice but to do it myself. I should have thought of it earlier, and I should have asked Andy to snap pictures of the insides of each vault while we were still there."

"Why do you care so much?"

"Because I was fond of Mr. Snail, my aunts' old butler. He was big and tough, and he looked like a hardened criminal. But in a world where nobody was nice to me, he was kind and caring. And he died trying to protect me. Now, someone has killed his brother. In a way, I feel that maybe I can pay him back by finding out what happened to his brother."

"The murderer could still be lurking around. It could be dangerous."

"That's why I'm glad you're here. You, and my gun." Margo grinned at him in the mirror.

"You said two things, Miss."

"Oh, yes. We were looking at the photographs that Andy took of the murder scene. He just got this fabulous new camera, and he went stir crazy with it. He took hundreds of photographs. I mean hundreds. He took some of the skeletons in the corner as well.

"So, I was looking at the photographs, and it seemed to me that one of the skeletons—well, they're all wearing habits, you know, priests' habits—it seemed that one of them had something sticking out of a pocket."

"You could have imagined it."

"Of course. But I couldn't stop thinking about it. There's another storm coming through tonight, and I was worried that whatever remains of the possible evidence will totally be washed away."

"I don't like it."

"I don't either, Brooks, but nor do I like the idea of someone running around killing people without getting caught."

"We'll have to hurry up if we want to stay ahead of the storm."

"Understood. I just wish I could have talked Sam into coming with us."

"And Andy?"
"Not Andy. I didn't want to ask him."

Chapter 27

Back at the Chapel—Saturday Afternoon

THE SOFT AFTERNOON DRIZZLE gave the decaying chapel an ominous look as it climbed out of the rising fog. Margo stuck close to Brooks and darted looks right and left, suspicious of the apparent calm in the clearing.

The Maritime Museum was closed. No flickering lights broke the approaching penumbra as they crossed the yard between the car and the buildings. The ground was wet, and her shoes kept slipping on the mud or getting sucked into it. Walking on the flagstones was no better. They were uneven and upended, and she stumbled, and Brooks had to grab her before she fell. She wondered why she hadn't thought to come in rubber waders instead of tennies.

She wiped the wet drops out of her eyes, and she entered the place hesitantly. There was still a pervasive smell of fresh kill and dry blood even though it had been hours since the body had been taken away. She shivered with foreboding. Now that she was there, surrounded by boarded-up windows and naked rafters, and decay and rot everywhere, she just wanted to get things done and get out.

A dark cloud sailed by overhead, and the sky rumbled. They walked silently to the back of the chapel, stepping over debris and fallen stones, and they reached the transept where the building opened its arms like a cross. Margo was about to turn to the right toward the vaults when Brooks grabbed her arm and put a finger on his lips. Margo held her breath and nodded. She had heard it too. There was someone else in the sanctuary, behind the altar, rummaging, looking for something. Above them, the sky rumbled again. The storm was getting closer.

Brooks looked like he had changed his mind. He tried to pull Margo toward the entrance—to retreat and get out of there—but they had come this far already. She had no intention of wimping out. Running away like a coward was out of the question.

She stared at the pile of discarded skeletons. There it was. Her eyes hadn't deceived her. In the darkest of the corners, something protruded from a monk's robe just like it had in the photographs, and Margo knew exactly what it was: a book of some kind. She had to get it at all costs.

Brooks looked at her in the eyes and started shaking his head mouthing no, no, but she was so close, she could almost touch it. She couldn't leave without it. She was sure that crouching quietly among the pews, she could hide until she got close enough. Then, she could grab the thing in two steps there, two steps back, and then they could take off—like gazelles—as fast as the wind.

Brooks pulled her back again, coaxing her toward the entrance, but Margo yanked her arm away. The thunder rumbled overhead, and a powerful stroke of lightning illuminated the chapel and shook it to its base. Margo and Brooks threw themselves down low by instinct. And then Margo—without any kind of warning—took off. She sprinted toward the skeletons, ran to the corner, and yanked on the book, pulling down a number of rotting skeletons from the pile. They came down with a thud and a cloud of thick, moist, stinky dust, and suddenly, the sound of rummaging behind the altar stopped. She had been heard.

Margo scampered back to where Brooks was crouching—looking angry and frustrated—and signaled that they had to go. They skirted the pews, going as low as they could, keeping to the ground. Then, they were at the end of the row of pews, and the last place where they could hide. From there on, they would be very visibly in the open, running away.

Brooks looked at her, and she nodded. He pulled at her, and in unison, they stood up and began running toward the big carved doors and the exit. Within two steps they had left the chapel behind and were now outside again, in the fresh, clean, breathable air—such a relief after all that rotting miasma. Margo briefly wondered whether they had even been in any kind of danger and whether they had been silly to run like that. But Brooks didn't seem to think so. He held her hand tight, and he ran steadily, not slowing down, not even for a heartbeat.

Above them, the night had crept in, and the continuously rising fog threatened to swallow the whole land around them. Between lightning strikes, the sky rumbled menacingly, and what was left of the moonlight among the clouds illuminated the dark buildings behind them. They looked more like figments of a nightmare than sacred buildings. The cypress trees moaned, their Spanish moss hanging like hair, looking like monsters trying to catch them, always just one step behind.

Meantime, the wind had picked up too and howled among the trees, and Margo held on to the wet book for dear life. That long run to the car seemed to be taking an eternity.

There was no way to know if they had been spotted and were being followed. The car was parked at the far end of the clearing, and the wet ground had turned to mud. They slipped and slid on the uneven ground, and Margo's shoes kept getting sucked down into the mud. Gratefully, she held onto Brooks with her one free hand, and with the other, she held the book to her chest.

Once close enough, Brooks pressed a button on the electronic car keys, and she heard the doors click open. It was pretty dark now and the outline of the chapel and the other buildings were washed out and blended into the penumbra.

As she turned around to take one last look behind her, Margo saw lightning hit the bell tower. The strike illuminated briefly the sky and the clearing, and she saw the trees swaying from side to side and branches and dead leaves flying in swirls, tossed up furiously by the wind. It was at that same moment that she saw someone running after them.

The figure, nothing more than a shadow, appeared out of the horizon and got bigger as it closed in on them. Suddenly, Margo screamed. She saw three, four, blasts of light, each followed by a twangy pop. They came closely one after the other, leaving behind a faint trail of smoky light. They were being shot at. Brooks, who probably didn't need to look at a gun to know what it sounded like when being fired, held her hand tightly and pulled. He never stopped running. He never looked back.

The car's headlights had been turned on with the remote-control ignition fob at the same time as the engine, and the headlights were so bright in the dark woods that they blinded her. She tried looking backward to see the murderer, but between being pulled along by Brooks and running for her life, she couldn't see a thing. Anger welled up inside her. She was right there, close enough to be at shooting distance, and yet unable to see the face of the shooter.

Wet and muddy, Margo hopped into the front seat of the car. Brooks was already reversing the Mercedes and turning it around. Mud splattered on the windshield, and he turned the wipers on. Whoever was after them must have run out of bullets because the shooting stopped, and as Brooks turned back onto the dirt road, Margo sighed with relief.

"That was close," she said, breathing deeply, waiting for her heart to stop hopping about in her chest.

"Did you get what you came for?" Brooks asked. He looked serious as he focused on the driving, but a tiny smile around his mouth told her that Brooks hadn't minded the excursion. He too enjoyed a touch of danger in his life from time to time.

"I sure did." Suddenly, unable to contain herself, Margo whooped with joy and looked at the leather-bound book in her hands.

"It's soaking wet. The pages will be stuck together."

"Yes. It will have to be dried before we can read it."

"That was kind of exciting," Brooks chuckled. "And we came out alive."

"Don't go saying that in public. We're going to get chewed out for putting our lives in danger."

Now out of peril, Brooks had slowed down some. The rain was coming down steadily now, and the tap-tap of the windshield wipers filled the contented silence in the car. Margo looked into the dark, relaxing, seeing nothing except for what the wide arc of the headlights illuminated in front of them: the muddy dirt road, the occasional set of eyes peering out from behind a bush. Here and there, though, a tiny, feeble light in the distance signaled that someone out there in the swamps lived in seclusion, not afraid of the dark or the loneliness.

Meantime, she noticed that Brooks had become serious again. All of a sudden, a viciously bright light hit the rearview mirror, and the interior of the Mercedes brightened up, showing the worried look in Brooks' eyes.

"What's wrong?" she asked him.

"Headlights behind us. Getting closer. We're being followed."

"Do you think it's him?"

"Who else? It has to be. The headlights are enormous, powerful, and getting closer. He must be driving a truck. He must have been following us with his headlights off."

"Could he run us off the road?"

"He could try."

"And push us into the swamp?" Margo felt her voice crack. She had foolishly thought they were safe, and now the danger was creeping up on them again. Brooks was frowning.

"Absolutely. And nobody will find us alive because that swamp is full of alligators. Are you well buckled in?"

"Yes. You?"

"Always. Hold on tight."

Brooks sunk his foot on the accelerator, and the Mercedes sprinted forward skidding on the wet soil for just a second or two. Then, it took off. Brooks drove fast, and Margo watched the concentration on his face. Pearls of sweat lingered on his forehead and on his upper lip. She was hot too, sweating, with adrenaline coursing through her veins, and she wanted to turn the air conditioner on, but she was scared to distract him. She held on tight as they careened on the wet, muddy road, still too far from town to be safe.

"How far are we?" Brooks asked.

Margo looked at the GPS. "Almost at Fisherman's Wharf. You can turn onto I-49 from there if you want. It's better paved and less dangerous."

"Is there a police station in Fisherman's Wharf?"

"I don't think so. What do you have in mind?"

"Don't worry. Just sit tight."

Brooks took the sharp right that got them off the dirt road, and the back of the car skidded badly sending up a wall of mud that splattered on the rear window. By now the truck was right on them, breathing down their necks. But the Mercedes was a good car, and Brooks a good driver. He recovered from the slide, straightened the car, and Margo finally dared to take a breath.

They were close to home now. They zoomed by the last houses of Fisherman's Wharf, dark and sleepy except for the bars where disappointed fishermen drank away the sorrows of another bad day's catch. Then, in rapid succession, the Marina with its fancy boats, and the multicolored lights of the pier that reflected on the shimmering waters. Then, the dark hills of the Golf Club.

"Call Sam," Brooks told her. "Tell him we're coming."

The truck knew it was its last chance to kill. Finally, having caught up with the Mercedes, it lurched forward and bumped into them, and the car was tossed forward, airborne for a second or two. There was no time to talk, and Margo just put her hand in front of her, instinctively protecting her face. The second bump came right after the first, and she heard the sickening crunch of metal from the rear, and her neck felt like it had snapped. She looked to the side and saw Brooks, unaffected, steadfastly barreling ahead: one purpose, one goal. His hand was on the horn now, honking nonstop. They had arrived at the outskirts of Half Moon Bay.

It seemed like a lifetime had passed by them already, but it was still early evening. It hadn't even rained in Half Moon Bay. The streets were all dry. Margo saw people look up and stare at them surprised as they barreled through the streets, running red lights. She had tried to call Sam, but the phone had fallen out of her hand when they got hit from behind, and then suddenly, there was no more time.

Brooks honked the horn furiously as he approached Independence Park. Margo gasped when she saw what he was doing. She was going to complain, but her throat was dry, and her voice died in her mouth. Brooks jumped the curb and started driving through the park. Bewildered, she watched the Opera House, lighted up like a Christmas tree, pass by on her right. She remembered there was some sort of function tonight. Well-dressed people turned around and watched the car zoom by, banging into benches and bumping on toys that had been left behind by the children running to safety.

To her left, the fountain was on, bubbling and gurgling cheerfully as usual. She held her breath, terrified of hurting anyone. In the hot summertime, children usually played by the fountain until late into the night. But they were scattering now, running out of the way. Suddenly, she was so thankful that Brooks was still pressing that horn like his life depended on it, scaring innocent bystanders out of their way.

And then—with an enormous bang—they stopped. They were in front of the police station. Everyone on duty had rushed outside, alerted by the hullabaloo. Brooks hadn't been able to slow down properly, so it was with a huge thump that he had driven against the steps, climbing the first one with the front wheel of the passenger side.

The truck had also jumped the curb, and it passed close to them. They heard a couple of parting gunshots, but at that speed, and having to drive at the same time, Margo was sure the murderer would have been unable to hit them. But she ducked anyway, still under the influence of the adrenaline.

In slow motion, still dazzled by the chase and the unexpected realization that she was still alive and not broken, she saw Sam running down the stairs, putting his gun away, and helping her get out of the car and stand up. Her whole body was shaking, and she wondered if she was going to have a nervous breakdown. But then she remembered the book she had rescued and decided that she was too excited to have that nervous breakdown. Maybe later. When she looked at Sam and reassured him that she was fine, she blurted out, "You're not going to believe what happened."

Later that night, much, much, later, Margo lay in her bed absentmindedly rubbing Ice and Fenway, unable to sleep. It had finally started to rain. Sometimes she heard a police siren, or a foghorn coming in from the dark waters of Shark Bayou, but basically, Half Moon Bay slumbered, safe from the storm. The cats purred, sleeping happily next to her.

Downstairs, Lucy was still fussing at Brooks, blaming him, angry that he had dared to put her life in danger. Bless her heart, Lucy was like a mother to all of them, keeping the order, keeping everyone true and honest, even though she was the youngest of them all.

A warm feeling of fondness filled Margo's heart, thankful to Brooks for always being there to protect her, and thankful to Lucy whom she loved like a sister, and who was always ready to take care of her.

Margo rolled to her side and said her prayers. Then she sighed contentedly, hugged her precious cats, and finally went to sleep.

Chapter 28

Madame Mansard on Sunday Morning

MADAME MANSARD FINISHED HER CROISSANT and her coffee and put the blue envelope with the invitation next to her empty cup. You have been summoned by the spirits, the card inside it said in italics on a background of stars and astrological symbology. How pedestrian, she thought and shrugged. Why did she care what these people were like? She should only worry about the outcome of the séance.

Madame Mansard walked to her bedroom. She brushed her teeth again, retouched her makeup, and decided she looked reputable enough for church. On her way out, she stopped in front of the painting—as she always did—an enlarged, framed copy of the photograph of *The Golden Gift Of Silence* that had appeared in the Veranda magazine a couple of years earlier, and looked at the evil-looking little girl that stared back at her with beady eyes, holding her malevolent looking sack-cloth doll. Then she touched the cross hanging from a chain from her neck.

The cross had been in her family for generations, handed from grandmother to mother, and then to daughter. And yet the little girl in the painting was wearing the same exact cross—her cross. With a unique, medieval shape and design, sprinkled generously with diamonds and precious stones, it was recognizable a mile away. The Gold Princess had been given to her by her mother for her First Communion, more than sixty years earlier. So, then what was this irreplaceable gaudy piece doing around the neck of a long-dead child in a painting, here in Half Moon Bay of all places, halfway around the world from her home in Japan?

It had all begun one innocent morning as she was drinking her breakfast coffee, thumbing through a home decorators' magazine that she subscribed to, and saw the glossy photograph of the painting with the child wearing her necklace. It was impossible to be mistaken. It was the same one.

She contacted the magazine right away, curious about the painting, and corresponded with several people, none of whom knew much of anything. But then the letters began arriving. They were always the same, with more or less variation. At first, they were polite, asking her about her cross, wanting to know more. Then the letters became ruder, more menacing. Someone in Half Moon Bay knew she was connected to the painting somehow, and wanted to know why. But how would she know? At any rate, that was how her curiosity became an obsession. And that was why she had come to Half Moon Bay.

Madame Mansard went to the back of the apartment and knocked at Haruki's room. She sighed, worried. Still no answer. She opened the door and peeked inside, hoping against all hope that he should be there. But he wasn't. Yuna wasn't in her room either. They'd been gone three days now. And she had the horrible feeling that something had happened to them.

She had to talk to someone. She couldn't bear this burden alone any longer. She paced up and down, wondering what to do, who to turn to. And then, she had an idea.

Chapter 29

Sunday Mass

MARGO SAT QUIETLY IN HER PEW with her legs crossed, swinging one foot nonchalantly back and forth, waiting for the people to arrive. Nothing as spiritually inspiring and comforting as sitting quietly in your favorite church while empty, right? She inhaled the ever-present aroma of incense that always lingered in the air and tried to get herself into a spiritual mood. But her mind was restless.

Dropped off early by Lucy and Brooks who attended the Presbyterian Church on the other side of town, she waited for eleven o'clock, turning the Missal in her hands, opening it and closing it again, unable to focus on the words. Who killed old Snail? She stared for a while at the stained-glass window over the altar, bursting with color and with the glorious sunlight that was pouring through it. She was going to have to buy a new car.

She resisted the urge to take her cellphone out and look at cars. She tried to focus on the Missal that was—once more—open on her lap. But her mind strayed again. There had been someone rummaging behind the altar in the chapel. Why? So maybe "it" was not in the vaults after all. But behind the altar?

Her train of thoughts was interrupted. People were beginning to walk through the door, with that soft chatter accompanied by the kind of respect that people adopt when they enter a church, or a hospital, or a funeral home. High heels clicked on the marble flagstones and echoed in the large empty space.

There was Mimi, arriving with Dr. Gabe. Mimi, Renata's pretty, plump, middle-aged mom—and owner of the Pirate Bay Inn and Hotel—

had always come across as an enigma. She was exhaustingly kind to Margo and insisted on always giving her a hug and a peck on the cheeks. It was uncomfortably awkward, to say the least. When Mimi sighted Margo, her face lit up with apparent pleasure, and she sent her a kiss with her fingertips. Margo gave her a quick smile in return and wiggled her fingers.

For a while, strangers trickled in, and she lost interest, lost in her thoughts again. The recurring theme here was the ship in the bottle, so they had to redouble their efforts to find it. And whoever had it had to be the killer.

She saw Renata come in with her boyfriend, that politician, and head straight to her mother's side. Renata was a devastatingly beautiful young woman of mixed heritage. Her raven black curls reached to her shoulders, not as tight as her mother's but obviously natural, not permed. She also had an enviable figure. No wonder Jack had been so in love with her. Well, seemed to be, anyway.

Renata never said hello, usually passing by her without acknowledging her presence, as if they had never, ever, seen each other before. She had been unable to forgive Margo for losing Jack—she presumed—but it hadn't been Margo's fault. Jack was fickle and unreliable. In the end, he had joined the army against everyone's better judgment, was sent to a warzone, and was lost in action. How was any of that her fault?

The organist began playing, and she took a couple of deep breaths to chase away the resentment Renata always brought up in her. The choir was on vacation, ergo so was she. It was a strange feeling to be sitting in a pew instead of in the choir loft, singing. She recognized the Bach Prelude and Fugue that the organist was beating on with a vengeance. He was so loud and vigorous that the parishioners went silent. Margo looked at her watch. Five past eleven. Father Armand was running late, which was truly not like him.

She looked around. Should she be worried? The church was full, and the expectation could be felt in the air like a living thing. Children were becoming rowdy and a baby started to cry.

The minutes ticked by and people were getting restless. Should she go and look for him? She was about to get up and check things out for herself when an old woman, who she had never seen before, sat down next to her. There was actually no space left, so she felt mildly annoyed when the woman sort of pushed her way in, but there were no more seats available, so she gestured to others in the pew to scoot over.

She tried to feel charitable toward the woman and turned to her to give her a smile. But when she looked at her, she saw that the woman's eyes were swollen with tears, and she held a wrinkled handkerchief in her gloved hand that she kept dabbing her eyes with.

"Are you all right?" she asked, suddenly feeling guilty for her unkind thoughts. The woman nodded and pointedly looked away, so Margo decided to not intrude and leave her alone.

Finally, Father Armand appeared. As always, a collective sigh from the female audience welcomed him. Because let's face it, Father Armand—despite being in his late forties or early fifties—was extremely handsome. He was tall, and his chiseled features, his abundant, well-cut hair, and those penetrating eyes made many a middle-aged woman swoon.

Margot shook her head. It never ceased to surprise her. But of course, Father Armand was completely oblivious to the fact that he looked like a movie star and that most of the female population of Half Moon Bay was in love with him. Margo chuckled to herself. The women flocked to him for advice—for advice on anything, on everything, probably as an excuse to see him, to spend time with him. He held their hands in comfort. He put an arm on their shoulders when they needed advice, and he hugged them compassionately when they cried, always having a never-ending stock of pristine white handkerchiefs that smelled of lavender for this purpose, which they took gratefully and probably never gave back.

But his sermons were always wonderful. There was never a time that Margo stepped out of that church without her spiritual wounds having been healed. He was a kind man, and despite his lack of experience in the material world, his advice was always surprisingly modern and to the point.

After Mass, Father Armand stood at the doors of St. Quintian's and one by one shook the hands of his parishioners, greeting every one of them by name, always asking some personal question. Has your foot healed well, my son? Or, how's that baby coming along? Or even, how many puppies did Daisy end up having?

So, Margo stayed behind to talk to him.

"I didn't see you back there," he said, closing the doors behind him with a deep, echoing boom. "Is everything all right?"

"Oh, yes. I just have so much to tell you."

"You have perfect timing, Margo dear because I need to talk to you as well. I was just thinking about paying you a visit this afternoon. Why don't we go see if Madame Mouton remembered to bake something on this lovely Sunday?" Father Armand rubbed his hands together with anticipation and Margo chuckled. That was his one weakness: good food.

Margo followed Father Armand to the back of the church, where a discrete door led to his private quarters. The smell of pecan pie assaulted her senses as soon as she entered the hallway. Madame Mouton rushed out to greet them and informed them that she had just pulled the tiny pies from the oven.

"We'll sit outside in the garden," he told her. "And we'll eat our pies out there if you don't mind." Madame Mouton beamed at him and offered to make some *café au lait* if someone was interested. She rushed back to the kitchen to make it, and Father Armand led Margo to his miniature private garden, with its benches, its statuary of marble saints and angels, and a tiny gurgling fountain set in the back of the garden.

Margo could hardly contain herself, and she began telling her news before they even sat down. She told Father Armand about how she went to the Maritime Museum on Friday with Saffron and met the naval officer, who told them about the Decepción and the Concepción, and the missing treasure. Then she talked about the young woman they found dead in the chapel next to the museum, and how she seemed to be Asian and nobody knew where she had come from. And how she wore foreign clothes and was murdered with a sword or a knife, but that they didn't know yet.

Madame Mouton came out with the bite-sized pecan pies on a tray and a huge pot of coffee, and Margo thanked her and popped a pie in her mouth, and kept right on talking. She told Father Armand how Andy, the deputy, had taken hundreds of pictures of the crime scene, and she saw something that looked like a book, and she had to go back and get it, and she and Brooks were almost shot and almost run off the road, right into the swamps where the alligators would have eaten them alive.

Father Armand held a tiny pie in his hand through all this and was so enthralled that he never got to swallow it. Madame Mouton had stopped watering the flowers and dusting up a storm around them, and she too stood mesmerized, listening to Margo's adventures.

In the end, Father Armand swallowed the pie and drank some of his coffee. He seemed very pensive. Finally, he got up, thanked Madame Mouton for the wonderful pastries, and asked Margo if she had ever seen his fish.

"They are in the back of the garden, in the fountain. Let me show you. It's time to feed them." Margo watched him eye Madame Mouton.

"Are you worried that she's listening in?"

"Yes. Maybe," he whispered discreetly. "She's a bit of a gossip, and I have something to tell you that I rather she didn't hear. Let's sit by the fountain. On that bench. I'll make a show of feeding the fish, and we can talk."

"You sound very mysterious." She walked over to the fountain where a dozen or so tiny multicolored fish frolicked among the lily pads while father Armand fed them pellets from the pockets of his soutane.

"Well, Margo, something happened, and I feel I ought to tell someone."

"Okay, you know you can tell me."

Father Armand looked up at the sky and seemed distracted by some birds flying overhead. Then he shook his head.

"I might as well start at the beginning. Someone came to see me early this morning. We talked extensively. Now, you know that I can't divulge anything told me in the confessional, but we never made it there. We sat on the sofa in my office, and I held her hand, and we conversed."

"In which case, you can tell someone."

"Yes. It's a thin line, though. Some priests might consider that a confession, but today, I choose not to."

"Father Armand, what is it? You're worrying me." Margo sat down on the bench and made sure Madame Mouton was out of hearing.

"She had a strange story to tell. She came to Half Moon Bay because she has been receiving threatening letters. Not quite hate mail, but some ugly mail. It concerns a family secret that she knows exists but doesn't know the context of."

"Yes?"

"Well, she came with a young man and a young woman, her relatives. The young Japanese man is almost completely deaf. His sister is his identical twin."

Margo inhaled deeply and her hand flew to her mouth. "The young Asian in the morgue," she said.

"Yes, possibly. They disappeared a few nights ago, and she hesitated to go to the police. I got the feeling that the young people set out to do something they shouldn't have been doing, and she didn't want to get in trouble or didn't want them to get in trouble."

"I see. What was she doing in a derelict, abandoned chapel anyway?"

"Exactly. So, I told her that the police usually don't look for missing persons until 72 hours had passed. That is correct, right?"

"Right. The police assume that by then most people return home voluntarily. If they haven't been kidnapped or murdered or something." Margo hadn't intended for her words to sound so bitter.

"Poor young woman. Nobody should have to die young, not alone like that." Father Armand patted her hand kindly. "I didn't want the gossip train to get to this poor woman before the police have a chance to talk to her. I could be wrong. And of course, there's the case of the young man who, being deaf, could be in a world of trouble. Madame told me their knowledge of English is very basic, which is not good. And she's terribly worried about them."

"Did she tell you her name, or where she's staying?"

"She's staying at some fancy apartments. The Belleview. Yes, that's it. She did tell me her name. It starts with an M, and that's all I can say, but they will remember her. Very tall, very foreign. Wears unusual clothes."

"Was she wearing gloves and carried a handkerchief in her hand?"

"Yes, gloves. I gave her the handkerchief myself."

"She sat next to me during mass. Her eyes were swollen with tears."

"Poor woman. She seemed very fond of the young relatives."

"Okay, I'll tell Sam."

"Don't tell him I told you?"

"Of course not." Margo got up to leave. They walked slowly toward the back gate. Father Armand walked with his hands clasped behind his back, and his soutane moving elegantly with his steps. On the way out, Margo picked up another pecan pie from the garden table and popped it in her mouth. Madame Mouton had disappeared into the house.

She was anxious to go tell Sam what she had just learned, but it was obvious that Father Armand still had something to say. They stood by the low wrought iron gate for a minute or two. She watched Father Armand put his hands in his pockets and then look up at the sky and count the clouds as they sailed by. Finally, it seemed like he had made up his mind.

"There's something else," he said, hesitantly. "I've been thinking about the statue of that sailor in the chapel, and the model of the Concepción in his hand."

"Yes?"

"Well, when I was in seminary, we had to read all kinds of books written by explorers and evangelists, and it so happened that once my assignment was to read this book called *Life Of A Christian Man Among The Beasts of Cap-Saint-Marc*. It was a horrible book written by one Monsignor Lafontaine, the Abbot of St. Adelelmus of Flanders. The one I told you about."

Margo looked at Father Armand with confusion. "The one that moved here from Haiti during the revolution?" she asked, trying to remember what all Father Armand had told her.

"Yes. Him. He was a piece of work. He believed in the most brutal punishments and disciplines for the poor black slaves that ran his plantations. And he loved to write with a luxury of details about everything he did to them. He was a sadistic butcher. It made me so sick that I couldn't finish the book, and I failed the assignment.

"When I heard about the murder of the old man down by the beach, I decided to read the Monsignor's autobiography. I inherited the library, you see. I would have never voluntarily acquired one of his books if I could help it. But there it sat, on the shelves, and I felt that there was a connection."

Margo nodded and switched to standing on her other foot. The story was getting too long, and she could hardly wait to go seė Sam. But Father Armand seemed to be in no hurry. She stuck her hands in her pockets and ordered herself to be more patient.

"So, I got the book down and started reading it. He kept a record of his life in Saint-Domingue, the weeks he spent in hiding in his secret passages, and the way he escaped and arrived at Louisiana. That's as far as I've gotten.

"But I can see that you're in a hurry. I'll get to the point. I think I know why there was someone rummaging behind the altar. I might even know why the young Asian woman got murdered."

"Why, do you think?" Margo asked with curiosity. "Why?"

"Because they were looking for the secret passage, of course. Just like we were."

"I guess it's possible. So, we have at least two people, one of them is our dead girl. Either they went there together and turned on each other, or they both happened to have arrived there at the same time. Anyway, one surprised the other, got in an argument, and they pulled their knives out."

"Seems like it. Anyone who knows his history would be aware of the secret passages in old churches and plantations. They were built for protection. Some were used by white families to escape being lynched by angry black slaves. Some provided escape routes for runaway slaves. And many Catholic priests owed their lives to them when they were persecuted. That's how our evil Monsignor escaped being lynched."

Margo nodded with enthusiasm. It made sense. It really did.

"That confirms our suspicion that a mechanism opens a door behind the altar. And that the door leads to a passage. But a hidden passage is no motive for murder, Father."

"It is, if the murderer thinks that there's a buried treasure involved. Now, we just have to figure out how to open it without bringing the roof down on our heads."

"What else does the book say?"

"That's about it. He talks about converting the existing caves into a usable tunnel. Technical stuff. But Margo, I tell you, he was a horrible man. I'm sorry for the monks that must have endured such an evil man's presence among them. Those old stories of children and animals disappearing from the neighboring towns were probably true. It gives me nightmares to think about them."

Margo put her hands on her ears, horrified, and shook her head.

"You're not going to tell me stories, Father Armand, are you? I couldn't bear it."

"Don't worry, Margo dear. I wouldn't do that to you. Now run along. Go tell Sam about that young woman, and whenever you have some time, let's get together and figure out how to get that door opened. And by the way, that wet book that you mentioned? I'd suggest you take it to Dr. Gabe. I've heard that he can do wonders restoring old books. He might be able to help you."

All that was very interesting, Margo thought as she walked slowly, leaving the church behind. But in no way did it explain the surreal nature of the cold blue light under the fissure behind the crumbling altar. Nor the feeling that this wasn't the first murder that had ever been committed there.

Chapter 30

Monsignor Lafontaine's Diary

FATHER ARMAND, ONCE HAVING STARTED READING the renegade priest's journal, had to admit to himself that he was curious as to how the story would evolve. Monsignor's diary was—after all—a historic document full of interesting facts about early life in Half Moon Bay, and he had to confess that the old goat was a good writer.

Eh bien! Mass was over, Margo was gone, and he had the afternoon off. No commitments, no visits, nothing that would interrupt a quiet afternoon of good reading.

He rubbed his hands together with glee and rushed to his office. There, he opened the cabinet that hid his beloved Glenfiddich Single Malt Scotch from Madame Mouton—who insisted on running his life with a tyrannical hand—and he poured himself the usual two fingerfuls, smiling at the prospect of the quiet afternoon. Then, he walked to the window and sat in the armchair, the big, comfortable one. Holding the whisky in one hand, he started turning the pages of the journal, and read on where he had left the other day.

1 March

Today I went to visit the Regnards, whom I haven't seen since we disembarked—to thank them again for saving my life—and I discovered something rather odd, something plutôt étrange, as they say. I saw the painting, and I found out something very interesting indeed.

But let me begin at the beginning. It was my first free day, as I've been extremely busy rebuilding the monastery, my new domain.

After careful consideration, I decided to leave my dog Bastien in the care of the herbalist at the monastery. My dear companion is getting old, and he'd rather sun himself in the gardens and watch the butterflies flit about him than go on a brisk adventure with his master.

I rode into town early afternoon. Half Moon Bay is but a collection of random plantation homes and slave quarters that dot the sugarcane and cotton fields. Had things gone differently, I would have much preferred to go back to civilization, to go back to France.

De toute façon, here I was, knocking on the gates of their spacious plantation home, surprised that no slave came running out to take my horse. I stood there for a while, with the sun burning the cloth of the habit on my back, and I stared up at the open windows of the home but saw no movement among the white curtains that billowed in the breeze.

I tied up Rodrigo, my horse, and walked the perimeter of Regnard Mound. The trees and the shrubbery seemed dry, and the kitchen garden that had been a point of pride upon my first arrival seemed to have been abandoned. Likewise, there was no one working the fields as far as the eye could see even though it was not a Sunday, and so, not really knowing what to do, I walked back to where I had tied Rodrigo to a post and decided to go back home. But Rodrigo was thirsty. He stared at me with defeat in his eyes when he saw me drink from my flask, so *que diable,* I thought I'd try knocking again.

Finally, after what seemed like an eternity, a young black woman opened the door. I could tell she was flustered, and when she saw my habit, she became very apologetic. *Bondye Bon,* she said, she hadn't heard me knock. *Entrez, s'il vous plaît,* and she would call Barthol *tout de suite* to take care of the horse.

The reception was a far cry from my first day at Regnard Mound when we had just touched land and were brought here with great fanfare and rejoicing. Our adventures had preceded us somehow, and we were fêted and welcomed. I remembered that as I had walked down the gangplank behind Madame the Judge's widow not such a long time ago, I had been surprised by all the locals—freeds and slaves—that had come out for our arrival.

Of course, there was the awkward moment when Madame the Judge's widow had to explain to her cousin, who came out to greet us, what the Captain had done to her daughter, and to the villain that had defiled her and left her with child. But still, there was much cheering, and much good food and drink.

I did hear later that the Captain of the ship didn't live very long after his arrival to Half Moon Bay. In a moment of anger, the Regnard cousin, who was so hopeful to sell his fair cousin in marriage, chopped the Captain's head off and placed it on a stake—holding him personally responsible for her lost virtue—right in the middle of town, in front of the church and the courthouse.

So, knowing that Rodrigo my horse would be well cared for, I entered the cavernous house, as silent as a tomb. I stood, not having been invited to sit anywhere, and I paced for a while. My footsteps echoed on the parquet as I walked. No dog came to bark at me, *pa gen okenn moun rive.*

Finally, I heard footsteps and got excited. Domine Miserere! I didn't really want to ride back to the monastery on the same day. It was a long and arduous ride full of hidden dangers where clumps of grass hid pockets of water where a man and his horse could easily get swallowed up. And, according to the locals, get eaten by giant *kayiman.* Footsteps meant that there was hope to stay the night and eat and drink some decent fare. The thought of the porridges prepared by Father Bernard nauseated me. Rather, I envisioned some *vyann kochon,* some *poul,* and a bottle of decent wine. And so, I smiled a friendly smile when I noticed that it was Madame, the Judge's widow, that came to say hello.

"My friend, *zanmi mwen,* how good to see you."

"Thank you for receiving me, Madame. I trust all's well? The house feels very quiet."

"All is well, Monsignor, but so much has happened. *Ou ta renmen kèk diven?*"

"Yes, please. Some wine would be very welcome. It's been a long day, and so hot for March."

I followed Madame across the hallway, and we entered a large round room, unfinished, still under construction, but of magnificent proportions. There, an enormous marble fireplace took place of honor. Two leather chairs, puffed up with pillows, sat in front of the silent fireplace, and above it, hung the abomination. Because what else could you call it?

"I see Madame managed to save the painting," I said, surprised, wishing it had fallen overboard.

"Yes," Madame answered sadly. She too would have probably loved to leave it behind. Then she laughed, making a dismissive gesture with her hands. "I had to. I had no choice."

"That sounds most mysterious," I said. I couldn't help myself. What could have been so important about this hideous thing that it warranted travels across the ocean, to be brought here, of all places, and over the lives of her own daughter and her unborn grandchild?

"Oh, I suppose I can tell you, Monsignor. You're a priest after all. But please, let's sit." Madame rang a cord suspended from the ceiling and the same young black girl came rushing in. "Aimée, bring us some refreshments, would you?" Then she turned toward me and asked if I remembered Aimée from the sea voyage. But, of course, I didn't.

We made small talk until the lemonade arrived, together with some rhum and small pasties. "You were telling me about the painting, Madame," I reminded her.

"Yes, the painting. My daughter and that Boukeman mulatto, remember him? They had squirreled away an enormous amount of riches. Don't ask me where it came from. He, being part of the slave collective, knew what was going to happen before we did, and he wanted to be prepared. By the time the revolution unraveled, he had quite a treasure accumulated, and he had this painting done."

I winced. It was almost too horrible to look at. Its primitive brushstrokes were full of evil, and I imagined that the rusty red that had been painted over the rag doll's mouth had been painted in blood. But I forced myself to remain calm. "But what does it mean?" I couldn't help asking.

"It's a warning to never tell. And it's the clue to the hiding place of the treasure." Madame looked away. "Terrible, isn't it?"

"Indeed, but what is the warning about?"

"Jacques Boukeman knew something about my husband the Judge, and this painting was a reminder that if he surrendered Boukeman to the authorities, he would talk, and tell everyone what the Judge had done."

"But how could he get away with all this? How did you allow it to happen?"

"How could I have prevented it? Do you remember when the Captain of the ship threw Boukeman and my daughter overboard? I lost them, but they left the painting behind. All that money, all those years of hard work, of tolerating that noxious climate and the horrible people of the island, all that is in that painting, but nobody knows what it means."

Madame then put her head in her hands and started weeping. It was very uncomfortable. I thought about putting my arm around her shoulder, but that might have been seen as inappropriate, so I made comforting noises, but all the while I couldn't take my eyes off the abomination. It told about an enormous treasure, but where? Where?

That night, Madame's cousin, the young Regnard had dinner with us, in a cavernous dining hall at a table that could have seated twenty, but where only the three of us ate, but young Regnard was in a foul mood, so we didn't talk much. I was just grateful to have a place to spend the night and have a decent dinner, so I said the Blessing, and then kept to myself.

Much later, when everyone in the house slept, I took a small, slender candle and tiptoed downstairs making sure not to be seen. I found my way eventually after roaming around the quiet darkness and slipped into the round room where the abomination hung in place of prominence.

I stood in front of it for a very long time and this idea slowly began forming in my mind. I want this painting, I told myself, and I have to figure out how to take possession of it. Needless to say, I won't be able to sleep a wink.

2 March

We had breakfast outside, on the lawn. A last remnant of cold air swept through the fields, and we sat shivering in the cold, sipping on hot coffee and *rhum*. I was going to ask why we were outdoors on such an inclement morning, but I soon realized that Madame wanted to talk, and she wanted to do so privately.

"You asked me what Jacques Boukeman held against us. I had considered taking the secret to my grave, but it's an ugly secret that weighs heavily on my heart, and I can't keep it to myself any longer."

"Madame, you know you can tell me anything, and in complete confidence. Unburden yourself," I told her and touched her hand lightly in a gesture of comfort. I was excited, hoping to hear more about the treasure. But what she told me knocked me off my feet. It was not at all what I thought. Not even close. This is what she said:

"In 1788, my husband purchased a large tract of land around the area of Cap-Saint-Marc. This was added to the coffee and sugar plantations he already owned, and it made him a very rich man.

"On the new piece of land, there was a large plantation house with several adjacent buildings, one of which was a boiling house, where the sugar cane was converted to sugar crystals. My husband, to learn about this new boiling system, began spending more and more time away from the house.

"I don't really know when I began realizing that he was never home. We were never too close, my husband and I, and often only saw each other for a few meals a week, or when we entertained. I commented on it to my housekeeper, and we began counting the time he spent away.

"At first it was days, but days turned to weeks and I began to worry. Our sons were coming home less frequently as well, and my housekeeper convinced me that there was a mystery that needed to be solved. If my housekeeper knew where they went and what they did—and she might have—she never told me. Maybe it was her way to warn me that I had to do something about it.

"You'll laugh at me, Monsignor, but one day I disguised myself as a slave team manager and followed them at a distance. If anyone saw me, I could always tell them I was lost, and heading for one of the many other plantations.

"I wish now that I had never followed them. I left the horse hidden behind some shrubbery and running from bush to bush—to hide myself, you understand—I made it to the house and waited until I felt that it was safe to enter.

"I found myself in a large, spacious hallway devoid of furniture. There was nobody in the room, and I turned around and around wondering what I should do next.

"I was about to leave, thinking that I had made a mistake, and my husband and sons had taken a different route without my noticing. My hand was on the door frame, and I was already stepping over the threshold when an inhuman scream pierced the silence. Imagine Monsignor. I didn't know what to think. Had it been a figment of my imagination? Had I gone mad? Whatever that scream had been, it filled me with fear and I turned to run away. But as I looked back one last time, I noticed what I hadn't seen before: a staircase of the same stone as the inside of the house, so well disguised as to be practically invisible against the wall.

"Still I wanted to go home but then the screams began. They were relentless. They were like nothing I had ever heard before. They were the howls of human beings in pain. At that point, I couldn't leave anymore. I had to do something. How could I have walked out of that place knowing that someone was in terrible pain, and I had done nothing to help? Deep in my heart, I knew that this was where my husband and sons were, somewhere up there at the top of the stairs, and that I had to go and find out what they were doing. Because I knew, I just knew that those screams were not coming from them, but from strangers.

"I climbed the stairs, terrified, feeling like a coward because I wanted so badly to run away. But I continued going, following the screams, and found myself on the last story of the house, a large open area like the downstairs.

"What I saw there was worse than what I thought I would see. Along the walls were dozens of slaves, chained to the walls like animals. There were cages as well, and there were more slaves in them. And my husband and sons just stood there nonchalantly, conversing, doing nothing to help them.

"I didn't want to know then, and I don't want to know now what my husband and my beloved sons were doing there. I chose to leave because I couldn't confront what was in front of me. I ran out of there quietly, as fast as I dared, without calling attention to myself, and I prayed all the way home. And the screaming and the begging for mercy went on and on in my mind. And it has never stopped. Even today, if I close my eyes and forget myself, I hear the screaming and the begging for mercy. I thank God that I had but a brief glance at those unfortunate souls, but even so, I thought about ending my own life, thinking that this was something I would never forget nor be able to live with.

"I ran downstairs and jumped on the horse and galloped back home. And I must have screamed out loud myself at some point, and my husband and my sons must have seen me as I rode away, because when they came home, everything had changed. We never talked about it. It was as if a wall of ice had come between us, as if I had become a stranger to them. No more smiles from my sons, no more pecks on the cheeks, or the usual ou gade bèl, manman that they often greeted me with. Our life as a family was over.

"That night, the mulatto Jacques Boukeman boldly stepped into my sitting room uninvited, and he had never done that. He looked at me with revulsion. He told me that he knew everything. And then, the next night, the rebels came and broke into my house, and I overheard that my husband and my sons were all dead. And I've wondered in the small of the night when I can't sleep, whether it was he who betrayed us. That hatred with which the rebels tore down my house and pursued me could have only been caused by what my husband and my sons had done to their people. You know, Monsignor, I hope God will forgive me, but I felt relief that the slaves killed them. It was as it had to be. In a way, they avenged those of their kind that had been hurt by my family. They deserved to die. I have no tears for them.

"You know, Monsignor, people who attended parties at our home were wined and dined with the choicest foods and wines, on the finest china, linens, and silver imaginable. My husband charmed them, titillated them, regaled them with stories, and was ever the perfect host. My sons were beautiful, and rich women vied for their attention, so they would be willing to marry their daughters. Who would have thought that such monsters existed behind their façade of gentility?"

Domine Miserere! There was no stopping the flood of her words. She continued complaining for a while, and all I could say was oui, Madame, oui, but deep down, if I had had a gold coin for each time I had heard a similar sob story, I would be such a rich man. But then I had to rub my chin and wonder. Actually, there might be a way to become that rich man. And as Madame continued to wallow in her self-pity, I made plans to get my hands on *The Golden Gift Of Silence*. And I couldn't help but smile.

Father Armand put the journal down and swallowed the rest of his whisky. Trust Monsignor Lafontaine to not only not pass moral judgment on Madame's confession, but cheerfully write on, ending the horrible tale with a determination to get his hands on the painting, so he could figure out where the treasure was. *Quel bâtard.* He put the journal down, disgusted. Then he had another shot of whisky, and needing to go for a walk to clear his head, he angrily slammed the door to his office behind him.

Chapter 31

Monday Meeting

MARGO ARRIVED LATE FOR THE MEETING. Now that she didn't have a car, she found that she was late for everything. She ran up the steps, said hello to Maurice at the front desk, and rushed to the conference room, banging the door open.

There was a time—not long ago—that Madeline, her sister in law, had been there for their Monday meetings, and so had Jack, her long lost love. Renata always came as well, at least when she knew that Jack would be there, and all of them, including Saffron and sometimes Andy, would try to solve the problems of the world. But now, Madeline was no longer interested in crime-solving. Her boys were growing up and needed constant supervision. Ever since the departure of Cousin Robert, his wife Madeline had been frosty to her—and who could blame her, seeing how now it was Margo who lived in the big house and Robert was gone—resentful despite the generous trust fund she had put in place for the boys, and the beautiful house she'd bought for her cousin's wife.

Jack was gone too. God only knew where he was these days. A Captain in dress blues had shown up one day at his uncle's front door with a chaplain and rung the doorbell. The uncle had been dreading the arrival of bad news every day as much as she had.

The uncle said he knew immediately that something was wrong. The CNO—the casualty notification officer, he told Margo—said his spiel, but he never heard a word. His universe had been shattered. Then the chaplain hugged him and tried to comfort him, but what comfort could there be when Jack was his only family left?

And then, it turned out that the Army had made a mistake, and Jack wasn't dead but missing. Now, if you knew Jack, you knew that that could mean anything. Point was that he was never heard from again. Maybe the Army had been right in the first place, and Jack was dead after all.

Margo said hello and went to claim her coffee and her beignet, and then sat down next to Saffron, who patted the seat she had been saving for her.

"Sorry, I'm late."

"That's okay," said Sam. I was just telling Saffron about the foreigner who came to identify our Jane Doe."

"The young Asian woman?"

"Yes. She was Japanese. Actually, part Japanese. Her name was Yuna. Yuna Yoshida. Poor old woman. She was heartbroken. She said she had raised young Yuna after an accident killed her parents. That's all I could get out of her."

"Did she know what she was doing in the chapel?"

"She said that someone had been following them for days. She thought it was maybe the person who had been sending her the hate mail, so, when Yuna offered to find out who the person was, she thought it was a great idea. But she warned the young woman to be careful. It sounded dangerous.

"Now, the old relative and this Yuna Yoshida had been accompanied to Louisiana by another relative, Yuna's twin brother Haruki. Haruki is almost completely deaf and mute. He reads lips well, but his English is very limited. The young man went missing at the same time as his dead sister. The relative seemed to think that he might have wanted to accompany her to protect her. But we won't know more until we find him."

"Bummer. So, we still don't know who she met. Did Yuna tell the relative anything?"

"She said she didn't."

"They must have driven."

"Yes, they had a rental car."

"In the relative's name?"

"Yes, of course. It's gone, but we have the license plate and make of the car, and we'll find it sooner or later."

"Drat. It will probably tell us nothing."

"At least we're pretty certain that the same person killed her and old Snail," added Andy.

"Anyone have anything else?" asked Sam. Everyone looked glum. He got up from his chair and started pacing. He scratched his head. "So tell me, someone, what do an old ex-convict and a young Japanese tourist have in common?"

Saffron got up and walked to where Sam was. She started counting on her fingers. "We know there is a ship—called the Decepción or the Concepción—that used to be in a bottle that's broken."

"Yes," said Margo, excited. "The murderer took the ship and also went to the Public Library for information on the secret. And he went to the Maritime Museum looking to find out more."

"Hold on, Margo. The officer in charge of the museum could be the murderer. He might be more interested in the secret, or the treasure, or whatever than he let on. And he was right there. "Can't eliminate him."

"Guys, guys," said Saffron lifting another finger up high. "There's also the painting, *The Golden Gift Of Silence*, which probably still hangs in the judge's library." She looked at Margo poignantly. "You and I are going to visit Jefferson Renard's house tomorrow and ask him if that painting still exists."

"I can't tomorrow. Beatrice, your psychic is coming tomorrow, you said. Or is that off?"

"Shoot, I forgot all about the séance. Let's go see him this afternoon then."

"Okay. So, Saffron, should we have a gathering for the people coming? Like a meet and greet?"

"How should I know? I can ask Beatrice what she would prefer. Maybe a small cocktail party."

"Girls, girls," growled Sam impatiently. "Can we please focus on the murders?"

"Oh, okay," Saffron said, and she shrugged. "So, one, we have the ship. Two, the painting. And three, the hate mail."

"Why the hate mail?"

"Because that was why she came to Half Moon Bay. Wasn't that what she told Sam?"

Margo jumped up. "Of course," she said. "That's what she told Father Armand. She came to Half Moon Bay because of some threatening letters she was getting from someone who lives here in town concerning a family secret that she had no idea about."

The friends all turned to look at her surprised. She quickly answered, "But you didn't hear it from me."

Chapter 32

Dr. Gabe and the Book—Monday Afternoon

MARGO LOOKED AT HER WATCH and decided she had time to visit Dr. Gabe before meeting with Saffron. After calling the hospital and assuring herself that he would be there, she set off walking.

The St. Hildegard Memorial Hospital of Half Moon Bay stood right behind St. Quintian's Church, connected by a pleasant, stone-flagged path surrounded by well-kept gardens, and remained as cheerfully beautiful as it had been in Colonial times. Once full of nuns and novices, it had been a teaching convent where—unlike teaching convents of the time where discipline was imparted with cruelty and without regret—the nuns had happily remained kind and understanding of the droves of orphans and poor children who were lucky enough to go to St. Hildegard's school.

Sadly, though, one day the convent ran out of novices. Times had changed, and young girls lost interest in dedicating their lives to religion. One by one, the nuns that remained got old and died, and soon the convent was left empty.

Then, someone had the brilliant idea of converting the building into a hospital. The rooms—left the way they had been originally—were large and spacious, and the windows were kept open almost all year round. Pristine white curtains billowed in the wind, and from the rooms, you could clearly hear the chirping of the birds and the squeals of the children playing in the playground of the elementary school around the corner. This was not a hospital visited by death, but one loved by life. Patients were cured at a surprisingly high rate, which the locals attributed to the protection of St. Hildegard, Half Moon Bay's unofficial Patron Saint.

The early afternoon was hot, with a sticky breeze coming in from the bay. Independence Park was full of trees and plenty of shade. Margo wished she had the time to sit on a bench and sip on a soda, or a lemonade. These were the last days of summer holidays, and there were children squealing with delight, and dogs barking, and nannies pushing strollers everywhere, and as usual, a long waiting line in front of the cotton candy cart and the Cajun Dog stand.

Dr. Gabe Gutierrez had his offices on the first floor of the hospital. She followed the signs to his office and found herself at the end of a hallway, facing a lovely, old fashioned set of French doors with beveled window panes to her left, and she entered.

The reception was empty and quiet, but the curtains in the large windows had been opened, and the sun shone onto the rust-colored carpeting with buoyant enthusiasm making the room look friendly and welcoming. To one corner, a set of children's toys, small tables with chairs, and a child-sized bookcase full of books, reminded her that Dr. Gabe was a pediatrician.

She stood in the middle of the room wondering what to do. After some hesitation, she sat down in one of the armchairs and decided to wait. Parenting magazines filled the low table in front of her. They competed for space with Good Housekeeping, Gardening, and all those subjects someone thought were appropriate for mothers of sick children.

The bushes outside of the doctor's office rustled in the gentle breeze, and she sat back and leaned her head against the back of the chair. The mellow quiet was making her sleepy. She touched the book in her lap with her eyes closed. It had made her purse so heavy. She remembered the chapel, and that pile of bones she desecrated by pulling the book out of a skeleton's embrace and making the whole tower of bones collapse. She hoped that what was in it was worth everything she had done to obtain it.

Finally, when she was beginning to doze off, the office door opened, and a young woman pushing a stroller came out, followed by Dr. Gabe who noticed her and smiled.

"Come in. Margo Fontaine, right? Mimi has told me a lot about you." He placed his arm on her shoulder and sort of pushed her into the room and closed the door behind them. It was awkward.

"What did she tell you about me?" she asked, annoyed.

"Oh, you know. Nothing much. Anyway, sit down, sit down. Father Armand warned me that you had an assignment for me."

"Yes, a book. I think it's really old. And it's soaking wet. I wrapped it in a towel. I really didn't know what else to do with it. I briefly considered drying it with my hairdryer, but I've been too busy."

"Wow, I sure am glad you didn't do that. May I see it?" Dr. Gabe extended his hand and waited for Margo to be ready to relinquish her treasure to him. He laughed. "It's okay, Margo. I promise to take good care of it. Let's see what we've got here." He unwrapped the book carefully and turned it all around, examining the corners, opening the cover gently. The cover had dried already in uneven patches and was beginning to peel.

"I thought maybe I should wipe it down with petroleum jelly, you know, like Vaseline, or with some olive oil or something," Margo said, "because the outside is beginning to crack."

"Goodness gracious, I sure am glad you didn't do that. It could have turned the leather binding into something as hard as wood. Leather is skin. Well, it's dead skin, but it still needs to breathe. Covering it with oil wouldn't have allowed that. There's something called Restoration Leather Conditioner. It's specially made for this."

"How about the inside? The pages are all stuck together. Can that be fixed?"

"Of course. The best thing would be to use a vacuum freeze dryer. The hospital purchased one at the end of 2005 when Hurricane Katrina flooded the basement where the historical records of the convent were kept. Of course, if we hadn't been storing St. Hildegard's journals down there, nobody would have bothered. But now we do have one, sitting unplugged and gathering dust."

"And the vacuum freezer will dry the book?"

"It should. We place the book in the vacuum chamber frozen. The vacuum is pulled and the heat is introduced. The book will dry while it remains frozen at a temperature below 32°F or 0°C. The ice crystals will vaporize without melting, causing no additional swelling or distortion."

"Umm," Margo said and frowned, feeling confused.

"It's complicated," said Dr. Gabe, and he chuckled. "I can explain better."

"Umm, no, no. It's okay. How about the cover?"

"The binding? I'll take it off if you don't mind. And I promise to be careful. I'll put it back on, and you'll never know it had been damaged, to look at it."

"I guess it's okay. I thought it would be an easy process."

"But it is easy. And it won't take very long. Give me a couple of days and you'll have your book back."

"So how come you know so much about this?"

"I'm a book lover. Always have been. My dad used to have a used book store. That's where I spent my days after school, sitting at his desk, reading instead of doing my homework." Dr. Gabe shook his head and smiled. "When Katrina flooded South Louisiana, I was an intern here. I saw the devastation and cried over all the magnificent old books that had been stored in the basement. When I finally managed to talk the City Council into calling for a fundraiser and we bought the machine, I learned how to use it. And now, I'm the resident expert in old book restoration." Dr. Gabe smiled. "So many precious books have been lost throughout history, that the few we have left, we have to take good care of them, right?"

Dr. Gabe stood up, and Margo knew it was time to go. Dr. Gabe looked at his watch and apologized. "Sorry to cut this short, my dear, but I have an appointment. I'll see you in a couple of days, yes?"

Margo nodded and left with a heavy heart. She hoped the book would be okay. All of a sudden it just seemed so important to keep it safe.

Chapter 33

Margo and Saffron in Regnard Mound— Monday Afternoon

MARGO LOOKED AROUND and saw Saffron's white Mercedes, waiting for her at the curb. She hurried down the steps and jumped into the car.

"Thank you so much for picking me up," she said.

"You need to get a new car."

"I know. I'll have time after the séance. In the meantime, I rely on the kindness of strangers."

"Is he nice?"

"Who?

"Dr. Gabe, of course."

"Oh, yes. Very nice, very avuncular. And, he says he can fix the book."

"That's awesome. At least you will not have put your life in danger for nothing."

"True, but, it's possible that we won't find anything interesting in it, anything that pertains to this case anyway."

"Hey, have you noticed that Dr. Gabe's dating Mimi?"

"Yes, I saw them in church together, holding hands, no less. But he seems more excited about it than Mimi. Besides, isn't Mimi like ten years older than he is?"

"Regardless. She's getting old. It's a good thing she has someone."

Margo nodded. "Does Jefferson Renard know we're coming?"

"Yes, I just got off the phone with him. Renata is there as well. He didn't sound too excited."

"I haven't opened the library doors since my uncle passed," Jefferson Renard said when he had heard them out. They hadn't been asked to sit, so they stood in the ornate hallway filled to the brim with antique tables, mirrors in gold-leafed frames, and tons of imposing paintings. Margo gulped. The place was like a museum. She quietly admired an Ingraham Mantel Clock with red marble inlays, a blush-and-ivory Royal Worcester vase, and some other pieces she didn't recognize, and those beautiful Persian rugs all over the floor. She loved Persian rugs.

Renata—Mimi's daughter—kept staring at Saffron and Margo with hostility, as if hating the intrusion. But Margo knew it was the unforgiving bitterness of losing Jack to her, and not the intrusion, that bothered Renata so much.

"Please follow me," Jefferson finally said, and he told the butler who'd been standing unobtrusively in a corner that they would be in Grand-père's library, should he be needed.

Jefferson Renard's mansion had to be the biggest house in Half Moon Bay, and the most richly furnished. He was the last descendant of a renowned family of judges and politicians and probably held himself at great pressure to get married and have heirs. And, by the way he ogled Renata, Margo could tell that it was she that he wanted to have those descendants with.

Unlike Margo's house, Jefferson Renard's was a true plantation home, complete with colonnades, balconies with wrought-iron banisters, and wrap-around porches. Generations of rich Renards must have scoured the world for all the unique and exquisite pieces her eyes could see in every corner and on every surface.

They passed the foyer and continued through a warren of more or less intimidatingly extravagant rooms and hallways, off of which wooden doors probably led to more warrens of extravagantly rich rooms and hallways. Every wall she could see was covered with portraits, seascapes, landscapes, and ornate mirrors. And everywhere they walked, these fine rugs covered the floors and kept their steps from echoing into the vast beyond.

"Regnard Mound Plantation is a rare example of local architecture influenced by early settlers from France and the West Indies," recited Jefferson Renard as if he were giving them a tour.

"The family once owned about 900 acres that stretched all the way to the Mississippi River. At one time, our plantation was almost as large as the one fenced in by Francesc Fontayn." He nodded toward Margo in acknowledgment of her heritage.

While Jefferson Renard and his entourage continued the tour, Margo stopped to catch her breath by a series of floor-to-ceiling windows that gave a ravishing view of the garden, with its miniature bridge, a few old-fashioned benches under the magnolia trees, and even a pond where ducks swam placidly back and forth.

"The main house was built around 1790 as a small settler's house," she heard Jefferson continue, and she hurried to catch up with them. "But as Half Moon Bay became more prosperous, so did the family. With help from the income of the family coffee and sugar cane plantations of Saint-Domingue, the house was enlarged and renovated extensively at the turn of the 19th century.

"In time, the land was sold, but most of the furnishings in the house remain original. Whatever has fallen into disrepair, I've had restored in as much as funds have allowed me. Eventually, I expect to leave all this to my own children, and hope they will carry on the preservation of this magnificent building."

At the end of the hallway, they stopped by a locked door and waited. "The housekeeper will be here shortly."

To make polite conversation, Margo asked about the book one of his ancestors had written, the Pirate Treasures: From Haiti To Half Moon Bay.

"Oh, yes. Of course, I've heard of it. It was all Grand-père ever wanted to talk about. Especially later in life when he became senile."

"Do you still have it?"

"I have no idea. I really never bothered to look for it. I felt like I knew the book by heart anyway after all those years of listening to the stories over and over again, so there didn't seem to be any point in reading it. But if we still have it, it could be anywhere. There are thousands of books in there. You'll see for yourself in a minute."

The housekeeper had finally managed to find the right key in her enormous key ring, and Jefferson Renard opened with a grandiose flourish the two wings of the door that led to Grand-père's magnificent library.

Margo's breath got caught in her chest. The library was circular, and the dome of its ceiling reached almost to the sky. Every inch of the walls was covered with shelves of books. And every inch left over was covered in rose-colored marble: floors, columns, pedestals. Jefferson had been right. It would take years to locate one single book among the thousands upon thousands in front of her. In the center of the room, a larger than life-sized marble statue of a bearded man showed the giant bent down on one knee—muscles bulging—holding up the earth on his back.

Margo got stuck in front of the statue and stared in awe. She heard Jefferson Renard step to her side. "It's Atlas, the Titan god of endurance and astronomy, condemned to hold up the sky for all eternity. It's a beauty, isn't it? It kind of makes you face your mortality." Jefferson Renard sighed, and Margo looked at him surprised. In spite of his short stature, his thick, foggy glasses, and his receding hairline, she got the sudden feeling that there was more to him that the simple politician. Then, Jefferson moved away and the moment passed.

She approached the others. They were all standing in front of an enormous canvas where a maleficent looking young girl held an ugly sack-cloth doll in her hand and stared down at the group from over the fireplace mantel. There was so much evil emanating from the painting that Margo shivered. No wonder the library door was locked.

"I wanted to burn the damned thing, or give it away, but the terms of the will are clear. The painting will remain here until the treasure has been found."

"What treasure?"

"I have no idea, but I'm sure it's just a bunch of bull."

"Could you get rid of it anyway?"

"Not under any circumstance. The family trust that governs my life and my every move insists that I keep it here if I want to live in the house.

Therefore, I keep this room locked, so I don't have to come across these two by mistake."

"So, this is the famous *Golden Gift Of Silence,* isn't it? We saw this painting in an old newspaper. Look." Margo took the paper out of her handbag. It had been placed in a transparent plastic envelope to protect it.

Jefferson took the plastic envelope and looked at it. "The Daily States. Hmm. I've never seen this before. Where did you get it?"

"Oh, from someone who didn't need it anymore. Look at the photograph. It's old and grainy, but look, you can see the painting well enough to recognize it, and you can see that there's a glass bottle with a ship in it. It's that ship that we're interested in seeing."

Jefferson turned around suddenly and looked at the fireplace. "Well, I'll be," he said, sounding puzzled. "Where's the ship?" He walked quickly to the door and told the housekeeper he needed some help. "Marie, have you seen the bottle that was there on the mantel above the fireplace? You know, the one with the ship in it?" The housekeeper looked flustered and shook her head. Then everyone, as if by accord, walked around the library looking for the missing item. But it was pointless. The ship in the bottle was gone.

"I don't understand," Jefferson said. "It's always been here," he said, patting the empty spot. "Ever since I can remember."

The group was silent on the way back to the front door. Jefferson looked like he was deep in thought, and Renata eyed Margo with malice. They were saying their good-byes, telling Jefferson thank you so much, and so sorry about your ship, when Margo noticed some unusual blue envelopes on the side table by the door. Nosy, because she couldn't help herself, she looked at them. They were addressed one to Jefferson and one to Renata, and the sender was Beatrice Saint-Clair.

"Do y'all know Beatrice?"

"Yes, umm, we do kind of," said Renata, squirming uncomfortably.

"Did she invite you both to the séance?"

"Why do you ask, Margo, and how is it any of your business?"

"Y'all might want to open those letters and read about the change of address," Saffron said flippantly.

"And why's that?"

"Because I can't have the séance at my house. So, it's going to be at hers." And she pointed a thumb at Margo.

When they stepped out of the house, the stars had already come out, and they twinkled faintly in the brightly lit horizon. Lights were on in the park, and in the boulevard, and the repetitive music from the singing fountain wafted their way. People were still out and about, but their noises were muted, unwinding the day. It was a lovely night for a walk. The breeze was soft and cool, and the rhythmic toss of the waves as they hit the shore and retreated, permeated the seaside town with a mesmerizing magic ambiance. There was so much to think about, and Margo couldn't stand the thought of having to sit in a car again.

"Would you mind terribly if I decided to walk home?"

"Why would I mind?"

"Because you'll probably think it's not safe. I don't want you to worry."

"I promise not to worry. But why would you want to walk? It's so far."

"Oh, no more than twenty minutes. It's a lovely night, and I miss sitting by the water and smelling the ocean breeze."

"In that case, why don't we drive to the Pirate Bay Hotel? Let's pick up some ice cream at the restaurant and walk down to the Marina. We can sit outside on a bench on the pier and watch the boats for a while, and then I'll let you walk home from there."

Margo laughed. "Sounds perfect."

Later, they stood on the veranda of the Pirate Bay, leaning on the banister and watching the people come and go on the Boardwalk, chasing kids and dogs, while they waited for Manuel to bring their ice cream out. The hotel was still packed even though the holiday season was just about over, and music poured out from the bar, keeping life busy and exciting. Tables on the veranda were full of people drinking, eating, chatting, and waiters and waitresses bustled about with trays full of stuff. Humanity seemed compelled to flock to the ocean side. Every year, more tourists came, and they stayed longer.

"There are several things that bother me about this whole thing," Margo said as they strolled down to the Marina holding their ice cream bowls. "For example, the death of the old man."

"What about it?"

"For one thing, how did he know there was a ship in a bottle? Did someone tell him in prison? Did he hear someone mention it? Did he read about it?"

"He could have read about it."

"I don't know, Saffron. It's too much of a coincidence that he was Mr. Snail's brother."

"I grant you that that is strange. Maybe the butler heard something and mentioned it to the brother. You know, as families do, shooting the breeze."

"And when he got out, he came to check it out, or something like it?"

"Maybe he came looking for his brother. Didn't know he was dead."

"Maybe. And now that he's dead as well, we'll never know." Margo licked the cold creamy ice cream off the spoon and stared out at the water. Some of the yachts were hosting parties. You could see the people dancing from where they stood, and the music carried to shore in ragged snippets, competing with the music from the bar.

"Why kill him, you know? He was just a run-down old man. Why bother killing him over a ship in a bottle. It couldn't have been that valuable."

"And then it broke and it became less valuable, I guess."

"Yes. But listen. You have to have a truly worthwhile reason to want to have a rendezvous out there. Way out there. And then to kill that person? Not only do you risk being found out, but it's not that easy to kill a human being. It might seem easy on TV, and it does happen occasionally, but it takes a lot of evil, or hatred, or determination, to kill, just like that."

"I know. I agree with you that it makes no sense. Unless there's really a treasure, of course."

"Or unless the murderer thinks there's really a treasure. But there are no treasures left in Half Moon Bay. There's nothing new left to discover.

You know that. This town—having been a haven for pirates—has been gone over with a fine, fine-tooth comb. What there was to be discovered, was found a long time ago."

Margo licked her ice cream some more. The idea was forming in her head that they had neglected one very important step in the investigation. They hadn't checked the first crime scene thoroughly enough, and she should go back and take a look at it for herself.

"How are we going to discover who did it? We don't have any clues."

"I have no idea, Saffron, but we forget that the assailant in the second murder was wounded as well. There were two distinct blood types on the floor, and Yuna's combat knife had blood on it, and it was not hers."

"I'd forgotten that. I'll call the doctors, vets, and pharmacies again, to see if there's any update on someone with a festering knife wound, either looking for medical help, or for wound-cleaning and bandaging supplies. There's a slight chance that by now that wound has gotten infected if it hasn't been cleaned properly."

"Thanks, Saffron. I think I'll go back to the first crime scene to see if we missed something."

"Don't do that. I can't let you go alone."

"I won't go alone. I was thinking of hiring Manny to row me out there. He loves an adventure, and—like any teenager—he can probably use some spending money."

"You will promise to take care of yourself, Margo, won't you?"

"I promise I will. Please don't worry about me."

Margo watched Saffron head back to her car, and she started walking on the waterfront. She watched the pedestrians stroll along the Boardwalk, their children still full of energy, skipping, and hopping despite the lateness of the hour. This time of the year, the breeze was cool and pleasant at night. No wonder people didn't want to go home. There was magic in the air, with the lights of the anchored yachts twinkling in the night, reflecting on the shimmering water, the faint music in the distance, even the muted sounds of the cars coming and going on the almost empty streets. It was the perfect night for a stroll. It was the perfect night to stay up late.

She stopped to lean against a lamp post across the street from her house and closed her eyes. You could hear the surf as it hit the sand and it frothed away. She wished she didn't have to go inside either.

Chapter 34

Marie Regrets

IT HAD BEEN A LONG DAY. Marie's feet were swollen again, and they were hurting. She slowly walked to the back of the house and sat down in the kitchen to have a cup of tea.

She knew she was in trouble, and the money she had been given to turn the other way was burning in her pocket like live fire. She had been unable to spend it because of her feelings of guilt.

When she heard Monsieur Renard telling the guests that the library had been sealed since his uncle's death, she panicked. Because during a house party, she had allowed one person in. Nobody else had the keys to the library except for her. Whenever the cleaning crews came to do the big room, she let them in, and she stood by the door supervising. So, if something was missing, the police would eventually figure out that she had been responsible. What to do?

First thing next morning, she was going to go to the police station and confess. It was better than being caught.

She tried to remember the person she let in. But she couldn't, not really. The house had been full of people, an important party. They came and went. Waiters had been hired for the night. There was no way she could possibly remember, not after all this time. Except that it was a man. Of that she was sure. Well, almost sure.

But Marie gave things some further thought and decided that a trip to the police would be premature. Even though Monsieur Renard was displeased that the bottle was gone, he didn't seem too angry. No need to stir the pot. Maybe it would be better to wait and see what happened. Yes. That was the prudent thing to do. She would wait and see what happened. Oh dear, she thought to herself. What have I done?

Chapter 35

Back to the Beach—Tuesday Morning

TUESDAY MORNING, MARGO HAD A HARD TIME getting out of bed. The sun was shining by droves through the sheer curtains into her second-floor bedroom, and Ice and Fenway were sprawled on the comforter—purring—unwilling to wake up and get going, and she too wished that she could spend the morning in bed. Monday had been so long and so exhausting, that one good night of sleep hadn't been enough to bring her usual perky energy back.

But she told Manny to be ready to leave first thing in the morning, so she struggled out of bed, got dressed, grabbed her backpack, and headed downstairs. Waving Lucy's and Brooks' objections away, she gulped her coffee down and opened the front door.

The fresh, salty air of the early morning woke her up. No cars drove by on the empty street as she crossed over to the Boardwalk. She turned around and looked at the house. Upstairs in her bedroom window sill, the two little faces of Ice and Fenway stared down at her, probably wondering why she had had to leave so early.

Except for some joggers, and for a couple of old-timers walking their dogs, the Boardwalk was quiet. Trash that hadn't been picked up yet, dotted the ample street, and trash cans that lined this end of the Boardwalk were brimming full.

She opened the paper bag Lucy had pressed into her hand and saw that she had packed a sandwich, a tangerine, and a small juice. Sweet Lucy. She nibbled on the bread stuffed thickly with sliced turkey, cheese, and tomatoes on mayonnaise as she headed for the Marina. The Sandwich

Terns were out in force, filling the air with their raucous gwit-gwit, and taking turns to plunge dive into the water for breakfast fish.

She threw her empty paper bag in a trash can and followed the Boardwalk to the end where the Marina began, where Manny would be waiting for her. Here in the Marina, crews wearing orange vests were cleaning up the pier and the sand on the beach, emptying trash cans and straightening upturned beach chairs and tables. Out in the bay, you could see the dozens of fishing boats accompanied by the gulls that habitually circled them, hoping for a few discarded fish.

She turned into the Marina and sighted Manny standing upright in his boat, waving both arms at her with enthusiasm. Manny, young, friendly, adventure-loving, and always full of enthusiasm. You had to like Manny. His boat was his life, in spite of his mother's constant begging him to study mon fils, so you won't be a loser like your père. But Manny just gave her a hug and told her he loved her—or so she had heard—and kept on doing what he loved to do best.

It would have been easier to drive, but after looking at Saffron's photographs, Margo was pretty sure the murderer came from the sea.

"Why the sea?" asked Saffron.

"For one thing, because of the way Mr. Snail fell. Looking at the water, watching the murderer walk away, then being stabbed, falling backward. Don't you think?"

"I don't know."

"I don't either. It's just a hunch."

"We should have checked for tire marks and footsteps, Margo, shouldn't we have?"

"Absolutely. But Sam was the one in charge, and he should have known better."

"You would think."

Manny navigated expertly the quiet waters off Half Moon Bay. They crossed the bay, parallel to the Boardwalk, and Manny piloted the boat around the rocky outcrop like he had done it many times before. For a fleeting second Margo wondered if the young Manny would have been capable of murdering an old man in cold blood, but quickly shooed the thought out of her mind. Manny was too kind and friendly to do an old man harm.

"Manny," she said anyway, "you do know someone was murdered on the stretch of beach we're heading to, right?"

"Oh yes, Miss Margo. Everyone knows."

"And you're really good at finding your way around here. These are dangerous waters where these rocks sit under the water."

"Yes, they are, but my dad and I used to come this way all the time. I know every single one of them where they are."

"Do you ever come out here?"

"No, not since my dad passed. It makes me sad. I only came today because you needed me to."

"Do you know anyone who comes out here?"

"Some of the high schoolers party out here, but they drive, as far as I know."

Margo sighed. No, Manny wouldn't be capable. "Tell me something, have you brought anyone else out here lately?"

"No."

"Do you know anyone else with a boat who would have brought the murderer out here?"

"No, Miss. Really. If I had heard, I would have told Sheriff Sam already."

"Okay, Manny. If you do hear something or remember something, make sure and tell Sam about it."

Margo watched the shore as they approached. The water was choppy out here, not like within the confines of the bay itself, that was protected by breakers. Her stomach felt queasy from the tossing about, and she almost threw up overboard.

They stopped a couple of feet from the shore and jumped into the water. They struggled to pull the little boat onto the sand, and Margo sure was grateful to have worn shorts and slip-on tennies.

They waded in the freezing-cold water. Then, something else occurred to Margo.

"Tell me, Manny, if I were to come ashore with a small boat, could I do it anywhere along this stretch?"

"No, Miss Margo, not anywhere. This is where I would do it."

"How come?"

"It's the only spot where the sand declines gently toward the deep. At any other spot, the shore drops so fast, so deep, that just one person manning the boat alone would be unable to pull it ashore by himself."

"Oh."

"And if you don't pull it out, it will float away."

"Oh, I see. So, this is where we should start looking, and head toward the murder scene."

"Yes, I would think so. Follow me."

"I should be the one walking in the front. I'm the one looking for clues."

"Yes. But I'm the one making sure that you don't step on a snake." He chuckled. "Some of them are hard to see. They blend in too well."

The shrubs were dry. Margo looked around for dry vomit, wondering if the lack thereof meant that the boat's pilot was a seasoned sailor. While the wind had swept the sand one way and the other—making all footsteps disappear—there was the need to look around carefully.

"This is the logical route," Manny was saying. "There's a path of sorts already, so he might have walked this way."

"Tell me, Manny, why do you keep calling the murderer he?"

"Well, Miss, because I can't imagine a lady shoving a knife into the side of a sick old man."

"How do you know he was sick?"

"My uncle saw him at Thirsty's. He was a regular mess."

Margo stopped and grabbed Manny's arm to make him stop and look at her. "Did he tell your uncle why he was in town?"

"Yes, he told everyone. He said he was about to win the lottery. He seemed very pleased with himself, *mon oncle* said. He had a traveling bag full of money. I'm surprised he didn't get murdered for it."

"So, he had a lot of money, huh?"

"That's what mon oncle said. He was going to meet someone who was going to give him the keys to some treasure in exchange for the money."

"Did he say who?"

"No. He said, person. Not man, not woman. Just person."

"But did your uncle actually see the money?"

"Mais oui. The old man took a wad out and paid for a round for all the people there."

"So, someone could have followed him out to steal his money. It was all gone when we found him."

"But, all the way out here, Miss? Plenty of places where he could have offed him close to Thirsty's. Why the need to come all the way out here?"

"You're right, Manny. In that case, the only reason to come out here would have been to make the exchange. To pick up whatever he was buying. Without being seen."

Margo stepped the trail behind Manny, letting him do the watching for dangerous reptiles while she walked almost doubled over, looking for clues. Frustrated that there was nothing to be found, she carried on, trying not to feel discouraged. There was nothing. Absolutely nothing except for the sand—always blowing, getting into your nose and your teeth—and the shrubbery, dry, coastal, generic shrubbery.

They reached the scene of the crime that had all but blended into the scenery already, and Margo shielded her eyes with the palm of her hand and looked around. It was turning into a hot day, for sure. No trace of fall in the air yet. She scrunched her eyes and stared into the monochromatic vegetation around her, hoping for a spot of color that would stand out, or a discarded piece of evidence.

"What are you looking for exactly?" asked Manny.

"I'm not sure. I was hoping to find something that would point me to the killer."

"All I see is a patch of dark sand," he said. "If it was here, it's gone now."

Margo picked up a dry branch and poked about the dark patch. "This is where he got knifed and bled out." She bent down and picked up a small piece of metal that could be anything, and she placed it in an evidence baggie. She poked some more and found another shard of glass.

"Is that what you were looking for?" asked Manny. He walked over to Margo and stared at the shard of glass.

"It's a piece of the broken bottle. It could have a print or at least a partial print." She quickly grabbed it with another evidence baggie before Manny could touch it. She looked around for the next half hour, inspecting every inch of the crime scene and the surrounding area, but there was nothing else to be found. Then, she looked at Manny, surprised that she hadn't thought about it before.

"Manny, will your boat be safe for another half hour? Will the tide pull it out to sea?"

"Not yet it won't, not if we hurry up. Why?"

"Because, did you ever hear that a pig stole the dead man's arm and took it to its lair?"

Manny suddenly went pale and looked like he was about to throw up. "I sure didn't. Why did you have to tell me that?"

"Come on, Manny, follow me. I'll tell you on the way."

This time, it was Margo who walked ahead. She struggled to walk fast in the sand, which was very difficult with her wet tennies, and when they left the seaside and they could already see ze promontoire where the Parrot Joe Shack sat, she took a quick left and began to climb toward Old Town.

"Where are we going, Miss Margo? I'm worried about my boat."

"We're almost there. And I promise that if something happens to your boat and it gets pulled out to sea, I'll buy you a brand new one."

"But where are we going?"

"Remember those caves behind Old Town? Where all the local kids go hunting for treasure?"

"Yeah, I've been there."

"Well, I think that that's where the wild pig took the arm. It's the only place where you could hide anything."

"You mean that arm?" Manny looked yellow again.

"Yes, that arm. I don't know how on earth nobody thought to go look for it. But it must be in one of those caves."

"And how are we going to find it?"

"By the smell of course," Margo said cheerfully, and she turned around surprised. Manny was vomiting into the bushes.

Chapter 36

The Arm and Other Stuff

"THE PROBLEM, AS I SEE IT, Manny, is that the clues are too scarce, and they all seem to point in different directions."

"What do you mean?"

"Well, the old man gets murdered. They steal his money and disappear with the ship."

"The one in the bottle?"

"Right. It can't be worth that much. It's just the carving of a random ship built inside a bottle. Sailors used to make those all the time back when they spent months at sea. Yet someone stole it from the Judge's house and tried to sell it to the old man. Something went sour, the guy gets knifed, and the murderer disappears with the loot."

"So, for whatever reason, the old man wanted it, but the murderer wanted it more, and he refused to turn it over, right?"

"Seems like it."

They continued on toward the cave formation, passing through clumps of sea rocket, camphor daisy, and seaside purslane.

The midmorning heat beat down on Margo's head and turned every step she took into an effort. The temperature had to be in the mid to high nineties by now. Not a cloud in the sky. And not a drop of water left in her canteen, either. She looked at Manny and saw that he didn't seem to be affected by the heat at all.

They stepped over uneven clumps of Caminada sea oats that ran parallel to the waterfront, planted with the purpose of helping the coastal restoration efforts. They looked healthy and thriving in the hot and humid climate. But with Louisiana's coastline losing wetlands at a rate of 16.57 square miles a year—the equivalent of a football field of coast every hour—those Caminada sea oats were going to have to work extra hard to make a dent.

She wiped the sweat off her brow with her arm. It ran in trickles down her face and her neck, and it got in her eyes, making them burn.

"So, what happened next?"

"What happened was that Saffron and I went to the Maritime Museum, and we ended up discovering a second corpse in the chapel next door." Margo looked at Manny and saw he was turning green and yellow again. "Don't worry, kid, I'll spare you the details. Point is that both victims were killed with some exotic knife that the coroner was not familiar with, probably with the same one."

At the top of the gentle incline, Margo looked up, relieved, happy to be done with the sand dunes. A series of shallow caves, probably dug out by the tides at one time long ago, stood in random formation in front of them. Their entrances were mostly covered in invasive ivy and equally invasive Purple Wisteria: those lush climbing plants with clusters of flowers that everyone likes to have in their yard, but if left to grow wild, have a fondness for choking everything they grow on. Impenetrable mounds of wild blackberries and climbing roses with sharp, vicious-looking thorns dotted the landscape. They walked from one cave entrance to the next, and Margo sniffed the air. Then, she stopped Manny.

"Here we are. This one stinks."

"Do you think the pig's still here?"

"I don't know, Manny, but we could stay at the mouth of the cave and make noise to give it a chance to run away."

"How are we going to do that?"

"Well, you whistle and I clap, real loud. Do you know how to whistle?"

"Of course, I do."

"On the count of three, then."

Margo and Manny clapped, whistled and yelled, but there was no sign of the wild pig. They threw pebbles into the mouth of the hollow space as far as they could, but when there was no wild rush, they decided it was safe to enter. They pushed aside the hanging curtain of wisteria and entered cautiously. The cavern wasn't wide, but it was long, and it got lower the further in you ventured. After a few steps, they had to bend over.

This was an ideal place for a lair, but the animal had probably been scared away by the dogs the other day and never dared to come back. There was no apparent fresh burrowing.

"Don't look so scared, Manny. It's gone."

"I am scared. Didn't you hear about that lady last year who was walking her dog close to Old Town? She was mauled by one of them pigs. She barely made it, and the dog died."

"The pig probably felt threatened by the dog. But an attack like that is an exception. The pigs mind their own business and just want to be left alone." Margo grabbed Manny's arm and pulled him deeper into the cave.

Even after all this time, the air in the cave was stale and heavy with unpleasant odors. Manny walked with his hand in front of his nose and looked like he wanted to run away. But Margo held him firmly by the arm.

They found the rotting limb in a corner, among a cloud of bugs that hung on like groupies. But there wasn't much left of it except for the bones sticking out from what remained of the skin, and the fabric that had covered some of the arm.

Margo squatted in front of the remains, holding a handkerchief in front of her nose. There had to be a clue here. She poked at the metacarpals and the phalanges with the stick she was still holding.

"Point the flashlight this way," she told Manny. "I think I see something."

"What is it, Miss Margo?" he asked, approaching her and pointing the light at the bony hand.

"Look here, between the fingers. I think it's a strip of cord. A blue cord."

"You're not going to touch that, are you?"

"Of course not." Margo took her phone out and took a number of photographs from different angles. "Now watch this." She pulled an evidence baggie from her backpack, wrapped it over her hand, and gingerly pulled the strip of fabric. Then, with a deft twist of her wrist, she turned the baggie around and sealed it. "And that's how you pick up evidence without touching it." And Manny was duly impressed.

Once outside in the fresh air, they both looked closely at the strip of yarn. It was rough and unusual looking. Neither Manny nor Margo had any idea what it was. She was going to have to ponder on that, see if she could figure it out.

They walked back to the murder scene and looked around some more, but there really was nothing else to find, and remembering the boat on the sand and the potentially rising tide, they hurried back to find that the water was almost ready to claim the little boat.

On the way back, Margo was pensive. The boat was rocked from side to side by the incoming tide, and she held on tight to its sides so she wouldn't fall overboard. They had to hurry up with their investigation. Pretty soon, the State Police bullies would descend on Sam, take things over like bulldozers, and mow down anyone who got in their way. And especially that Bergeron guy, the one that liked to shove everyone around, what was his name? He was the worst. For some reason, he hated Sam and hated all of Half Moon Bay.

They had to hurry up and solve the crimes, or else.

Chapter 37

Beatrice in Half Moon Bay

MARGO WALKED ALONG THE BOARDWALK—heading home—hands in pockets, head down, kicking stray pebbles to the side of the road. On the beach, children screamed with delight chasing waves and building sandcastles. And out there somewhere, a murderer lived his life unaffected by his deeds, assured that he was going to escape punishment.

It annoyed her that he was probably gloating. It had been two weeks now, and two murders, and they had no clue who he was, or what had motivated him to kill. On TV, the perps were always apprehended by the end of the show, but in real life, it was different. A minute police department, and a sheriff that wasn't all that good at solving murders, and what did they have? Absolutely nothing.

As usual, walking along the beach made her pensive, and she wondered where life would have taken her had her mother not died so young. She would have never come to live in Half Moon Bay, never met her relatives, never made friends, never seen her best friend Jenny dead in her arms, nor ever had any cats.

She ran across the boulevard, avoiding a couple of cars that zoomed by and honked their horn at her, and took the steps up to her front door two at a time. She was about to stick the keys in the door when it opened by itself, and a startled Lucy explained—breathlessly—that they had forgotten that Beatrice the medium was arriving today.

"And she showed up, and look, here's her luggage, and she went to the beach, and she is sitting on that bench. You can see her from here."

Lucy extended an arm and pointed toward the bay where benches were placed scattered along the sand with a view of the water.

"And this is her luggage?" Margo asked, looking forlornly at the two pieces of luggage, incongruous, unmatching, and way too big, sitting to one side of the entrance.

"Carpetbag?" Lucy asked.

"I think so. They look made of carpeting material. So why are they here and not in the hotel?"

"I have no idea. But she did give the impression that she thought she was staying here."

"Really? I don't recall having invited her to stay with us."

"So, what do we do?"

"We can't be rude, I guess. And we have plenty of rooms. Any of them made up for guests?"

"I can make one up in a half-hour. Shall I tell Brooks to bring her luggage upstairs?"

Lucy looked troubled, as troubled as Margo felt. Had Saffron discreetly decided not to mention this detail, or had she forgotten? "Lucy, I'll be right back. I'm going to talk to her. Get the room ready, just in case."

Margo ran recklessly back across the boulevard, again avoiding the zooming cars, the insults, and the honking of angry horns, while elevating a quick prayer to St. Dennis, the patron saint of frenzy, just in case.

Beatrice—unaware of Lucy's dilemma—sat in absolute repose, with her back to Margo, looking out to sea. As Margo approached, she saw the woman's long, wavy hair, moving softly in the breeze. She saw the woman breathe in hard as if she had sighed and felt like an intruder. For a second, Margo felt herself in her place—a newcomer, a stranger—probably surprised at the tranquility and the beauty of the little bay. She remembered her first time in Half Moon Bay, the aroma of the sea, the gentle breeze, the raucous cry of all those seabirds she didn't recognize, always circling overhead. And the muted sounds of happy people running on the beach, the dogs chasing children, the little boats bobbing on the water. So much happiness she had never known before. And they actually had palm trees. You wouldn't think they would grow in this part of the world, but the weather never got cold enough in the winter, so they thrived. And the beach looked like a tropical paradise.

She caught up with the stranger, went around the bench discreetly making enough noise to be heard, and planted herself in front of Beatrice.

"Bienvenue en Louisiane. My name is Margo Fontaine. You met my housekeeper, Lucy."

"Thank you, Margo Fontaine. My name is Beatrice Saint-Clair." She stuck an arm out and they shook hands. Then—as if she had received an electric shock—she looked at Margo, her eyes huge with surprise, and her hand went to her mouth. "Oh, no," she said, staring at Margo.

"What happened?" Margo sat down on the bench next to the stranger, and she stared back, worried.

"He's not dead. He's on his way back."

"What on earth do you mean, he's not dead?"

"I'm so sorry. It popped out of my mouth. It doesn't usually work this way."

"What doesn't, and who's not dead?"

"When I touched your hand, I got this image of a young soldier with a backpack, his hat in his hand, walking this way. Somehow I knew he was walking this way."

"That's not funny." Margo jumped up from the bench and twisted her hands. The image that jumped into her mind was horrifying. It was Jack, somewhere out there, still alive, God only knew in what kind of danger, doing his best to survive, struggling to make it home.

"Please don't be angry. I didn't mean to upset you. Sometimes images jump into my mind, and there's nothing really I can do about it."

"How did you know about Jack?"

"I tell you, it was an image that came to me."

"That would imply that you're actually psychic, and surely there's no such thing."

"I know. There's no such thing, and yet I get images sometimes, and they're usually right."

"Let's not talk about this," Margo said, her mood completely spoiled. She looked at the woman, not young but still lovely, with that long, flowing blond hair that billowed ever so slightly when the breeze touched it. She seemed to be telling the truth, but how could one know? "Lucy tells me you'll be staying with us."

"Yes, but apparently, I wasn't expected to, was I?"

"Never mind that. We'll be happy to have you. You must be tired after your trip. Why don't we go get you settled?"

"You must be tired too, after all that sailing and running after clues."

Margo stopped and stared at Beatrice. "How on earth would you?" she began, but Beatrice put a hand on her arm and told her, smiling, "Your housekeeper told me." The ice broken, they both laughed and walked companionably along the Boardwalk.

"Unusual last name, Saint-Clair. Where are you from, originally?"

"Actually, my ancestors come from Haiti, but I'm second-generation American, from Florida."

"With blonde hair and blue eyes?"

"My ancestors were mostly French, from Haiti, but French."

Margo grabbed Beatrice's arm to help her navigate the always wild traffic across the boulevard. "Big coincidence then, because we're investigating a couple of murders with Haitian undertones. You'll have to walk faster if you don't want to get run over."

"You're not from around here either, are you?"

"Not really. My mom was born here. She was a famous Opera singer. If you love Opera you might have heard of her, Nicola Fontaine. She sang all the big soprano roles in all the most important theatres, and I was born on the road. We never stayed anywhere for very long. We lived in hotels and patrons' mansions and stuff, but then she died and I came to meet her family—my family—and I made friends, and I stayed."

"Beautiful house."

"Thanks. My mom grew up in it. I had to get it back. But it was very run down. I'm slowly having it restored. It takes a long time."

Beatrice stopped in front of the house and looked at Margo. "It's very lonely, sometimes, isn't it?"

"Yes, it is." Margo sighed. "The house is full of memories that are part of me, but that I never took part in. It's hard to explain."

"And the soldier was your young man?"

"Yes, in another life a long time ago. I fell in love with him when I was a teenager, and it took me years to find him. But when I did, he left. He went to war."

"And now he's trying to come back to you."

"I hope not." Margo shook her head. She now had a new worst nightmare.

"Aren't you happy? Relieved?"

"No. I'm terrified. Because I'm in love with another man." Beatrice looked at her with understanding in her kind, blue eyes. Not wanting any pity, Margo quickly opened the door and went inside.

Chapter 38

Dinnertime Revelations

BROOKS ROSE TO THE OCCASION, and he appeared in the dining room dressed to the nines in his butler uniform. He was even wearing the white gloves. Margo giggled as she watched him bring in an enormous jug of Cajun Lemonade—garnished with sugarcane sticks—on a tray on which sat two tall glasses full of crushed ice. Then, with extreme concentration, he proceeded to pour the lemonade into the frosted glasses and dole them out.

She waited for Beatrice to take a big mouthful thinking that it was your common, garden variety lemonade, and she laughed with delight when she saw Beatrice's eyes open wide with surprise.

"This is the most delicious lemonade I've ever had," she said.

"So glad you like it. It's made with rum, lemonade concentrate, and club soda. And I think Brooks adds a touch of Tabasco sauce. Do you have anything similar in Haiti?"

"To be honest, I've never been, so I don't know. I've had a Haitian *Jacmel* a few times. It's made with Rhum Barbancourt, mango rum, Grand Marnier, and pineapple juice. As for food, the closest I've ever gotten to Haitian food was the stuff my *granmè* used to cook."

Lucy, too, was showing off. There was a dizzying sequence of gumbo, étouffée, boudin, and everything she managed to find in the refrigerator. Meantime, Margo kept an easygoing conversation with her unexpected guest and realized that she too was having a good time.

"So, anyway," said Beatrice after swallowing her last piece of boudin, "my granmè used to make these meat pies. Everybody in the Caribbean makes meat pies, but my granmè, she used to add a sliced hardboiled egg and some lime juice, and they were to die for. She used to roll out her own dough, and it was an all-day affair. You have no idea how hard it is until you have to do it yourself. But I, and I'm ashamed to admit it, I buy the frozen puff pastry already made, and that's how I make my meat pies."

"So, did your family pass down stories about Haiti?"

"Like folktales?"

"Yes."

"My granmè told me children's stories before bedtime when I was little. There was one about a neglected third daughter who became queen, and I think a boy who, in order to be allowed to marry the princess, had to go fetch four hairs from the devil's beard. Oh, and there's the man who was eaten by monsters because he didn't listen to his own dream, and the boy who got killed for eating his father's apple. Stories like that."

"I asked because I was wondering how much you knew about Haitian culture. This case that I'm working on includes a carved ship in a bottle and a painting with a sack-cloth doll whose mouth has been sewn closed shut with red thread."

Lucy came into the room with a pecan pie and behind her walked Brooks with fresh coffee. They moved outside to the veranda, and Brooks served the coffee.

"It sounds to me that the red thread sewing the mouth shut is a blood warning. The ship in the bottle, I don't know. Didn't sailors whittle those to combat the boredom of long stretches at sea? It might have no further meaning."

"So, the ship could just be a plain red herring."

"Yes, and the real clue could be hidden in the painting."

"May I ask you something? And will you answer me honestly?"

"Of course, my dear. What is it?"

Margo set her cup down on the table and looked at her hands. They were shaking. "This young soldier you saw in your vision, was it true?"

"Was it true that I had a vision about him?"

"Yes. I'm afraid I've heard all my life that psychics are charlatans. And I'm sorry, I don't mean to offend."

"You don't, my dear." Beatrice patted Margo's hand kindly. "I, myself never believed in them. Whenever I read news about someone foreseeing a future event, I always scoffed. I never believed in ESP or anything like that."

"But that's what you do now," Margo said, confused.

"Let me tell you something about myself," Beatrice started, and had a sip of her coffee. She looked sadly at the flowers growing in the yard, now falling into darkness as the sun was setting.

"Not that long ago, I was quite an ordinary person. I went to school, I got married, got pregnant. The usual. But my baby died. Then soon after, my husband died as well, and I struggled to get on with my life. I couldn't find a reason to continue living. But I did survive. Somehow.

"And then one day I started seeing things, hearing things. Like visions. I got very scared. I had just lost my husband and my baby, and the fear of death was still fresh in my heart. Of course, you don't know this yet because you're so young, but the first thing you think of when something unusual happens in your body, is that you must be very sick, and you're going to die." Beatrice laughed gently and smiled at Margo.

"But I hated the idea of going to the doctor. I refused to go. I didn't want to deal with any more bad news. Besides, in my family, we had always healed our own bodies naturally, with herbs, with teas. So, that's what I did. I tried everything."

"Did it help?"

"No, it didn't. The visions got worse. It was terrifying. I even thought I might be possessed by the devil. I had always been a good Christian girl, so the devil was always at the back of my mind.

"But eventually I gave in. I couldn't live like that any longer. First I went to my priest, who after many discussions assured me that I was not possessed by the devil. And he had a good friend, a doctor, who wanted me to have an MRI, to see inside my brain in case there was something there that shouldn't be there. They sort of bullied me into going, and I had the MRI done.

"To make a long story short, I have a brain tumor. It's growing, and it's pretty much inoperable. The surgeon said we could try to get it out anyway. What do I have to lose, right?

"But what's the point? Maybe if I had gone to the doctor sooner, who knows? I might have wanted to fight to stay alive. But it's too late."

"Please don't say that, Beatrice. You're still young. Surely you want to live?"

"Yes, I guess so. But I don't have the motivation. I'm tired of the pain, but I'm scared of the surgery. I guess it's easier not to fight it. It will be over soon enough."

"But isn't the pain going to get worse and worse if you don't do anything?"

"I'm not sure. Maybe God will spare me that part."

"Couldn't we do something?" Margo was distressed. Visions of her dead mother tried to break loose from her subconscious mind. But denial had buried them so deep that all they could do was lurk in there and threaten her. "You can't just give up. Maybe get a second opinion?" She grabbed Beatrice's hands. "If it's money that you need, I have plenty of it. We could go to the best specialists. And you wouldn't be alone. You could stay here with us until you recovered. We'll take good care of you, I promise."

Beatrice laughed softly. "You have a kind heart," she said. "But don't be so sad. It's the tumor that has given me this gift."

"What makes you think that?"

"It's somewhere in my temporal lobe. I get seizures that produce what my doctor is fond of calling hallucinations."

"But that's not all they are, are they?"

"No. They are true visions. Every single time they have corresponded with a real event. It's like when I shook your hand and suddenly I wasn't in the park anymore but walking on a dusty road next to this young man dressed as a soldier. It was so hot, and there was so much jungle around us, and I wanted to sit down so badly because I was so tired. And he said, no I can't sit down, not now. I have to hurry home. I have to see her one more time. And right as I was about to ask whom, the jungle vanished and I saw your worried face and I knew, just knew, that he was coming to see you. Now, if you'll excuse me, I better go to bed. I've had such a long day."

Later on, that night, when Margo dragged herself upstairs to go to sleep, she passed by her guest's bedroom to find out if Beatrice needed anything. She almost stepped into the room when she noticed that Beatrice was sitting at the vanity table and Lucy, her housekeeper, was brushing her long blonde hair. They were chatting away happily, so she decided not to interrupt. Beatrice's reflection in the mirror looked exhausted, but she was smiling. With a heavy heart, Margo left them alone and headed for her room instead. She tried very hard not to think of Jack because she was sure that she would cry.

Chapter 39

Dr. Gabe and the Abominable Book

DR. GABE PEELED ASIDE THE PAGES of the prayer book cautiously, making sure he didn't tear them. For all that it had been nestled in a priest's coarse robe for over 100 years, it had survived pretty well. It had been the leather cover and the thick robe that had kept it legible after all those years.

The information in it was sparse. It was a regular prayer book, illuminated in the old fashioned medieval style. On the first page, a shaking hand had written a few words on the flyleaf in the inexperienced handwriting of someone with little practice at writing.

"My friend, you have died but you shall find peace in Heaven. I'm placing your beloved prayer book in your pocket so that it shall be buried with you. Rest assured that after all the misery he has inflicted upon us, our Abbot has died of his wounds. Many died in the uprising, but he didn't survive to continue his evil deeds. The men and women responsible for putting an end to his reign of terror have vanished into the swamps as quietly as they had appeared, and nobody will ever know what all transpired here.

"So, rest in peace, my young friend. You and the others that died before your allotted time in suffering under his malevolent hands have been avenged. I'll see you soon on the other side."

Dr. Gabe continued thumbing carefully through the pages. He found another legible notation in faded black ink, one written by a different hand. The letters were so tiny and tightly written that he had to pull out a magnifying glass to be able to read them.

"*Deus misereatur nostri,*" he read out loud, enunciating carefully the unfamiliar words in Latin. "Monsignor Lafontaine is mad. It was the middle of the night and I couldn't sleep. I snuck out of the dormitories to enjoy the warm summer night, and I noticed the flickering of flames coming from the chapel. I rushed to it, thinking that it was a fire. But when I reached the chapel and looked through the open window, I realized that it was not a fire but the light of many candles instead, held by monks and by people I had never seen before. They were having a ceremony."

The next few words had melted into the page, their ink diluted by the rain. Frustrated, Dr. Gabe tried to turn the page in case the story continued on the next one, only to find that the following sheets were stuck together. He picked a scalpel out of a drawer and fiddled with the sheets, trying to separate them. He had to know how the little monk's adventure continued.

After a while, patience paid off, and Dr. Gabe managed to separate the pages. Anxiously, he read on.

'To my horror, Monsignor stood at the front of the altar dressed in some Pagan robe, holding up a long, murderous knife that was stained with what looked like blood. He was saying some sort of prayer in an unfamiliar language, and the people in the pews prayed with him. I had to rub my eyes to see if I was dreaming. I had to know.

'I moved to the other window, as close as I dared. Behind him, on the altar, I could clearly see the dead body of a child in a pool of blood. The shivers took hold of me, and I had to run to the bushes to throw up what little food I had consumed for dinner. I realized that the rumors were true. Monsignor had brought with him from Saint-Domingue a new type of Mass that was an abomination. It is said that for a price, Monsignor can make your desires come true, by sacrificing to a Pagan god. Until tonight I had never thought that this was anything but idle gossip.

'I wish I knew what to do. Some of our own monks were at the Mass. How can I know now who to trust, who to fear?'

The blood froze in Dr. Gabe's body. He didn't want to read any more of the young monk's notes, and he set the book aside. But curiosity got the best of him. He was a doctor after all, and scientific need to know gnawed at him. Finally, he put his paperwork away and picked up the book again.

Page after page, notes filled the narrow margins of the prayer book, but except for a word here and there, the sentences were illegible. Dr. Gabe slammed the desk with his fist. Here was a chance to peek through time into the secretive life of an ancient monastic order, and he was unable to do so.

Toward the end of the book, he found one more legible entry, written in apparent haste. His heart sunk with sadness when he realized that it was the story of the disturbing end of the young monk.

'He knows it was me,' he wrote. Dr. Gabe could almost feel the despair in the young man's heart. He knew that he was going to die, and he was afraid.

'I think he's known all along, but he didn't tell me so that he could toy with me. I've lived in fear. He wants me to go with him to the chapel tonight, just the two of us, and I'm so afraid that he will hurt me. But I'm also afraid to disobey. His punishments are so cruel and inhuman. He must have learned those in Saint-Domingue as well. I've prayed all night and all day but my soul can't find peace. What am I going to do?'

Dr. Gabe closed the book and sighed sadly. Poor child, he thought. Dead before his allotted time, but at least cherished enough by a friend to be buried with his beloved prayer book.

Chapter 40

Haruki—Wednesday Afternoon

WHILE MADAME MOUTON SLEPT restlessly on the couch, Haruki quietly slipped out of the apartment and headed downstairs. The upscale Belleview afforded Madame all the privacy she needed, but none of the solace for her sorrow after the death of Yuna.

Haruki exited the elevator and looked around. The porter at the front desk nodded to him, and he nodded back. Madame was probably not in any danger, but it was good to know that while he was not around, a barrier at the front door might provide her with a safety net against strangers.

A soft afternoon drizzle moistened his jet-black hair, but Haruki didn't mind. His soul was on fire ever since his sister had been murdered, and he felt oblivious against everything around him, except for the burning hatred that smoldered inside him.

He sat in the car for a few minutes, gathering his thoughts. He regretted not having gone with Yuna to meet the man when she had asked him to. He regretted not having followed her until it was too late. And he regretted not having let the police know when he found her body but running away instead. It was being unable to speak that so often got in the way of making the right decisions. He was shy, almost scared of strangers who were so often cruel, but he should have been there. Instead, he left her alone to die, and then he ran away.

He turned the car ignition on, and he set the GPS. It was too late for everything else, but it was not too late for a formal sendoff to her soul. He patted the backpack on the passenger seat to make sure that he had everything, and he began to drive.

Half Moon Bay was grey and gloomy, the skies overcast and heavy with rain, and the waters in the bay looked angry. Frothy waves slapped the shore restlessly as he took a left turn before the Marina and headed out of town.

Soon he left the Marina and the golf course in his rearview mirror, and a few minutes after that, the Fisherman's Wharf. For just a second he wondered whether fishing boats went out in this weather, but lack of interest in the subject veered his mind back toward his sister and the unlikely way in which she had been killed.

The soft afternoon drizzle soon turned into a steady shower. He turned the windshield wipers up higher, and the tack-tock of their rhythmic movement annoyed his train of thought, and he grunted with frustration.

Finally, he sighted the decaying chapel, climbing out of the rising fog. In the gloom, the chapel looked more forlorn than ever—an abandoned carcass—and it seemed to have decayed even further ever since he had been here just a handful of days earlier.

The Maritime Museum was closed. No flickering lights broke the approaching penumbra, no movement disturbed the solitude. Haruki parked close to the Museum entrance where there was a proper asphalt parking lot. He jumped out of the car impatiently, and held the backpack to his chest, protecting it from the rain, and hastily crossed the yard between the car and the buildings. The ground was wet, and as soon as he stepped off the asphalt, his shoes slipped on the mud, getting sucked into it. He tried walking on the flagstones, but that was no better. They were uneven and upended, and now almost completely covered by the sloshing mud.

At the gaping, open door of the chapel, he stopped and looked up at the sky. The rain wasn't going to stop any time soon. He shrugged hopelessly and wiped the wet drops out of his eyes.

Haruki entered the cavernous space with hesitant steps. Over the wet smell of rotting vegetation, there was still—surprisingly—a faint smell of fresh kill, and yet so many days had passed since his sister's death.

He shivered with dread, but honor and duty forced him to take those steps that he didn't want to take. He was looking for that dried puddle of blood at the back of the chapel where his sister had given her life for an impossible dream, and with the water and the tears running down his face, he took one step after the other, stepping over decay, over fallen stones and rotting wood, over dank, dirty water puddles, and finally found the spot where he had found his sister dead.

Dark clouds sailed by overhead darkening further the inside of the chapel, and the sky rumbled. What little daylight there was left was vanishing fast. He refused to look to his right, to the corner where the heap of skeletons had been tossed negligently as if they had been nothing more than a pile of wood. That was not what he was there for, and he looked away.

He put his backpack on a bench that received some protection from the rain, in a spot where the roofing hadn't collapsed completely.

Out of his backpack, he took out his black kimono, and changed into it, tying it with determination around his waist. *Matsugo-no-mizu* would be impossible. Yuna's body was not there for him to moisten her lips for the "Water of the Last Moment" ceremony, but Haruki improvised and he sprinkled some water on the wet puddle diluted with blood where his sister had lain. Then he covered the area with a piece of white paper to keep out the impure spirits of death. This was going to have to be the *Kamidana-fuji.*

Haruki glanced around and found a largish stone brick that he dragged next to the paper. He pulled out a handful of wilting flowers from his backpack and put them on the brick. This was the best he could do. He had no table, no bedside with deceased. But he put a couple of incense sticks in an incense holder, and a candle next to them, and he tried to light them with a match. They refused to catch fire. Grunting with exasperation, he watched them smoke and fizzle out over and over again, and he gave up. In his heart, those incense sticks—and that candle—were smoking gloriously, elevating their purifying aroma to the skies, and his sister surely knew that.

Finally, he pulled out of the backpack Yuna's favorite combat knife, and her prettiest kimono, and with shaking hands, and a sorrow that was piercing his heart, he placed them on the white paper. The knife should defend her from the evil spirits, and she would be dressed as a princess to go to Heaven. Then he sadly shook his head and told himself this was all he could do.

He was already walking back out of the chapel when he remembered the money for the River Crossing. He rushed back to the makeshift shrine and rummaged in his pockets until he found six coins for the crossing of the Sanzu River, the *Sanzu-no-kawa*. He hoped that Yuna would find a good spot to cross the river on the seventh day on her way to the afterlife. Indeed, there was nothing more he could do, except wish for the best. Whether she would cross on a bridge, a ford, or a place with a snake, would be up to how well she had lived her life. On the other bank of the Sanzu River, the demons Datsue-ba and Keneō would determine the weight of the bad things she had done in her life.

Haruki slowly walked back to the car. Whether his sister got cremated, or her body shipped to Japan, that was not his decision to make. But he had done everything in his power to give his sister's soul a proper sendoff. At least that.

Barely seeing the road through the tears that refused to stop falling, Haruki carefully drove back home.

Chapter 41

The Diary of a Murderer—Thursday Night

ALL IN ALL, IT HAD BEEN A GOOD DAY, Father Armand told himself. Visits to the sick, check. Review of the church budget, check. Polishing of the sermon for Sunday, check—and two days early at that. Everything was done, except feeding the fish.

He stepped out into the garden and admired the horizon, tinged with wild reds and oranges. It was a splendid sunset. God must love pretty sunsets. He sure sent many of them to South Louisiana.

The cicadas were chanting up a storm, and that made Father Armand think that rain was coming. In those little villages of the Amazon, when the *chicharras* sang, it meant that the rain was near. Those had been good years, the years he spent in the rainforest. Danger, adventure, wild rivers impossible to cross, headhunting natives salivating for a white priest's scalp, and all the kind people and the fun people that had made the first years of his priesthood so exciting. And so, the chicharras were singing.

He hurried to the fish, embarrassed that he had almost forgotten to feed them. What would the little dears do if he forgot about them, captives in a marble fountain, with nowhere to go? He picked a handful of food pellets out of the pocket of his soutane and spread them on the water. He thought that the fish looked up at him gratefully, and he talked to them, pretending that they understood each other. After a while, he told them good-night, and he headed back into the house.

Madame Mouton was gone—and he usually tried to stay in his office until she closed the doors behind her—but she had left some appetizing smells behind, and he changed his direction and set course toward the kitchen. Dear, much-feared Madame Mouton. She had left him a scrumptious looking meal on a tray, and he felt guilty for hiding from her. But it was that she just talked too much, and Heaven forbid he might say something he shouldn't have because by the next day it would be all over Half Moon Bay. She had that special technique for questioning him that made it very difficult to remain discreet.

But dinner looked good, and he poured himself a generous glass of local Muscat wine to drink with it. Then, as an afterthought, he remembered that he hadn't finished reading Monsignor Lafontaine's memoirs and ran back to his office to pick the old book up. He sat at the refectory table, and propping the book against the wine decanter, he began to read, between big, satisfied, gulps of soup.

26 March 1792

Brother Jehane is an extraordinary painter. I asked him to reproduce the large Madonna and Child in the refectory. He mumbled a lot to himself while he stared at it, then went off to mix his paints. After a while, he came back and managed to copy it onto another canvas, but with such perfection that it was impossible to tell which one was the original one, except for the wetness of the paint. Such is his natural ability. Not even the master who painted the original, not even he, himself would have noticed the difference.

This weekend I've invited myself to Regnard Mound, and I'll bring Brother Jehane as my servant. I'm very interested in showing him *The Golden Gift Of Silence.*

30 March

As I suspected, the household is still in a state of misery and dereliction. We arrived at Regnard Mound in the early afternoon and—like the last time—found the place deserted, not a laborer in sight. By now it's almost April, and the planting season has gone to waste. I'm beginning to suspect that the Regnards have fallen on difficult times and had to sell their slaves. Except for the same two—Aimée and Barthol—that I had encountered on my previous visit, I've seen nobody else.

Madame, the Judge's widow was gracious as usual. She feels lonely without her daughter and has—behind her cousin's back—sent messengers to all the Cayman Islands to see if anyone has sighted them. An impossible task, if you ask me. Probably easier to find a needle in a haystack than to find those two alive still among all the natives. But she was looking for encouragement, and encouragement was what she got. I told her all would be well, and God would grant her wish if she was generous to His Church, meaning me in this case, of course.

Domine Miserere! The cousin looks like a ghost. He has deteriorated. He has lost so much weight that his elegant clothes hang on him as they belonged to another man. He ate absentmindedly, barely saying a word or two, and when he was done, he just stood up and left the room without excusing himself or saying one word to us.

"This is the way it is these days, Monsignor. Please excuse him," the poor widow said. What could I say? I helped her find excuses for his behavior so she wouldn't have to feel ashamed, and we went into the library where Barthol served us an after-dinner drink, and we stared uncomfortably at each other for a while without having much of anything to say.

Gratefully, that was over, and it was bedtime. As I left the room, I glanced back at the abomination and told her in my mind that I had plans for her.

We waited impatiently for the house to quieten down, and then Brother Jehane and I snuck downstairs with our slender candlesticks, and we rambled around the house until we found the library. When I say ramble, that's what I really mean. This house is a maze of rooms and hallways and dead ends. Without a guide, it's just about impossible to memorize its layout.

Brother Jehane hadn't seen the abomination before, and he was shocked at the evil that emanates from her. I had an urge to tell him I told you so, but it was better not to carry a conversation, lest we be heard by someone. So, he examined the painting meticulously by moving the candlelight all over the canvas, examining it square by square, taking his time—and taking forever, until I thought that my legs were going to buckle under me, and I would have to sit down. Finally, I had to grumble a hurry now, Brother, for the love of God, and he nodded, took one last look, and we snuck back into my rooms.

"What do you think, Brother Jehane?" I asked. I was impatient.

"It can be done, Monsignor. I have everything I need to mix up the paints, and I can build a canvas of that same size. It can be done."

"Very well, then. Tomorrow night we'll go back to the library so you can make some sketches and measure the canvas."

"And then we go back home?"

"Yes. And we come back Thursday night. Madame has told me that they're going to New Orleans to celebrate Easter with friends and will be gone a few days. Their two slaves are going as well, and the house will be empty. How fast can you paint it, do you think?"

"I will need three full days, no more."

"Will that be enough to copy all the most minute details as well?"

"Yes, Monsignor. Three days."

And that's the plan. Not bad, *hein?* I must say, I'm going to bed grinning, and will probably have a hard time falling asleep tonight, with all the plans that keep running across my mind.

5 April at dawn

I've barely been able to sleep from the excitement. My old dog Bastien watches me despondently. He would have preferred to have a good night's sleep, with the candle lights off, and silence around him. But I spent most of the night pacing in my cell. Brother Jehane on the other hand is completely serene, probably sleeping like a child, unaware of the momentous event he's about to take part in. Never in his wildest dreams would he understand that he'll be conjuring up a treasure from a painting. He's a simple man with an impossible gift, but a rather limited imagination.

So, today is the big day. We plan to set out early. Brother Jehane has all his painting supplies packed, and me, I haven't been able to think of anything else. I wish Rodrigo my horse could fly. Ah! Brother Jehane calls. We're ready.

5 April at midnight

Disaster! The fool! What has he done? All has failed. We were expected. We were ambushed, beaten, and chased away like beggars. We had barely turned into the road that leads to Regnard Mound when a group of armed Regnard men jumped out from behind the bushes and surrounded us. There was nothing we could do, Brother Jehane and I, unarmed and outnumbered.

And now we'll never have another opportunity like this one, not now that Regnard has warned me that he'll be waiting for us if we attempt to go back.

I've been trying to piece together what happened, how it happened, not that it matters anymore, but only Brother Jehane and I knew what the plans were, and I sure didn't tell anyone.

So, I asked him nicely. I have to remind myself to play nice. These are dangerous times. A handful of monks have accused me of being too harsh, too cruel in my punishments, and I forget sometimes that this is not Cap-Saint-Marc, where I was truly the master of God's domain. Here I'm just one of them, they say, and compassion must be the word of God, and on and on they go, trying to turn me into a gentle soul. But I fear retaliation. Not all of these uncultivated peasant monks are as gentle as they would like others to think. Domine Miserere! I've seen the hatred with which they look at me, and they're quite fond of Brother Jehane. So, I play nice. But his treachery aches in my soul and desires deeply to be avenged.

How did it happen? I asked him over and over again, and he became a blabbering idiot and insisted that it had been an accident. It slipped out. He doesn't remember who heard him. He doesn't know who the traitor is, how would he know? Point is that someone deceived me by telling Regnard what my plans were. Someone in this monastery, who hated me enough to want to be rid of me. But I'll find out. I'm still the Abbot Primate of this monastery and have the authority to question, to investigate. I know how to make people talk. I know how to make them confess. I'll root out the evil ones, and as God is my witness, they will pay.

Father Armand skimmed through the next pages. He had no interest in finding out what punishment was meted out to the unfortunate Brother

Jehane. Monsignor was too fond of his methods of torture, savoring with cruelty the pain he caused.

And then suddenly, a few pages later, he saw Brother Jehane's name, mentioned but briefly. It was a short note on the monk's death, but it was a cryptic *eh bien, il est mort,* and nothing else.

Father Armand pushed away his empty dinner plate and poured himself another glass of wine. He kept turning the pages until he saw that Madame Regnard was mentioned again.

7 May 1794

I haven't been back to Half Moon Bay in a very long time. Two years, perhaps? Ever since Brother Jehane and I were ambushed by a posse of barbarians and chased out of Regnard Mound on the fateful day in which we were going to paint a copy of *The Golden Gift Of Silence.*

I've been asked to say Funeral Mass for Madame the Judge's widow's cousin, the younger Regnard: Fernand. I shouldn't go. What if someone knows that we were chased away like dogs with mange, betrayed, beaten, humiliated? What if he told someone? What if Madame remembers?

I've thought about it for a good while. Two things stayed in my mind. One, that I was offered generous remuneration for going, and I do need the money. The local priest is away on a pilgrimage, and Regnard was an important man. He needs an important funeral. Then there's the curiosity that has been burning inside me. I just want to know. Has the treasure been found? Has it? I still dream of it. I imagine everything I could have done with it. Go back to France, live like a human being again. I'm tired of these festering swamps and these sanctimonious monks, whose only interest is to pray, pray, pray, and stare at me with hatred.

I've commissioned a statue of the Blessed Virgin and have gifted her the treasure in promise, if I do find it. Maybe she'll help me find it. But for that, I have to go and talk to Madame, if she will see me.

9 May

I'll be setting out later today. It's Friday. I've been offered to stay at the priest's chambers behind the church. I'll settle in tonight, make myself comfortable, and ask around, find out how things are going in Half Moon Bay.

9 May, Midnight

The road was long. A soft drizzle accompanied us all the way. Rodrigo hated it. They've paved the trail to some extent in the last two years, so it wasn't too bad going all the way.

As soon as we got to the church—named for some reason after St. Quintian, an obscure saint that nobody has ever heard of—a young servant of the priest came running outside and promised to take good care of Rodrigo. He seems to like horses, and Rodrigo nuzzled his shoulder, so I can assume that they will become great friends.

The chambers are comfortable. Much more so than mine at the monastery. If this priest doesn't come back from his pilgrimage, I might be able to get transferred here. It's so much more civilized. I'll have to be charming to all so that they remember me fondly when they need a new priest.

The cook left me a big pot of gumbo and a bowl of fresh rice. The roux is dark and spicy, and it's thick with okra, chicken, shellfish, and the most important trinity of seasonings: the celery, the bell peppers, and the onions. I had forgotten how good a bowl of gumbo could be.

I'm tired and ready for bed. But I did want to write these few words. Tomorrow, I'll set out to *faire une reconnaissance,* as they say, and hope to come back with good news.

10 May

A lovely Saturday, and what a day it was. This used to be a small town, just two years ago. But how it has changed. I stepped out of the church and looked around, and I thought my eyes were deceiving me. I was standing facing a large piazza full of flowering trees. I think they call them Crepe Myrtles. There's a marketplace, and women with kerchiefs on their heads and aprons on their ample girths sell pots of honey, and sweet cakes and pasties, and you can find giant tubs full of flowers of all sorts and colors. I was so surprised that suddenly I was in danger of becoming a poet.

Anyway, because of my priest's habit—my soutane—I was recognized of course, and people walked up to me and welcomed me. It was a very pleasant morning. At a stall, some men invited me to eat and drink with them, and we sat down on some benches under an oak tree, and I told them all about the monastery.

And that's how I found out that Madame's the Judge's daughter and her mulatto husband had arrived in town not a fortnight earlier.

After the men left, I remained on the bench pondering on my future. It seems that things have become complicated, and now the prospect of the treasure seems farther away than ever. With the legitimate heirs back, there doesn't seem to be much point in pursuing this particular train of action.

The prospect of going back to France obsesses me more every day. It's obvious that there's nothing to gain by remaining in Louisiana. After all, I have family and connections back home. I could start over. Yes. I have some serious thinking to do.

11 May

Quae est in Gloria Dies Solis! What a day this has been. It started early with a vigorous breakfast prepared by the servant. Then, I asked him to help me dress. For those simple-minded people who think that the priest can just hop into his soutane and go, let me tell you, nothing is that easy in life.

Since the Eucharist is to be given during Fernand Regnard's Funeral Mass, I first put on my white floor-length linen alb, which symbolizes the purity of the priest, *sic in et sic porro*. Then, I put on my purple chasuble. I've always been partial to wearing a purple chasuble for a funeral over the traditional white or black because I look best in purple. My chasuble reaches almost to the floor, and it makes me look slightly taller and slightly more slender, and that's all good. Then I threw the stole over my shoulders and headed to the front of the church, to open the big wooden doors.

I thought there might be a gathering of enormous proportions in front of the church, with the wailing and the lamenting, and all that usually comes with the funeral of an important man, but I was met with silence. The piazza was empty except for me, a scraggly dog chasing a squirrel, and some birds fighting in the tree branches. I must admit to an ignorance of Cajun funerary customs, so I scratched my head in wonder, and I waited.

Very soon I heard music in the distance, slowly coming closer from the direction of the bay, and what sounded like horses' hooves clattering on the flagstones. I stared in that direction, and finally, I saw what was going on. Four black horses harnessed to a black carriage sauntered in my direction, barely distinguishable in the distance. As they got closer, I noticed that they were wearing plumes of black feathers on their heads, and a black cloth on their backs, embroidered with the Regnard crest.

My servant came running out to see the parade, and he was the one who explained. They're coming from Master Regnard's home, he said. They must've hired a band to play for him, he added. He seemed very excited and jumped up and down when he saw the funerary procession getting closer. Wow, the Tous Saints band. They're pretty famous, Monsignor. I can see their colors!

As the funeral procession got closer, the music too became more audible. The brass band—all in black, purple, and gold uniform—played melancholic dirges and hymns that gave a somber air and lent a dignity to the event. Despite myself, I have to admit that I was entranced. Music has that effect on me.

People slowly got closer and filled the piazza, milling about, gossiping, greeting each other, excited that there was a fais do-do to break the monotony of their existence. Eventually, everyone entered the church. I saw Madame the Judge's widow walking right behind the hearse, her head and face covered with a black lacy veil. I wondered if she was smiling under that veil, knowing that now Regnard Mound was finally hers, but, clever woman. Under that veil, you couldn't tell.

Madame was accompanied by her daughter whom I remembered quite well, and the mulatto Boukeman, holding up a young child in his arms, all of them dressed in proper black. I nodded to them as they passed, and I was so worried for a second that a scandal would break out, that she would point a finger at me and tell the world what I had done, but Madame nodded back and even lifted her veil ever so slightly to give me a tight little smile. It seemed like I was safe.

After Mass, the march proceeded to the cemetery, and to the family mausoleum which had obviously been whitewashed and prepared for the arrival of Fernand Regnard, who died in the flower of his youth, I still didn't know how.

People on the streets joined in and followed the mourners to the cemetery. The brass band played a couple more hymns, but with a more upbeat tone, and many people surrounded them merrily and danced. It was quite inappropriate.

Then, the band members approached Madame and spoke to her quietly, tipped their hats courteously, and left the cemetery. Most of the mourners and the curious left with them, following the music that had now become wild and cheerful. Someone was playing the drums, someone else, the tambourines. Then, with a whole lot of fanfare and excitement, they vanished into the heart of the city, leaving me alone with Madame, with her daughter, and with Boukeman, still holding the child.

Madame drew me to a bench under a Magnolia tree and asked me to sit. I was expecting the worse, but soon realized that she knew nothing about what had transpired between her cousin, his men, and me. Here's what I remember of the conversation, *plus ou moins*.

"You never came back, Monsignor," she said. "And I missed your company."

"Please forgive me Madame, but these have been busy times."

"I understand, Monsignor, but I needed someone to talk to, and I would have welcomed your wisdom and your kind words."

"Is it too late to talk, then?" I had to ask. My heart was pounding. There was no telling what she had in mind.

"No, not really. But as you see, things have changed again. I have my daughter back. Messengers I sent out a long time ago—remember?—came back with the news that they had been sighted, and I sent for them. It's a miracle. I have my daughter back."

"I'm so happy for you, Madame. It's a shame that you had to lose one family member to gain another one."

"Yes. That. You see, I had told Fernand not to agonize over the loss of his money because there were all these treasures that Boukeman had salvaged, and all we had to do was figure out how to find them."

"Oh, really?"

"But we couldn't. Only Boukeman knew the secret, and he was nowhere to be found."

"So, you did tell him about the treasure?"

"I ended up telling him, yes, because he needed the money. But something went terribly wrong."

"What did, Madame?"

"First, Monsignor, I must insist that this be a confession."

"As you wish. We'll treat this as a confession, Madame, and I'll never reveal what you tell me."

"Thank you, Monsignor. It all started when I told Fernand about the chests of gold and jewelry that Boukeman said he had stashed away. I always had a feeling that most of that was stolen from other rich plantation owners. Remember the stories of how the slaves went from house to house, lynching the French men, and stealing their belongings?"

"I remember only too well. They almost lynched me as well."

"Yes. They set fire to the plantations and massacred all the women as well, except the ones who were willing to marry the black men. Remember those stories?"

"How could I forget, Madame?"

"Well, I never had the courage to ask him exactly where all that came from. Boukeman is an angry man. He's resentful and quick to take offense. And I'm scared of him."

"I don't blame you, Madame. Monsieur Boukeman does look somewhat cantankerous."

"So, I watched Fernand's decline—you know, always worried, always grumbling about the loss of crops or the loss of workers—already his slaves had run away, incensed by the fervor of freedom and, between us, Monsignor, Fernand was not a violent man, not like his cousin the Judge, and I suppose that emboldened them."

"So, you figure that they weren't scared of being pursued and brought to justice?"

"Quite. So, one day they took off, and that was that. Because of this, and because Fernand didn't have it in him to chase them down and punish them, he hired hands to plant the fields and all that. Someone had to take care of the crops. Plenty of young, strong men without jobs around here. But a few bad growing seasons, too many hurricanes one after the other, and before long, he was a man on the brink of poverty. He declined so fast. You saw him, Monsignor. Barely interested in eating, no energy to show even the smallest token of politeness."

"Yes. I did think that he was ill, perhaps."

"He was one step away from being ruined. So, we began searching for the treasure, trying to decipher the painting, looking for hidden words, for clues.

"By the time Boukeman and my daughter came to Half Moon Bay, Fernand had given up all hope. He was a broken man. Imagine the joy, the sudden hope of seeing Boukeman. He was family now. Surely, he would help, for the sake of his own child. So, we explained to him what the situation was, and we begged for financial help."

"And how did he react?"

"He was surprised that we went to him for help. I don't think he was very fond of us, and who could blame him. Anyway, he was adamant. He had nothing, he kept saying. He was as poor as we were. He offered to help in the fields, but money there was none.

"Fernand didn't believe him. Day by day, animosity grew between them. They began to bicker and to threaten each other. When they drank, they hated each other even more. One day, things got out of hand, and Fernand came into the drawing-room with a gun. He tried to shoot Boukeman, but the gun didn't go off. At this, Boukeman, furious, jumped up and attacked Fernand, who stumbled backward near the fireplace, and as he fell, he hit his head on the cantilevered marble hearth and was instantly dead."

"So, that's how he died?"

"Yes, but don't go thinking it wasn't an accident. I was there, and I saw it. Imagine the shock. We didn't know what to do. It had been an unprovoked attack from a drunk and desperate Fernand, and I swear—even though it's a sin to take His name in vain—but I swear to you that there had been no intention from the part of Boukeman to kill my cousin.

"My daughter became hysterical. If we told the truth, her husband—I guess I should call him that—he would be dragged away by an angry mob and lynched. When I saw that despair, those tears, I decided to lie. Since everyone knew that Fernand had taken to drinking, I spread the word that he fell, drunk, to his death."

"Madame," I told her, shocked almost beyond words. "I don't know what to tell you. I'm so very sorry for everything you've gone through. What will happen now?"

Of course, my heart thumping even harder, I imagined Madame in charge of the treasure. Surely Boukeman would tell her the truth now, right? And Madame was fond of me and would probably be amenable to sharing her wealth with the church and all that, or at least giving me enough to make my way back home.

"Well, Monsignor, you would have thought that this would be the end of our troubles. But not at all. The thing is that Boukeman was telling the truth. There's no treasure."

"What, *ça n'est pas possible!* But how can that be?" I exclaimed and jumped up from the bench, but quickly disguised my disappointment and sat back down next to Madame.

"No, seriously. There's no treasure. It was left behind in Saint-Domingue. Last-minute—and thinking that sooner or later he would go back—Boukeman decided to leave the treasure behind. Safer than bringing it onto a ship where the possessions of a black man would be easily confiscated. So, he left it all in your church, hidden in that space you have under the altar."

"But how would he have known about it? I never told anyone."

"In a way, you did, Monsignor. Boukeman followed you one day when you snuck out to check that you were leaving nothing important behind. Because it was empty, you didn't have a reason to go back and check it again. And because the enclosure was marble, the treasure would be safe forever. It would not rot, or burn down until it was recovered."

"And when did he tell you this?"

"After Fernand's death. He said he had told my cousin, but Fernand had refused to believe him."

"This is a catastrophe," I told her, feeling the devastation of the death of my dreams.

"It is, Monsignor. We can never go back to Saint-Domingue for it. We'll be lynched. I'm sure nothing has changed."

"So, we have to allow the treasure to remain lost forever?" At this point, I wanted to put my head in my hands and cry. Goodbye dreams of going back to France. I was to be an outcast forever, and a poor one at that.

"I'm afraid so."

"What will you do now?"

"Boukeman says he will rebuild the plantation. He says he can succeed, and he asked us to have faith in him."

"Oh, Madame," I told her. "You have no idea how sad this makes me."

And this was my day. Tomorrow I go back to the monastery. Downtrodden and without faith in the future. It's all over now. *Tout est fini.*

Father Armand snapped the book shut. It all made sense now. The sailor holding the ship up to the Virgin Mary in the chapel was the gift Monsignor Lafontaine had originally promised her: a marble statue and the riches—symbolized by the ship in the bottle—being handed to her, a plea for help in exchange for a treasure. It had nothing to do with what he had suspected at the beginning: that the ship would show the doorway to a secret passage. He would have to tell Margo that he was mistaken. But he was curious about the figure kneeling in front of her. It could possibly be the Monsignor himself, portrayed as the traveler.

Then he thought about the treasure, everything Boukeman, and his allies had plundered from the neighboring plantations. He wondered if it still lay where it had been originally hidden, all these two hundred years later.

He didn't mind that Monsignor Lafontaine never found it. He wouldn't have deserved it. Although everyone kept saying that God worked in mysterious ways, too often the spoils went to the rich and the powerful, and the rest of humanity—the one that most often suffered—was left with nothing.

Suddenly the pointlessness of the murders hit him, and a small groan of anguish came out of his mouth. *Humana cupiditas.* Indeed, how true.

He looked at his watch. Too late to visit Margo's house. But this couldn't wait. He couldn't just sit on this news and not share it. He wouldn't be able to sleep a wink.

He decided to drive by Margo's house and see if her lights were still on. He wouldn't knock or anything. Just a quick look-see. He picked up his keys in a hurry, grabbed the book, and slammed the door shut behind him.

Chapter 42

The Séance—Thursday Night

LIKE A MASTER OF CEREMONIES, Brooks opened wide the doors to the octagonal room, and the guests entered one by one. At night, the room had acquired a more somber air. Maybe it was the hundreds of candles that Brooks and Lucy had lighted, or maybe it was the ancestors, whose portraits seemed to be imbued with life in the flickering light of the candles as they looked down on the guests.

Margo approached one of the windows and drew the dark red velvet drapes aside. In this magical light, the drapes looked like cascades of blood, adding to the otherworldly ambiance of the room. Outside, the midnight moon had come up, and you could see its sliver shining in between the twisted limbs of the oak trees. A steady drizzle peppered the window panes.

The round table had been covered with a brocade cloth that shone in all the shades of the rainbow. As requested, Lucy had found and placed a large glass fishbowl in the center of the table, where it mirrored in miniature all the comings and goings of the people.

Margo wondered if Beatrice would tell everyone where to sit, but the guests seemed to have an idea of their own, and each went directly to a spot as if it had been preordained.

Outside, in the double parlor, the CD playing Beethoven piano sonatas had stopped, and the house fell into silence. Everyone was in awe of the moment, and the guests quietly settled into their places around the table.

Beatrice stood behind her chair and held on to the back with a tight grip. Her knuckles had gone white. Her walking stick leaned against the side of the table, and her long, wavy blonde hair shone like a halo around her worried face.

"I'm here because you all desperately need help. This evening must not be taken lightly. We play with life and death when we attempt to contact those on the other side." Beatrice lifted a slender hand as if to stop someone from interrupting here. "I know it's something we shouldn't be doing, but every one of you has reached a turning point, and let's face it. Sometimes we can't resolve things on our own. Sometimes we need help. Maybe that help will come tonight. Maybe it won't. But let's enter this gathering with serious intent. There is nothing to fear. Monsters won't materialize out of the fog. Faces won't appear overhead, and probably the table won't wobble. More often than not, that's just to make scary movies even scarier.

"And now, let us pray."

Beatrice bent her head forward and closed her eyes. Margo, surprised, couldn't help but stare at the guests as they all obediently inclined their heads and listened.

"In the name of God, Jesus Christ, The Great Brotherhood of Light, the Angels, the Archangels, and all the Saints, please protect us from the forces of Evil during this session. Let there be nothing but Good around us, and let us only communicate with Entities of The Light. Amen."

Of course, nobody in the room but her knew that Beatrice had a brain tumor that was killing her. Nobody knew that neither doctors, priests, nor spiritualists, had been able to explain her gifts. And nobody probably understood the true nature of her prayer. Racked by doubts that she might be possessed by the Devil, Beatrice tried to help others while pushing all evil out of her life.

The gentle rain from earlier was quickly becoming a downpour. Beatrice sat with her back against the window, but Margo, sitting more or less across Beatrice, was facing the window. Through the slit in between the two panels of drapes, she saw a burst of lightning illuminate the penumbra, and the twisted limbs of the oak trees outside all of a sudden looked like arms of monsters reaching to her, trying to come in. Then a rumble shook the house, and the water inside the fishbowl trembled.

She hadn't noticed that Beatrice hadn't opened her eyes. She sat across from her, pale, ethereal, and as still as death itself. A soft moan came out of her mouth, and the hair on Margo's back stood up. Then she opened her eyes and looked at the guests and smiled.

"*Ob causam accersistis me?* Why have you called on me?"

Beatrice proceeded to put her hair up into a bun, slowly, determinedly, with deliberate, youthful movements, digging hairpins out of pockets Margo hadn't noticed she had. Her face had gone through a subtle transformation. It became more elongated, younger, much younger. Her nose more prominent, her cheekbones higher, and her eyes more slanted, darker. And Margo wondered if it was the flickering candlelight and the mystical ambiance that were making her see things. But then Beatrice stood up and pulled her back up straight, and Margo realized that it was not her imagination. This was a different Beatrice from the older, weaker one that had sat down painstakingly a bare few minutes ago.

"Hold hands tight, carissimi, the new Beatrice said. "Hic me tecum. Don't let me go." The group quickly scooted the chairs over and closed the space left by Beatrice's departure. Even with the smattering of Latin, everyone knew that if they broke the circle, the illusion of the new Beatrice would go away.

Beatrice strolled around the room, leaving her walking stick leaning against the table. Her steps were strong and obviously pain-free. She was a young woman again, full of vitality and spunk. There was a rosy flush to her cheeks, and her eyes sparkled with mischief. All of a sudden, the scent of gardenias pervaded the room and a gust of fresh air rushed through in a wave and made the candle flames shimmer, go out for a second and come back.

She walked to the drapes and turned around to face them.

"I know what every one of you wants. I have the answer that you seek. But don't blame me if it's not what you hoped for."

She took a few steps toward Madame Mansard and put her hands on the old woman's shoulder.

"Why were you taken away, Avia, torn away from your true family? Why did your mother run? Was it that your mother held a secret she couldn't tell? I can call her and ask her." The apparition began humming with eyes closed, and Madame Mansard's face became a rictus of horror. Her head shook vehemently.

"Don't ask her," she pleaded. "I don't want to know." Poor Madame Mansard's voice had become weak and infantile as if she had regressed to childhood.

"But she wants you to know, Avia. She wants you to know that the body is under the gardenias." Beatrice's laughter fell over the room like crystal chips into a glass bowl. "Don't break the circle, carissimi, if you don't want to see me go." She walked to the fireplace and touched one of the candlesticks with her fingertips. "Everything has changed, and yet nothing has changed," she said and went back to Madame Mansard who was shaking like an autumn leaf. Everyone's eyes were glued to Beatrice as she strolled around the room, this Beatrice who was not Beatrice, who was making Madame Mansard whimper.

"But it's the cross you truly want to know about, isn't it?" She leaned gracefully over the old woman's head and touched the golden cross embedded with diamonds that hung from her neck on a thick golden chain. "It's beautiful. It's very old. It's older than all your ancestors. It's older than this house. All the women in your family have worn this. Before you die you will give it to your youngest granddaughter, but the one who really wanted it is gone, isn't that right? And yet why do you doubt? Are you its rightful heir? Or was it stolen from the rightful heir when your mother buried the body under the gardenias? That is your true question, isn't it?"

Madame Mansard was crying now. "Is my mother really in the room?" she asked in her little girl voice.

"Yes, carissima, she is. She wants you to stop crying now. She says she did it for you because she loves you. And she wants you to know that she didn't steal the necklace. It's rightfully yours."

The storm beat down on the roof, and the chandelier swayed from side to side above their heads. The gusts of wind had intensified, and the guests all looked at each other worried, but they continued clasping each other's hands tightly.

Beatrice walked over to the young Japanese man sitting next to Madame Mansard. He hadn't said a word all night.

"Worry not, Catulaster," Beatrice told him, whispering in his ear, loud enough for everyone to hear. She ruffled his hair fondly and she smiled. "Before the night is over, you will be avenged." Haruki shook his head from side to side. He tried to vocalize his denial, but only a guttural sound came out of his throat.

"It's all right, Catulaster. We understand. You did everything you could. Nobody will blame you." She patted his head one more time and walked on. She looked around and chuckled. "Who would like to be next?" Then she set her eyes on Jefferson Renard and walked straight toward him.

"Ah! *Ex vetustissimis artis*. You're the politician, aren't you? Your *Avus* says hello."

"Beg pardon?" Jefferson croaked, barely audibly. "What is an avus?"

"That's your venerable grandfather, the Judge."

"Oh no, is he here?"

Beatrice chuckled again and her voice changed. It had become deep and shaky, like an old man's voice. Her face changed too, and bushy eyebrows and numerous faint wrinkles seemed to supersede Beatrice's lovely face.

"I want to know what you've done with your grandmother's pearls, you ruffian. Who told you that you could take them?"

Jefferson looked at Renata in panic, and Margo looked from one to the other, surprised at all the private information that Beatrice was handing out so freely. The circle was never broken, but she did see the look of fear in Renata's eyes. She was effectively wearing a string of pearls interspersed with what looked like rubies and emeralds. It was probably a priceless piece of jewelry, and oddly she felt as one with the indignant grandfather. Those extravagantly beautiful pearls, around Renata's neck? Seriously?

"I'm sorry Grand-père. I gave them to Renata. I want to ask her to become my wife."

Margo's eyes went straight back to Renata and saw the shock in her eyes. It was obvious that this was news to her. Then, to everyone's surprise, the face of the grandfather vanished, and the younger Beatrice took his place.

"Do you believe in me now, politician?"

"Yes. I'm so sorry. Yes, I believe in you."

"The tree branch broke twice. Once when that ship sailed, and once again when the body was buried under the gardenias. And yet here you are. You need to learn your true history. You have retributions to make. And you have to tell that woman with the pearls that you're not who you are pretending to be."

"I will. I swear I will." Jefferson was shocked. Sweat was pouring down his forehead and he moved his face close to his arm and wiped the sweat off on the sleeves of his shirt without breaking the circle.

"Does this answer your question?"

"Yes, it does. I think I've always known."

"Very well, then."

Beatrice walked to the fireplace. The logs were burning, but Margo didn't remember ever asking anyone to light them. After all, it was the middle of August, the hottest month of the year in Half Moon Bay. Beatrice opened her hands and looked at the head of a faded dry rose that had appeared in them. Margo, mesmerized, watched as she crushed it languidly in her hand and brought it to her nose and inhaled. Suddenly, the fragrant scent of tea roses pervaded the room as if they had been in a botanical garden. "*Ex odore rosae,*" she said sadly and threw the crushed petals into the fire.

"You, Margo Fontaine," she said and her hand waved gracefully at the air, "you will find him eventually. That is a promise. I close my eyes and I can see her. She's wearing a beautiful blood-red gown. *Rubea sicut sanguis* it is. She doesn't know that she's in danger. He's hounding her, so she quickly takes her long black gloves out of her purse and puts them on. She doesn't want you to see the marks on her wrists."

Margo, horrified, jumped up and tried to tear her hands away from Jefferson Renard and Saffron, who were holding them tight. But Beatrice turned to face her and bellowed, raising an arm and pointing it at her.

"You sit down. I'm not finished."

Margo, shocked, sat back down. All of a sudden, the candles flickered, and out of thin air, more rose petals materialized and they twirled in the air around and around like a tornado, carrying the scent of tea roses, whipping them into a frenzy.

"Everyone must sit," she repeated loudly, and she took a few steps. When she turned back to face Margo, she was still angry. "He must be stopped, or else he will do it again." Beatrice looked furious, shaking. "He followed her. He waited for her to be done singing, and then he followed her to the back alley, where the stage door was open. She recognized him, and she tried to run, but those heels, the high, slender heels of her pretty shoes, they got stuck in the grate and she couldn't move. She tried to take them off but it was too late. Nobody helped her. She died alone."

Margo thought she heard someone scream, but it was her own screaming. It was years of memories repressed that came back to her in a flood. She tried to stop them because they hurt so much. She tried to push them back into oblivion where they had lived so long, but they refused. She saw her mother's dead body, finally, the way she had really found it, with the knife stuck in her chest.

Years of repressed tears fell down her face, down onto her chest, her blouse, and then down into her lap.

"*Ne clamet,* carissima, because you will find him, and he will pay." Beatrice approached Margo and bent her head toward hers, gently, lovingly, and their faces touched, and she could smell her mother's perfume, and Margo felt for a second that it wasn't Beatrice holding her, but it was Nicola, her mother, telling her that she loved her. "Ne clamet, carissima," her mother was telling her in that soft, sweet, loving voice. "It will be all right."

"I'm tired, carissimi, I need to sit." Beatrice walked to where she had left her chair and dragged it slowly to the fireplace, where she sat down with a grunt. She approached her hands to the fire as if she was warming them. "I just need to rest."

Everyone was silent as Beatrice sat with her head down. The fire crackled and illuminated her lovely face, and at times it was the face of the old, exhausted Beatrice, at other times the face of that new one that could see into people's soul.

Everyone waited, respectfully. Meantime, the storm had intensified, and gusts of fat raindrops splashed against the windows and sounded like pebbles thrown by a giant hand. Lighting flashed across the sky, and Margo counted, one, two, three—as she always did—trying to calculate the distance while she waited for her heart to stop pounding, and for the pain to go away.

Finally, Beatrice got up from her chair. She went straight for her cane and eased her weight on it. She was not the young woman anymore. She was old, much older than Beatrice. Her hair had become white, and wrinkles covered her face. She stooped as she slowly approached Renata.

"You called me because you needed me. I could take the cards out and read them to you, and tell you that there's a man in your dreams who's holding a knife. I could also tell you that there's a body under the gardenia bushes.

"It wasn't Avia's mother who did the killing. She just did the digging. It is the man in your dreams who murdered her husband and wanted to murder her child. He was jealous. He wanted her for himself, but she loved her husband. Avia's grandmother was a faithful wife, but the man refused to accept that and killed her husband. But instead of giving in to him, she ran away, to the other side of the world, and took Avia with her.

"That man in your dreams is a memory. It's not your story but theirs. You need to burn that book. That book was his. Le livre des trésors. That treasure was his obsession. The day you brought that book into your house, you brought part of his evil spirit with you. The day you burn that book, you will sleep again. These are not your secrets, and you shouldn't have to be burdened by them.

"Don't look so sad, carissima. I see a good life ahead for you. You will prosper."

"But the letters, Beatrice."

"The letters. Yes." Beatrice sighed. She sat down again. "Stay away from me. These are my secrets."

"Yes," Renata whispered. "They scare me."

"I know. But he'll stop. He promises he'll stop. Won't you, now?" Beatrice was standing again and was walking directly at Harry Louvière, who was snarling, showing some ugly, sharp incisors. Almost behind him stood Jimmy Falgout, Saffron's assistant, a visible sheen of sweat on his face, his eyes wild with apprehension. He took a step back and stumbled on the cables of his recording equipment.

And then, chaos broke out. Everyone was talking at the same time. Harry Louvière tried to get up from his chair, but Madame Mansard and Renata held him down tight. Jimmy Falgout—trying to flee—was already at the door of the octagonal room when Brooks grabbed him and held his hands behind his back.

Meantime, Harry Louvière was growling obscenities. "Get away from me, witch," he spat at Beatrice. "Don't touch me. You know nothing."

"Oh, but I do. I know it all." Beatrice raised her walking stick and pointed it at Harry Louvière's chest with a trembling hand. Harry Louvière, stabbed with the stick, bent over and grunted with pain and tried to tear himself away from Renata and Madame Mansard. Beatrice took two more steps. She looked pale and exhausted, and Margo started walking toward her. She had to put an end to this madness.

She was about to call out for order. But suddenly, an unexpected shriek broke through the moment and everyone looked at each other, startled. An inhuman howl was coming out of Beatrice's throat.

"Interfector," she screamed to no one with a broken voice and pointed her stick into the empty air. "Obsecro te, Interfector. Obsecro te. This treasure has corrupted too many hearts and ruined too many lives. This has to stop with you." As Beatrice approached him, Harry managed to pull away from Renata and Madame Mansard, and he grabbed the walking stick and yanked it away from her. With all that was happening, the guests had let go of each other's hands, and the circle was broken.

By now, everyone's eyes were on Beatrice. There was something wrong with her. One of her hands went to her face, touching one side of it, poking. "Numbness," she said, surprised. "I don't understand." Then, her arms fell limp to her side, a blank look came over her, and she began to collapse as if in slow motion. Jimmy Falgout, who had been there to supervise the filming of the séance, made a move toward her, but Brooks held him tight.

"Let me help her," he told Brooks with despair in his voice. Someone has to do something." When Brooks let him go, he hurried toward the medium with extended arms, but he was too far. Saffron and Renata were much closer and ran to her, but they were too late as well. Beatrice lay sprawled on the floor, on that hard, wooden floor.

Margo hurried to the door and yelled for Lucy. "I need a pillow, a blanket, and an ambulance. Now." She rushed back to the room and told Beatrice that help was on the way. They placed the pillow under her head and covered her body with the blanket, and Beatrice smiled a sad, distant smile.

"Don't worry, carissima," she told Margo. "It will be all right." Then she closed her eyes.

The ambulance was there within minutes. The first responders packed her into it, attached an oxygen mask, and rushed away. It would have been nice to think that St. Hildegard would perform another miracle and allow Beatrice to live, but Margo knew what the others didn't, that Beatrice was living on borrowed time, and that unless that miracle was performed very soon, it would be too late, and she would die.

Chapter 43

Chaos and Accusations

AS THE AMBULANCE DISAPPEARED en route to St. Hildegard's, Margo quickly dialed Sam's number. He sounded sleepy and annoyed, and Margo had a hard time convincing him to get up. But when she told him what was going on, he grunted and said okay. He promised to bring Andy and Maurice with him. In the meantime, Brooks had been instructed to keep everyone calm. She didn't want any absconders.

She watched the ambulance with its revolving lights silently vanish around the corner, and with a heavy heart, she turned toward her house and looked up. The moon in the night sky, unperturbed by human suffering, had kept on moving across the horizon. Around her, all the houses were dark and quiet, unaware of the drama that had unfolded in her home tonight. Only the surf, roughed up by the stormy weather as it swooshed up and down the sandy shore, and the distant sound of a car or two, zooming by on the faraway highway.

She walked up the steps arm in arm with Saffron, who couldn't seem to stop crying. She thought about crying herself. Sorrow for Beatrice mingled with frustration in her heart.

One of those people in her house had to be the murderer, but which one? Madame Mansard, the foreigner—aloof and cold—who looked quite capable of murder. Was it her imagination or the old woman wasn't broken up by her young relative's demise? Where was the grief? Where was the sorrow? How about Haruki, the dead girl's dumb and deaf twin brother? He looked guilty as hell. But what was he guilty of? Murder?

Then there was the politician, who might or might not have known before tonight that he was not the rightful heir of Regnard Mound. Would keeping that secret be a reason to kill? If it was, then Renata—ambitious and calculating Renata—would have been cheerfully capable of offing anyone who got in her way.

And Harry Louvière, the most famous inhabitant of Half Moon Bay? Did he harbor a secret that must be kept quiet at all cost? If he had to, would he kill to keep it so?

And then she thought of Jimmy Falgout, who walked about as quietly as a ghost. Nobody ever remembered that Jimmy was there. He had a way of blending into the background that made people not notice him. And then she remembered being followed by a redheaded tall man. How scared she had been. She had no proof that it had been him, Jimmy, who had stalked her. But who else did she know who had red hair?

Once back inside the house, Margo told Saffron to go join the others in the octagonal room and to keep an eye on them, and she walked to the front window, where she could watch the street. She crossed and uncrossed her arms impatiently and waited. Why was Sam taking so long?

Beatrice's aggressive exchange with Harry Louvière really bothered her. It had seemed so contrived. Did Harry stage that little act to keep Beatrice from talking? That tousle over the cane could have very well caused her apparent stroke. And he had winced and doubled over in pain when Beatrice poked her stick at him. Was it because he was hurt? Was it because of a festering wound caused by Yuna's combat knife?

Nevertheless, she was trying to build a case on assumptions. The crucial piece of the puzzle was still missing. She pondered some more. It had been a most bizarre night. If Beatrice knew so much, how come she didn't finger the murderer? Or did she?

Frustrated that the police car hadn't appeared yet in front of her house, Margo walked away from the window. When she entered the octagonal room, the chandelier lights were back on, and Brooks and Lucy were serving drinks and passing around the trays of finger foods, those exquisite little *canapés au saumon fumé, au fromage et au concombre* that had all been prepared in advance for the party she thought they were going to have after the séance. Now they came in handy to keep her guests busy and in situ.

Margo looked at her watch impatiently. Come on Sam, she thought. They'll eat, and then they'll get impatient to leave. Especially Harry and Jimmy Falgout, who were constantly trying to sneak out.

She was about to call Sam on the phone again when she heard voices and echoing footsteps coming closer from the double parlor. Then, all of a sudden, there was Sam with Maurice, filling the doorway, in uniform, looking all official despite their sleepy faces and their uncombed hair. "Sorry it took me so long," Sam said. "I couldn't find Andy anywhere."

She sighed with relief. The atmosphere of resentment was thick in the air, and she was happy to relinquish responsibility. Sam stalked into the octagonal room like he owned the place and ordered everyone to sit. Maurice remained in the doorway—arms akimbo—blocking the only way out. Then, Sam demanded an explanation. Half a dozen voices rose in a frenzy of frustration, competing vociferously to tell him what had happened, and how they wanted to go home because they hadn't done anything wrong, and it all became a blur for a few minutes until Sam whistled sharply and told everyone to settle down.

Saffron abruptly stood up and walked over to him, pulled him to the side, and she whispered something in his ear. In the eerie silence, all you could hear was the scratching of the tree branches, beating against the windows of the octagonal room in the whistling wind, and that soft whisper. They all stared expectantly at Sam, their faces pale and worn out, wondering what Saffron was telling him.

"All right, then. Seems like we have a solution. Saffron filmed the séance so that she could use it for research purposes for her book. So everyone, remain in your seats while we set things up."

They all wiggled in their chairs, looking at each other suspiciously, waiting impatiently for Jimmy Falgout—now quiet and humbled—Brooks, and Saffron, to arrange things. A TV set was brought in on a serving tray with wheels, a cable was attached to it, and finally to the video camera that Jimmy had placed earlier on the fireplace mantel, semi-hidden among pots of flowers and family portraits. Nobody had noticed it.

Sam turned around to let Lucy know that he was ready for the lights to be turned out when he noticed Andy, standing to the side.

"There you are," he said. "Where have you been? I've been calling you for the last half hour."

"Sorry, Sam. My phone must have been off."

"I'm glad you're here. I think we're about to unmask the murderer."

Then, Lucy turned the lights off, and everyone stared at themselves on the TV screen as Beatrice began the séance.

The film began with Brooks opening the doors of the octagonal room. The guests filed in, one by one, hesitantly, fear, and expectation in their eyes that shone in the light of a hundred candles. The ancestors in their elaborate portraits, silent guardians, stared down at them from the penumbra.

Margo saw herself approach one of the windows and draw the dark red velvet drapes aside. Saffron fast-forwarded the film. Now everyone was sitting, staring at the crystal bowl full of trembling water in the center of the table.

Beatrice appeared next, pale in front of the camera, the dark shadows under her eyes starker and more visible in the uneven light. Still, Saffron kept her finger on the fast-forward button, but slower now. There was Beatrice, talking, her knuckles white, her walking stick leaning against the side of the table, and her long, wavy blonde hair shining like a halo around her worried face.

Then, Saffron stopped. "This is where it all begins," she said.

Margo saw everyone's head bent in prayer. The sound of the rumbling storm came through faintly in the film. The guests watched the TV screen with rapt attention. Ob causam accersistis me? Beatrice had asked, laughing wickedly.

Mesmerized, as she watched Beatrice metamorphose into a youthful woman, Margo had to admit that she had not imagined it. This was almost a different Beatrice from the one that had sat down painstakingly a bare few minutes ago. Even her voice was different.

She watched Madame Mansard as Beatrice told her that the body was under the gardenias. She saw the shock and the disgust in the old woman's face. Maybe the old girl didn't have the stomach for murder, after all.

That was when the storm got worse, and the unlit chandelier began swaying from side to side. Everyone—including herself—had stared at it, wondering if it would fall. But she had a feeling that there was something she had missed. Not everyone stared at the chandelier, did they now? One person had stared at Beatrice herself. She was going to have to watch the film again to be sure.

But the moment passed, and young Haruki was next. He hadn't said a word all night. He had looked startled and ill at ease. She had felt sadness for the young man who was barely able to hear and talk, but now she noticed that there was also enormous hatred in his expressions. You had to wonder what he was thinking.

"Worry not, Catulaster," Beatrice had told him, ruffling his hair as she smiled. "Before the night is over, you will be avenged." Yes, but what had that meant? Another murder?

Jefferson Renard was next. She saw him watch the approaching Beatrice with apprehension. He looked like a man who would have preferred to be somewhere else. The candlelight illuminated the beads of sweat that were running down his face. Then, Beatrice's features seemed to change again and her voice became deep and shaky, like an old man's voice. Poor politician. The look of panic and vulnerability said it all.

"Your Avus wants to know what you've done with your grandmother's pearls, you ruffian."

"I'm sorry Grand-père," Jefferson had blurted out meekly, and Beatrice had chuckled. Nope. Not a murderer.

Then came the fireplace scene, and Margo held her breath. She heard the crackling of the logs coming across clearly and remembered thinking that nobody had lighted them. It had been a deeply touching moment, though it was hard to express why it had been so: the fire illuminating Beatrice's sad face, her hair like a halo around her head. Knowing that Beatrice was already dying when that scene had been filmed, gave it a much more poignant meaning. She watched Beatrice open her hands and look at the dead rose that had appeared in them. There was such sorrow in her features as she crushed the dry rose languidly. Ex odore rosae, she had said. Did she know that she was dying?

When Beatrice turned around and walked toward her in the film, Saffron discreetly fast-forwarded it to where Beatrice sat back down, seemingly exhausted, skipping the scene of Margo's mother. Gritty gusts of fat raindrops splashed loudly against the windows, sounding like pebbles thrown by a giant hand.

Then, it was Renata's turn. Poor Renata. Her troubles were many. No wonder she had gone looking for a medium. For one, the man in her dreams holding a knife—who apparently caused the death of the man buried under the gardenias—was haunting her dreams. And then some horrible letters. They must have been really mean and nasty. Renata had whispered. "They scare me." And nothing scared Renata. Nothing. She knew it well enough.

And that was the moment. Everyone gasped and waited. Beatrice, walking directly at Harry Louvière, her cane raised, poking at him, and Harry struggling to wrestle the cane away from her. And there was Jimmy, approaching him from behind and deftly slipping something into his jacket pocket. Then, turning around to see if he had been observed. How had she missed that?

Finally, Beatrice, disoriented from the stroke, looking wild, looking confused, accusingly calling someone Interfector, waving her cane.

But no, wait. That was not what all had happened. In real life, she had missed it. But in film, it was so much more vivid. Hold on. The bow tie. Hadn't Mrs. T.—her favorite librarian—said that nobody wears bow ties anymore? The professor, giving a lecture on sunken treasures. Harry Louvière, the professor, the expert in obscure books about ships. Harry, who was in the best position to know about the Concepción and the Decepción. Harry, the Interfector?

Margo tried to think her theory through, but there was Andy asking what Interfector meant, and the hypnotic concentration with which she had been watching the screen was broken.

"What?" Sam asked harshly. Saffron stopped the film.

"Interfector," Andy repeated. "She called him Interfector. What does that mean?"

"I don't know," Sam told him, annoyed, and shrugged. "Someone look it up."

"Latin, right?" Saffron asked, taking her cell phone out to check the internet, but everyone knew it was Latin. "It means murderer. She called him a murderer." Saffron stood up, shocked, and stared at Sam. "Oh my God, she called Harry a murderer!" At a nod from Sam, she pressed play again.

The film was almost at its end. There was Harry Louvière, trying to pull himself away, but held tight by Madame Mansard and Renata's hands.

"Get away from me, witch. You know nothing," he had growled.

"Oh, but I do know. I know it all." And then Beatrice, raising her walking stick and poking at Harry's chest, and Harry doubling over, grunting with pain.

Within seconds, it was all over. Jimmy Falgout reaching out to grab her, Margo and Saffron, rushing to her, and in the last frames, Beatrice, having a stroke, sprawled on the floor, on that hard, wooden floor, dying, and a shadow, discreetly stepping away from her. A shadow whose face she couldn't see. Had her eyes deceived her? There had been another person in the room, standing close to the dying woman. Just a shadow, face turned away from the camera, moving fast. Someone not accounted for. What was he doing there?

There was an absolute silence in the room. Before Margo could finish thinking through her dilemma, Sam started walking toward Harry Louvière, handcuffs in his right hand, Harry the historian, the most famous man in Half Moon Bay, Harry, who looked like a trapped wild beast, darting glances one way and the other, searching for a way to escape.

But something just didn't add up. She was going to have to watch the film again.

Chapter 44

Reckoning

MEANTIME, FATHER ARMAND ZOOMED through Half Moon Bay, although that was an overstatement because it was only, what, four, five blocks? He was not a man given to feelings, or premonitions, or anything of the sort, but all of a sudden, he was in a hurry.

His windshield wipers screeched. The rain had passed, so he turned them off. In the middle of the night, with the street lights shining on the wet, oily puddles on the road in all the colors of the rainbow, and the lights from the yachts reflecting lazily on the waters of the bay, this was a lovely town. He'd almost forgotten what it looked like after 7 pm, accustomed to being home in his own cozy abode by the time the sun went down.

Anyway, here he was rushing down Jamaica. As soon as he turned right on Boardwalk, he realized it would be hard to park. A line of cars blocked his way, parked inconveniently in front of Margo's house, including a patrol car with its overhead strobe lights on. Well, there was no need to worry about Margo being awake. The whole town was visiting, apparently.

Remembering his urge to hurry, and trying not to feel offended for not having been invited, he double-parked as close to the front of the house as he could and turned the ignition off. He grabbed the book and got out of the car. All he could hope for was that they wouldn't think him a fool.

A rivulet of muddy rainwater ran down the street and circled his ankles. Father Armand winced. By the time he made it up the front stairs, he realized he had forgotten to put his shoes on and the hem of his pants, and his slippered feet, were soaking wet.

Something big was going on inside the house. He found the front door unlocked. It opened to the touch and he stuck his head into the silent room. The double parlor showed signs of a party. Jackets hanging on the coat rack, purses and shawls left behind on the chairs, and coffee tables full of abandoned plates and glasses. But there was nobody there.

He stepped in and walked around. It seemed like voices were coming from the back of the house, faintly, and he felt suddenly shy, hating to intrude when not invited. But he shrugged it off. This was important. He followed the sound of the conversation.

He walked by the main staircase, the one that climbed graciously in a curve, its carved handrail majestically polished. He looked up, distracted for a second by the beauty of the renovations. The ornate plasterwork had been repaired. He remembered that whole sections of the cornices had fallen off, leaving the raw wooden ceiling exposed. The decorative ceiling medallion that had almost rotted away had been replaced by a new one, enhanced with gold leaf and faded rose trim. As a lover of colonial architecture, he felt pleased by the changes.

Up on top of the stairs, Jenny's two cats stared down at him. They looked disconcerted but too afraid to come down and investigate. They watched him with big inquisitive eyes as he waved to them and kept on walking. Last time he looked up, they had stuck their little heads through the balusters, still looking at him.

The voices were getting louder. He passed the kitchens to his right, brightly lit, almost tiptoeing, feeling guilty for the intrusion. It was obvious that this was a party. Boxes, containers of food, bottles of drinks, and kettles on the stove, piles of plates, miles of silverware, all made him think there must be lots of people in the house.

He thought of coming back on the morrow, but he had advanced this far, so he might as well keep on going. And he remembered that he was in a hurry, and picked up his steps.

He turned the bend in the hallway and found himself at the end of the road. He'd never been this far into the house. It had to be the oldest wing. Remodeling here had been kept to a minimum. Portraits and faded landscapes in oil graced the sides of the hallway, dotted with small ornate tables with inlaid woods and marbles, and randomly placed elegant fancy chairs with brocade upholsteries. A series of long, threadbare Persian rugs covered the warped wood flooring. It creaked badly under his feet, and when he finally found the room where everyone was gathered, he realized that he had been heard.

He stepped into the octagonal room and stared at the gathering, surprised that they too were staring at him, shocked to see him there. Though there was so much he had planned to say, rehearsing it in the car, to excuse his most inappropriate midnight visit, his voice failed him. All he managed to say in the end was a non-sequitur: "I'm sorry, but there's no treasure after all."

Chapter 45

Promises

"SO, WHAT HAPPENED THEN?" Madeleine—Margo's estranged cousin asked, sitting at the edge of her seat in the octagonal room that had been turned back into a sitting room. Gone were the table, and the chairs, and the candlesticks, and all the remnants of the séance that had ended in such a tragedy. Ice sat very close to her and watch her curiously as she spoke. Fenway—as usual—sat in Margo's lap and allowed herself to be petted, as a special favor.

"We were all in shock. Imagine. Father Armand shows up in my house—in the middle of the night—wearing pajamas and soaking wet bedroom slippers. Everyone was floored."

"Never in my life," Margo's Aunt Beth exclaimed with indignation. She hit the floor with her walking stick to prove her point, making the cats twitch.

"At least he was dressed. And let me tell you, Aunt Beth, he was wearing the most exquisite black silk pajamas I've ever seen. His initial— the A for Armand—was embroidered on the breast pocket with gold thread. I know, because I had to get close to him to check it out. I couldn't believe my eyes."

"So, who did you say was the murderer, chérie?" Aunt Tilly asked, putting an open hand by her ear, eager to hear her answer better.

"Why Harry Louvière, right?" Aunt Tilly said. "Our most famous town member."

"I don't think so," retorted Aunt Beth, banging her stick on the floor again. "He's a wuss. He doesn't have it in him. He's all words."

"Sam, and everyone else, were convinced it was him," Margo said. "How so?"

"Well, he seemed to give himself away. He fell apart when he found out there was no treasure. He cried like a girl. Sam said he had suspected him from the start, but I don't know if that's true. You know Sam."

"And you never suspected him?"

"Not until he winced when Beatrice poked him with her stick. All along I had thought it was Jefferson Renard, just because he had so much to lose. But then Saffron's new assistant started stalking me, and I thought maybe it was him. And he was acting bizarre every time I saw him. And then everything fell into place in my mind, and I realized how wrong I had been, because I remembered seeing those yellow stains on his fingers, and his shaky hands and I figured that he must be on drugs. Always so nervous, so twitchy. And he always has a sweetly sick metallic smell."

"Did he ever tell you why he was stalking you?"

"Yes. And it was such a misunderstanding. He was on the shady side of town to buy drugs. When he saw me, he thought I was looking for him. He knows I'm a detective and Saffron's friend. At the séance, he slipped the drugs he was carrying into Harry's jacket pocket, just in case he was searched. Poor Harry, kept insisting they weren't his. But that's all been sorted out.

"And then, all of a sudden, Beatrice collapsed, and Father Armand showed up to confuse things even more, and you know the rest."

"But how did it happen, chérie?"

"It was when Father Armand stepped into the room and said, 'There's no treasure after all'. Harry crumbled. I mean, he literally fell apart. He fell on his knees and looked up at the ceiling, and tore at his hair, and he wailed. He just kept saying, *C'est pas possible,* c'est pas possible. Imagine what Sam and the others must have thought. This was the behavior of a guilty man. Anyway, he was so beaten down that within five minutes, Sam had bullied a confession out of him."

"Did he confess to the murders?"

"No, Aunt Beth. Not to the murders. It was the letters he had been sending to Renata."

"Why would he do that? I don't understand."

"Harry doesn't think like the rest of us, Aunt Beth. He wanted a confrontation of some sort to get information out of her."

"I remember Harry Louvière," Madeline said. "He went to school with us. He was so serious, always better dressed than any of us, and he loved to read. We partied, but he preferred to stay home and study. He didn't have many friends. Then he left to get his Master's degree, and when he came back to Half Moon Bay, he was already famous."

Margo put little Fenway gently on the floor. And she brushed the silky strands of fur stuck to her clothes.

"Let's go check on Lucy and that tea," She said, putting a hand on Madeleine's arm, and they got up and left the room. On their way to the kitchen, they peeked out of one of the hallway windows and stopped for a minute to watch Brooks in the yard, showing Madeleine's three boys how to use a bow and arrow. They were having a grand time, giggling excitedly, taking turns.

"Robert would be pleased to see them so grown up and so healthy," Madeleine said, smiling wistfully.

"And—you have to give it to them—so polite." Margo chuckled, still surprised at how well they had turned out. "I wonder where he is. Have you heard from him?"

"Not for a while," Madeleine said. "But I know him. He'll be back. He just has to find himself."

Chatting amicably, they continued to the kitchen. It was wonderful having her aunts and her cousin's wife visit. Margo almost choked up on the thought of finally having her family back.

After Lucy set them up with tea, and sandwiches, and all sorts of goodies, and Fenway was back comfortably in her lap, Margo finished telling Madeline and the aunts the rest of the events.

"What will happen now?" Madeline asked, sipping tea delicately out of an ancestor's bone china.

"Beatrice had brain surgery, and the doctors are discreetly optimistic. Perhaps St. Hildegard has performed another miracle after all. Madame Mansard went back to Japan. She didn't like being here so much. Too many skeeters, too much humidity."

"But she's the rightful heir to Jefferson Renard's estate, right?"

"That's true, but only up to a point. Don't forget that when Madame's mother left Louisiana, she forfeited her right to the estate. Besides, the will states clearly that only those willing to work for the betterment of society can live in the house and benefit from the legacy. Madame Mansard had no interest in that. She left happy and probably never looked back."

"And the young man left with her?"

"Haruki? Yes, of course. He was only here to protect her, she said."

"But Margo, who was the murderer? You still haven't said."

"The only person that nobody was watching. The only person who had access to all the information from day one. The only one who had the guts and the know-how to commit cold-blooded murder. Twice. Andy."

"Sam's deputy?"

"Yes."

"This is so complicated," complained aunt Tilly. She looked very confused.

Margo reached over and patted her hand.

"No, listen," she said. "Mr. Snail had come across that old newspaper that mentioned the treasure in the jail's library, the one I showed you. Right? He needed information about the article, so he called the newspaper. Jimmy Falgout—the redhead that stalked me—took the call. Yes?"

"Yes, dear."

"Jimmy thought he was a nutcase and ignored him. But when Madame Mansard called the newspaper to find information on the Golden Gift painting, and it was Jimmy who answered the phone, he figured that there could be something to the treasure after all."

"Oh, I think I understand now."

"Then, he got together with Andy, who went to high school with him, because he remembered that Andy's grandfather was a famous treasure diver and might have heard about the missing treasure. They had big plans together, Andy and Jimmy Falgout. But at the end of the day, Jimmy is a drug addict, unreliable, incapable of carrying out long term plans. So, Andy promised to share the treasure with him if he let him work alone."

"He probably had plans to kill Jimmy too," Madeleine said.

"It's very possible. Anyway, Andy began corresponding with Madame Mansard. All very innocently, of course. But he goaded her. He pointed out that Madame had been denied her rightful legacy, and wasn't she going to do something about it, and so on. Egged her on to come to Louisiana to stand up for what was rightfully hers."

"Why would he have done that?" asked Aunt Tilly, with her hand cupped around her ear.

"He knew she had the cross. Since the cross is also in the painting, he thought it might be part of the clue, so he wanted her here, hoping that Madame's knowledge of the past, and her cross—together with the ship in the bottle—would help him decipher the location of the treasure. Remember, Aunt Tilly, that it was because of the painting of the Golden Gift and the cross that she contacted the magazine? Andy needed her here."

"Well, he sure accomplished that," added Madeleine.

"Yes, he did. Andy is much more devious than he seems. He orchestrated the séance from behind the scenes to get everyone together in one place. Then he quietly stood in the darkness and listened. It was his last chance to find out something about the whereabouts of the treasure."

"How did you discover it was him, my dear?"

"When I watched the film, I noticed there was someone extra in the room. He approached Beatrice, maybe to threaten her or scare her, or even—who knows—to help her. And even though his face was turned against the camera, it was reflected in the large window in front of him, when the lightning struck. As plain as day. What was he doing there? He hadn't been invited. Sam said he had tried to get in touch with him but couldn't find him."

"He slipped in."

"He sure did."

"Did he confess?"

"Not yet. But there's enough evidence against him. I'm sure they will find the ship in his house. Plus, no doubt there will be a wound on him that hasn't had the time to heal. And think. Both murders were so precise and so cold-blooded. With his police training, Andy is much more capable of murder than these other weaker-minded civilians. Don't you think? But not to worry. Sam will bully the truth out of him. His feelings are very hurt. He was fond of Andy."

"I'm shocked."

"So was I. Then little fragments of clues started to pop into my mind. When we discovered the body on the beach, Andy had bent down and picked something up and slipped it into his pocket. Something small and blue. I'd forgotten that. Then, there was his change of attitude. When he found out that I had the newspaper article from the dead man's room, he grabbed my wrist aggressively and tried to bully me into giving it up. It was so unlike him."

"What about the young girl who was murdered?"

"Haruki said Yuna, the sister, became very interested in the treasure herself and ended up corresponding with Andy in private. Madame is wealthy in her own right, and Yuna had been waiting for a long time to be named her heir, but Madame was slow to make up her mind, so Yuna decided to hasten things along. They were negotiating a deal. She would provide information, he would make sure she got the cross."

"Sounds to me like she was very naïve," Madeleine said.

"I agree. Her mistake was that she didn't want to wait any longer. She teamed up with the first person who made her an offer not knowing that she was making a pact with the devil. And who would doubt Andy anyway? He's a police officer."

"Have you seen the cross?"

Madeleine nodded. "Oh, yes. Madame wears it all the time. It's a big heavy piece of gold incrusted with gems and diamonds. It must cost a king's ransom in today's market, plus its value as a historical artifact and a work of art. She told her brother that she planned to meet her contact, to talk to him. They had a disagreement and fought. Andy is a strong man, fueled by greed. Although he insists that it was an accident and that he never meant to hurt her, who will believe him? He had already killed the old man."

"Capable of killing a young girl. How appalling."

"Quite true," said Aunt Tilly.

Margo looked suddenly at the aunts, worried that details about the murders might have been too graphic for them. But, no. They were perfectly happy, eating their hearts out on tiny meat pies and cucumber sandwiches, following the gruesome story with delight.

"You know, Aunts Beth and Tilly, I was kind of hoping that you would know something about these portraits hanging on the wall."

"Oh, yes. We know them all. These are our ancestors. Isn't that Charlotte?" Aunt Beth asked as she pointed her cane at the painting of a lovely woman in a pink and lace taffeta dress smiling down at them with a knowing smile, and she nudged her sister to make her look.

"I think so, yes."

"Do you remember great aunt Charlotte? She was the one who ran away with that Spanish Toreador, what was his name?"

"Tito Santander," the aunts giggled. "The family was so embarrassed that they had to rename him, Don Jose, to make him sound more proper. That's him to her right, the one with the funny moustache and dressed in his pink *Traje de Luces,* his bullfighter's outfit."

"Yes, I remember," Aunt Tilly squealed with delight. "Your Grand-père Francois had to go all the way to New Orleans to fetch her. They were about to sail off to Spain, can you imagine the scandal that would have been?"

"No worse than the one about Micheline, your Grand-père Francois' cousin, the one that had the triplets out of wedlock with that slave Barrois, the one that ran away so that her brothers wouldn't hunt him down and kill him."

"What happened to the triplets, Aunt Beth?"

"Well, all I can tell you is that they were not blond and they didn't have blue eyes, if you know what I mean. They were shipped off to France to school when they got a little older, and nobody heard from them again."

"But no story is worse than the one of Marie des Pres and her husband Abelard. Those two over by the window, painted standing close together with so much love in their eyes as they stare at each other that you would think they remained together till the end of their lives. Well, let me tell you. Abelard hooked up with a girl in town, one of those kinds of girls— you know—and tried to get rid of Marie his wife who complained too much about his extra-marital adventures. Fed up, he paid some toughs who kidnapped her, didn't have the guts to kill her and locked her up alive in a coffin, and placed her in the family mausoleum. It was sheer luck that there was a funeral that same morning and they heard the poor Marie banging about in her coffin. She was rescued in the nick of time."

The aunts smiled at each other fondly.

"Those were good times," said Aunt Tilly.

"They were, indeed."

Thanks for reading! Please add a short review on Amazon,

and let me know what you thought!

To check out the first chapter of the next Margo Fontaine Mystery,

ALLIGATOR HUNT, *please read on.*

Don't miss the next Margo Fontaine Mystery:

Alligator Hunt

Introduction

The Storm

THERE WAS MUD EVERYWHERE on the feeder road. It must have rained heavily while he'd been gone. A series of lightning strikes illuminated the distant horizon and then subsided. Chris Mouton—feeling the drop in barometric pressure in his bones—drove as fast as he could, like a maniac, avoiding the potholes, scattering wet pebbles under the tires of his truck, hoping to make it to safety before the heavens opened up and drenched the world. But already the winds were picking up and trying to blow him off the road. He could feel the strength of the gusts beating down on his truck, making it shudder, and he held on to the steering wheel as well as his meager frame allowed him to.

He looked up at the blackening sky and frowned. It would be tight, but he might still make it. Judging by the distance of the lightning, and a lifetime of experience in the wild and inhospitable swamps of Louisiana, he calculated that he had enough time. But just barely. He dreaded the idea of being stuck in the middle of a storm out in the open. Once the deluge arrived, the roads would flood within minutes and become impassable. He could easily be swept away, big heavy truck or not. And it wasn't so much that he was afraid of dying by drowning—God knew that everyone must die somehow, sometime—but he couldn't bear the thought of not being in control of his own destiny. This was his life, his story, and he still had so much left to do. He would have to leave the dying for some other time. Right now, he needed to get home.

Suddenly, appearing out of nowhere, a scraggly brown dog ran across the road, right in front of the truck. He slammed on the brakes, startled, and the truck skidded to a stop. He had barely missed running the dog over. Poor beast. He felt a pang of sorrow for it, out in this weather, and he hoped dearly that it had a home, or at least a safe shelter, to run back to.

He took a few deep breaths and waited for his heart to stop pounding. Damned weather. It made you do stupid stuff. He should have been paying attention to the road, and he should have been wearing his seat belt.

He found the seat belt wedged behind the cushion, and he put it on. Minutes wasted—he grumbled—and the storm approaching fast. He looked around for the dog, but it had vanished. Nor was there another car on this stretch of the road as far as he could see. He hadn't passed one in forever. This was such a lonely place. Usually, he enjoyed the soothing solace of the empty road. But not on a day like this. Should he get in trouble this far from civilization, he would be on his own. He needed to be more cautious.

At the next intersection, he stopped, and with his left arm, wiped the fog off the windows and the moist sweat off his brow. He really didn't want to miss the turn-off toward Mudville. The wind was picking up big time now and already leaves and smaller branches were flying at his window like projectiles, swirling around the truck, blinding him, disorienting him.

Knowing in his guts that his turn-off should be but a few hundred feet ahead, he drove on watchfully, upper body leaning into the steering wheel, trying to see through the dust and the flying debris, face as close to the front windshield as possible. His anxiety level increased as he counted the distance from the last intersection in his head and almost forgot to breathe until he saw the dead tree leaning against the abandoned remnants of the rotting fence that was his landmark.

His body flooded with relief and he whooped out in joy. He would hate to have to admit out loud that he had felt some level of fear. But he was aware of that apprehension, that unease that always lurked in his restless soul whether he took his medication or not. He felt safer, no, he needed to be alone among the trees and the swamps out where no other humans lived. And so, he was ever so glad to be getting close to home.

Within minutes he was at the next turn-off, and he couldn't help smiling when he saw his shack, its rusted aluminum roofing peeking out from behind the clumps of trees and overgrown bamboo. Yup, it was still there, shaking under the onslaught of the approaching storm.

He had heard on the radio earlier that the tropical storm would become a hurricane by the time it landed, and he didn't doubt it. Already the gusts of wind came with brief, violent showers that pounced on the ground with peppered force, and disappeared within seconds, as fast as they had come, followed by that howling wind that put the fear of God into your bones.

As pleased as he was to be finally home, he cursed under his breath that he had wasted precious time. He hesitated. Didn't seem like he would have a chance to board up the windows. Didn't seem like he would even have the chance to unload the plywood for them from the bed of the truck. Shoot, he told himself, I'm too late.

He jumped out of his truck and ran to the door. He brushed away the swirling leaves that hit his face and got into his beard. He had to hurry. At least he should close the windows properly and fasten those worthless outdoor wooden shutters that were probably going to blow away at the first gust of wind unless they were boarded up.

He looked up at the sky, at a straggling flock of squawking birds flying away in a rush, and at the dark, angry clouds accumulating with a vengeance over his head. The weather looked threatening, but it was still holding. He decided that he would put up as many boards as possible before the full strength of the hurricane winds came his way and he picked up some heavy-duty leather gloves and began unloading the truck.

Chris worked hard. He worked fast. Years of experience made the process automatic. He had the tools, he had the knowledge, and the anxiety gave him a speed he rarely experienced. He was usually more of a laid-back beer drinker who took his time to accomplish stuff. But he loved his shack, and today, anxiety lent him wings.

His shack—his home—was in a small clearing surrounded by forest lands, and swamps, and gigantic centenarian trees that had already been saplings when the French had stepped foot in Louisiana for the first time in the year 1717 or so. Its lonely location was its safety, but it was what made it so vulnerable as well. A fire, a bad storm, and out there, nobody would ever find out that someone might have lived in that secluded shack and died.

Before he finished nailing up the last board, he turned around toward the thick of the shrubbery, thinking that he had heard something, but there wasn't anything there. Just a quick light brown shadow that seemed to whizz by, and then nothing. Some wild animal, running from the storm. He had no neighbors, and he lived alone. Nobody ever came all the way out there into this Southern nothingness but him. Or his brother, when he needed something. Of course, there wasn't anyone there.

Pleasantly surprised that the weather had held long enough, he finished nailing on his last plywood board and walked to the house, fighting the wind. He thought he heard a small girl crying out a name repeatedly like she was calling for her cat or her dog, and he turned to look toward the swamp, startled, but nothing. Of course, nothing. He was imagining things again. That was what always happened when he stopped taking his pills. Or was it because of the pills? Chris shook his head and went into the house, locking all the locks on the door behind him. Then he walked from window to window, testing each one of them, making sure that they were all secure.

But he couldn't stop thinking of the little girl. Was she real, or was she a ghost? Was she out there? Was she lost? Did she need help? He couldn't let it go. By habit, he walked to the window to look out, but it was boarded. He shrugged. There was no way to look out. He would just have to let it go. He took a beer out of the refrigerator and pulled the tab off. The cold froth sprinkled his face, and he laughed. It was always that same excitement, opening a can of beer.

He pretended to forget the little girl and drank his beer, but he drank it down fast, in big gulps. He couldn't get her out of his mind. He decided he was going to go outside and see, real quick, make sure that she wasn't lost, or in some kind of trouble. He couldn't just sit down and enjoy his hurricane in peace when there could be someone out there needing help, now could he?

When he stepped through the door, it slammed against the wall behind him, almost blew off its hinges. The wind had picked up tremendously. It was going to be a big one, they said. Everyone get out while you can, they had said. But Chris was going nowhere. He had survived every major hurricane that had struck South Louisiana in this same shack ever since he had been a kid, and he wasn't about to run now. No, sir. He had enough beer for two weeks at least, plenty of dried meats, and a larder full of canned goods big enough to feed him for two straight years. Then, there was all that bottled water, and of course his beloved generator. That blessed thing had been his paw-paw's, and it was still running as good as it had back when. Yup. He wasn't going nowhere.

He stepped onto the front porch and admired the all-powerful strength of the storm, feeling it in his bones, in his soul, sheltered in a corner from the worst of it. He inhaled with his eyes closed. The air smelled of rain. It smelled of impending storm.

The bushes and the weeds shuddered under the onslaught of the wind, and soon, huge fat drops of water began plopping on their big shiny leaves, making drip-drip sounds before they slipped onto the wet ground. He opened his eyes, amazed and humbled by the power of nature. Smaller trees were bending over, from side to side, as if following a rhythm of their own, left and right, left and right. Soon the dancing would be over, and they would be torn out of the ground and thrown aside like so much refuse. Bigger trees would lean over for a while, and after they could lean no more, they would get picked up by the hurricane winds and pulled out of the ground. They would twirl around and around in their own tornado, their roots dangling about them, flinging the dirt and the worms, and the ants and everything else that lived on that tree, onto the ground, and the wind wouldn't stop until everything was dead. Dead. He had seen that before, so many times.

Then he heard the cry again, and it startled him out of his complacency. He squinted toward the thick of the forest, trying to see through the gathering darkness. This time he knew he hadn't imagined it. It had been loud enough to be heard over the howling wind, and he knew exactly where it had come from, too. He patted his side where he carried the gun in its holster and picked up the machete from the floor by the front door, and with his courage right where it belonged, he started walking that way.

Things scratched his face as they were blown by the wind. Some of them even hurt. Pecans, small twigs, pinecones, God knew what else. But he didn't falter. He brushed his face. He was going to find out what was going on. And if someone out there was in trouble, he was going to do something about it. His conscience wouldn't allow him anything less.

He followed the path, cutting shrubs down with his machete where he had to. He knew his way around every bush, every swampy puddle, every cypress tree. And on he went, obsessed, bowing his head against the wind. Within minutes, a complete darkness fell, and he unhooked his flashlight from his belt. Not that it was going to be needed much, because lightning kept striking methodically, sort of keeping the way in front of him illumined. With that and the flashlight, he would be okay. Besides, it wasn't like he could ever get lost, right?

The wind was intense. The rain was pouring so hard now that he could barely see two feet in front of him. The full force of the hurricane had arrived. The sludge under his feet quickly became deep and slippery, and it sucked him down, turning every step into a struggle with the muddy ground that was trying to swallow him.

Then, suddenly, a small tree, a sapling, got uprooted, lifted into the air and tossed right in front of him, barely missing him. And then another one. And then, whole clumps of vegetation flew in front of his eyes, and he knew that if he didn't move, he would be next.

This was not good. Maybe he had been too hasty. He hadn't heard the cry in a while. For all he knew, he had imagined hearing the voice. Wouldn't have been the first time either. He stopped. This was ridiculous. He was going to go back home. But where was he? How far had he walked? He turned about, suddenly disoriented. He looked around to see which way he had come from. The trees were all so tall, so dense, and the wet night so disorienting, that he felt suddenly lost. And that howling wind!

He sighed with despair, turning around and around, trying so hard not to panic, thinking about what to do next, when he saw it. He didn't believe it, but he did see it. An enormous alligator, white as a demon ghost, shining as if it was made of light, slowly making its way through the trees, barely a few feet from him. He stopped and stood still, scared to breathe. He had never seen any gator this big in his whole long life. Gaping, he watched as the beast made its progress slowly heading away from him, never looking his way. But that was not what took his breath away, no. It was what the alligator had in its mouth. The unholy creature was dragging the body of a man, his blood obscenely red against the maw of the shiny white beast.

Chris finally reacted and took his gun out and got ready to shoot, but his guts failed him. Before he knew what he was doing, he realized he was running away, running as fast as the wind, as fast as he had ever run before. The man had been alive, God, absolve me, he would never forget, and he would never be able to forgive himself. The man had been alive, and—like a coward—he had run away.

About the Author

Agnes Makóczy is a freelance writer and adventure traveler. She's the author of the Margo Fontaine Mysteries, a series that takes place in the fictional seaside town of Half Moon Bay, in South Louisiana.

Ms. Makóczy loves to write. She carries her computer everywhere and finds inspiration for her stories in the places she travels to. After brief attempts at Romance Novels and one Health book, she's had to face the truth: she loves writing Murder Mysteries the best.

To read about her other books and upcoming works, please visit:

www.agnes-makoczy.com